'I like it when you
wondered why the fir
spoken all night should b

'Then let me kiss you a

Before she had any ide
her up into his arms, his li   passionate possession of
her mouth as he carried her across to the bed. His mouth
moved with devastating persuasion over the slender
column of her throat and reached the lace-trimmed neckline
of her négligé.

Catherine had thought there was nothing left that could
shock her, but when she saw that he planned to take off not
only her robe but also her nightgown, she fought away the
debilitating waves of pleasure and sat bolt upright. Since
babyhood, she had never been wholly naked in front of a
man, and she could not quite believe that the Captain's
authoritative gestures meant what they seemed to mean.
She clutched at the padded lapels of his dressing-gown as
she struggled to give voice to her objections.

Unfortunately, coherence once again eluded her.
'Captain Moreton!' she stuttered. 'My nightgown!'

Jasmine Cresswell was born in England and, before her marriage, worked for the Foreign Office. In 1961 she was assigned to the British Embassy in Rio de Janeiro, Brazil, where she met her husband, another expatriate Britisher. They flew to the United States the day after their marriage on a 'temporary' assignment that has lasted twenty-two years. They have four children and now live in Denver, Colorado.

Jasmine started writing after her attempt at a doctoral degree in history had been frustrated for the third time by her husband being transferred by his company. Writing was the only career she could think of that could be taken anywhere in the world, without needing permission from anybody!

The Moreton Scandal is Jasmine Cresswell's tenth Masquerade Historical Romance.

THE MORETON SCANDAL

Jasmine Cresswell

MILLS & BOON LIMITED
15–16 BROOK'S MEWS
LONDON W1A 1DR

First published in Great Britain 1986
by Mills & Boon Limited

© Jasmine Cresswell 1986

Australian copyright 1986
Philippine copyright 1986

ISBN 0 263 75399 9

Set in 9½ on 10 pt Linotron Times
04–0586–86,800

Photoset by Rowland Phototypesetting Limited,
Bury St Edmunds, Suffolk
Made and printed in Great Britain by
Cox & Wyman Limited, Reading

CHAPTER
ONE

THE ROSE velvet curtains in Lady Annabelle's bedroom were tightly closed, but at the first hint of daylight, Captain Moreton woke up. The habits of the past seven years, he had discovered, were not easily changed.

For a moment he did not remember that he was back in London and his body tensed, alert to the possibility of danger. Nowadays, he slept little, and despite the long sea voyage home, he had almost forgotten how to relax. He had spent too much time exploring the dense rain-forests and sunswept plateaux of South America, where relaxation was a luxury not offered to those men who planned to survive. Having seen what happened to Europeans who allowed their concentration to wander, he had found it a powerful lesson. He had no intention of ending his life tied to four wooden stakes, stretched out over an Indian camp fire.

A frisson, not of fear but of preparedness, snaked down his spine and he stirred warily. His movements brought the smooth, warm curve of Annabelle's hip more closely against his side, and awareness of his real surroundings immediately returned.

As he leaned back against the scented, lace-edged pillows, restlessness gripped him at once and he turned to examine the woman lying beside him. His habitually harsh expression took on a gleam of tolerant affection as he ran his hand over the plump perfection of her body. Lady Annabelle had been a delightful, inventive lover and he was grateful to her for the hours of mindless enjoyment she had provided. He had not expected his first weeks back in London to be so painless.

He felt the bitter memories begin to push at the edge of his consciousness but, with the ease of long practice, he thrust them aside. He looked again at Annabelle, admiring the delectable swell of her bosom. Even in sleep her body projected a latent sensuality. She was only twenty-three, which was young to be a widow and very young to have acquired such an intriguing repertoire of sexual variations. He knew that her husband, the elderly Lord Brigham, had died after less than a year of marriage. Probably of terminal exhaustion, the Captain reflected cynically, at least if last night's activities were typical of what Annabelle demanded in her bed.

The lazy wandering of his hands gradually became more purposeful, and Annabelle stirred pleasurably beneath his skilful touch. Her russet hair splayed out on the pillow as she turned, still half-asleep, and pressed an eager kiss against his mouth.

'You have beautiful hair,' he murmured, and she accepted the praise with a little wriggle of satisfaction. She was still not sufficiently awake to answer him with words, but her body was already soft with welcome and he responded expertly to her unspoken request for physical gratification.

He ran his fingers through the ringlets clustered at the nape of her neck and deliberately forced himself to compare her chestnut curls to his memory of Diane de Verette's dark, gleaming tresses. As he had expected, his recollection of Diane made him feel anger rather than grief. What a fool he had been seven years ago, he thought with a sudden flare of bitter self-mockery.

He became aware of the increasing urgency of Annabelle's kisses, and moved swiftly to possess her, suppressed anger giving fire to his actions. Their bodies pressed ever closer together and, for a little while, he was able to lose himself in the pleasures of their union. Then, all too soon, it was over. Annabelle still clung to his neck, and her hands stroked his chest as she gave little murmurs of contentment, but he was overcome by the familiar, haunting sensation of loneliness. Silently he rolled to the far side of the bed, unable to tolerate the intimacy of their bodies when his mind felt so far away.

Annabelle did not seem in the least aware of his mental withdrawal, or if she was aware of it, she considered it irrelevant to her mood. She reached out, touching the patch of black silk that covered his left eye. He sighed inwardly, steeling himself for the inevitable questions. Tact was not one of her more prominent virtues, and her curiosity surpassed that of most women.

'How did you lose your eye, William?' she asked. Her voice, normally high-pitched and a little breathless, was still languid with the aftermath of satisfied passion.

'I haven't lost it,' he replied, managing to keep all trace of impatience out of his voice. He had learned from experience that his eye-patch represented an irresistible topic of conversation for the women he took to his bed, and he had almost learned not to resent their questions.

'I have merely lost my sight in that eye and the power of movement, that is all.'

'Then there is no real reason why you should not take the patch off, is there?'

He had no intention of explaining about the pain that followed upon prolonged exposure to the light. 'It is more comfortable to keep my eye covered,' he said.

'Do you never take it off, then?' Her curiosity was not at all appeased by his brief answers.

'When I bathe, and when I sleep alone.'

She giggled, then moved back towards him, snuggling contentedly against his powerful shoulders. Fashion decreed that aristocratic skin should be soft and white, but she found the sight of his dark, tanned body exceptionally erotic. 'I'll wager that you do not often sleep by yourself,' she said coyly.

'No. I have found that the night is not a good time to be alone.'

Her fingers continued to stroke the edges of the silk eye-patch, straying to the taut ribbon that kept it in place. His lips tightened, but he did not say anything as he covered her hand with his own, then guided her fingers to a new resting-place on the flat, muscled surface of his ribcage.

'If you cannot keep your hands still, my sweet, there are better places for you to caress than the top of my eyebrow,' he said lightly.

'You are changing the subject again,' she replied, pouting reproachfully. 'You will never talk about how you were wounded, William. Please tell me how you lost the sight in your eye. Does it still hurt?'

'It happened at Waterloo,' he said curtly. 'And, I promise you, the injury is no longer in the least painful. My wounds, such as they were, all healed long ago.'

'I didn't know that you had fought at Waterloo,' she breathed. 'How brave you must be to have taken part in such a terrible battle! Oh, how I wish I had been there to tend to your wounds! But, of course, I was only fifteen and still in the schoolroom.'

'Believe me, even if you had left the schoolroom, you would not have enjoyed the experience. Waterloo was no place for romantics who imagined themselves to be ministering angels.' As soon as he had spoken, he regretted his sarcasm. She did not deserve to receive the sharp edge of his tongue, and in any case she was not capable of understanding his irony. Feeling contrite, he raised himself on one elbow and dropped a quick, light kiss on her rosy cheek.

'The truth is, my dear Annabelle, that I did nothing more dramatic during the battle than carry messages from one command-post to another. It is difficult to portray myself as a hero simply because I didn't have the good sense to cover my head whan a couple of powder-kegs exploded at my feet.'

He tossed back the bedcovers while he was still speaking, and pulled on the dressing-gown one of the servants had thoughtfully provided. His actions were jerky and impatient. He would never have guessed that a simple eye-patch could exert such universal fascination. During his travels across South America he had enjoyed the company of more women than he cared to remember. But whether they spoke English or Portuguese or Spanish, whether they were aristocrats or peasants, they had always asked the same questions. Sometimes he thought that if he ever did decide to marry, he would search for a woman who either had been born dumb or had lost the power of speech. Since true communication between men and women was evidently impossible, perhaps total silence was the most sensible goal for a man to strive for.

Only Diane de Verette had been different. She had never pestered him for details of what he had done at Waterloo, neither had she ever asked him why he kept his eye permanently covered. But her silence, the Captain reminded himself sardonically, had not been caused by sensitivity to his innermost feelings. It had been caused by indifference, or perhaps by fear that any intimacy between them would make her own deception more likely to be discovered.

He walked across to the windows, angered by the degree of bitterness his memories could still arouse. In the past seven years he had not allowed himself to think very often of Diane de Verette. Since the time that she had betrayed him, since the bleak day when he learned how she had successfully tricked his brother into marriage, he had accepted that life was much easier to endure if it contained no threat of emotion.

He had also learned that Fate was a capricious mistress, determined to smile lavishly on those people who were most indifferent to her charms. When he left Lisbon and sailed to take command of the troops guarding Napoleon on the island of St Helena, he had not cared whether he lived or died. Ironically, his cool, unemotional leadership of the soldiers stationed on that isolated hell-hole had won him nothing but praise. Promotion had been his for the taking. Instead, at the end of his three-year tour of duty, he had resigned his commission. He had travelled to South America for no more compelling reason than the fact that he did not much care to return to England, and South America was relatively near.

He had pursued the rumours of buried treasure and fabulous wealth to be found in the emerald-fields of La Plata, that huge area west of Brazil, merely because such a pursuit gave an appearance of purpose to his self-imposed exile. Once, in the days when Diane had been promised as his wife, he had possessed nothing but the income from a modest country estate inherited from his father. With a slight, self-mocking smile, he remembered now he had longed to possess a fortune so great that he could shower priceless gifts at Diane's elegant, silk-slippered feet. Now, when riches meant little to him, he had become the possessor of a fortune more vast than any in his wildest fantasies.

His expression tightened into a mask of cold cynicism. He had quickly learned that almost anything and anybody could be bought with sufficient money. The most sensitive conscience, it seemed, could be soothed by a large enough infusion of golden guineas, and every door in London, however exclusive, was wide open with welcome.

The trend of his thoughts was becoming fruitless and he cut it off abruptly. It was, he decided, time to give Annabelle her farewell gift and be on his way. He had spent far too long with the Foreign Secretary, explaining the volatile situation in South America, and particularly in Brazil, which had recently declared its independence from Portugal. Civic duty was all very fine, but a visit to his family was well overdue. With sudden decisiveness the Captain drew back the curtains, allowing the morning sunshine to stream into the room.

'Oh lud, William, did you have to do that? It cannot be past nine o'clock and we were not in bed a minute before two!'

'I'm sorry,' he said, adjusting one of the curtains so that the light no longer fell directly on Annabelle's face. 'But it is a good day for travelling, and I must make an early start.'

'Oh, William, surely you could stay with me for another few days? You have only just arrived in London, and we could have so much more fun together!'

'I'm sure we could!' He smiled at her engagingly but immediately turned back to look out of the window, and she sensed that he had forgotten her presence almost as soon as he turned away.

'I'm afraid it isn't possible for me to remain in town,' he said when he finally faced her again. 'I returned from the Americas nearly a month ago, and I have not yet visited any of my family. They knew that it was necessary for me to spend time settling my affairs in London after such a long absence, but now it is more than high time for me to pay them all a visit. My mother, especially . . .' His voice tailed away. 'In any event, it is a long ride to my brother's estate in

Suffolk, and he is expecting me at Wellespont by tomorrow evening at the latest.'

She pouted again. 'Oh lud! Brothers and mothers are such a bore! Couldn't you tell them that you need to confer longer with your man of business or some such tale?'

'Yes, I could tell them that.'

'Then why don't you?'

His smile suddenly hardened a fraction. 'Because it would not be true, my dear, and I am not fond of lying.'

'Oh la! A little stretching of the truth would hurt nobody, and there is so much we could do to amuse ourselves!'

'You are probably right. Nevertheless, with deep regret, I repeat that I must leave you this morning.'

His professions of regret were entirely genuine, although they centred on his reluctance to meet his family rather than on his desire to remain with Annabelle. Despite weeks of bracing self-lectures, he was still not ready to face the fact that within less than thirty-six hours he would see Diane again for the first time since she had left his ship in Lisbon. By tomorrow afternoon he would be at Wellespont. Tomorrow evening he would have to sit down at the dinner-table with his former fiancée, who was now his brother's wife. And the mother of his brother's children. A flash of pain, quickly repressed, stabbed him. No, he thought bitterly, he was definitely not ready to meet his two young nephews—who ought to have been his sons.

Swinging abruptly on his heel, the Captain walked over to the dressing-room, where his evening cape lay tossed carelessly over the chaise-longue. He rummaged in the pocket concealed in the silken lining and extracted a small velvet case, grimacing faintly as he replaced the cloak. He reflected, with a brief awareness of irony, that there was something to be said for the Indian custom of keeping the women in a separate hut and sending them back there the moment sexual gratification was complete. Personal experience had repeatedly proved to him that the night of passion was a great deal more appealing than the conversation which followed the morning after.

'I have a small trinket for you,' he said, returning to the bedroom and allowing none of his distaste to show. He held

out the box and she took it eagerly, her eyes gleaming with
the uninhibited greediness of a young child.

'Oh, William, a present! How lovely!' She quickly
opened the box and stared round-eyed at the gaudy chain of
gold-linked emeralds. 'Oh, they are beautiful, simply
beautiful!'

She bounded out of the bed, indifferent to her naked-
ness, and rushed to the looking-glass in the corner of the
room. She dangled the necklace against her throat, her pink
cheeks darkening with pleasure. The stones looked good
against her pale skin, he thought absently, but they clashed
badly with her china-blue eyes.

Annabelle flung her arms around the Captain's neck and
kissed him fervently. The green fire, he reflected cynically,
was working its usual morning magic. It was amazing how
even the most devastated female heart seemed to recover in
the presence of an emerald necklace.

'Dearest William, your gift is divine! The jewels are
divine! I shall wear them tonight at the Debenhams' ball.
They will be perfect with my new dress. It is bronze silk, you
know.' She whirled back to stare at herself in the mirror,
her bosom heaving with excitement.

A tiny frown suddenly marred the smoothness of her
forehead. 'But my new evening shoes are silver, and so is
my stole! They will look terrible with all this gold! What on
earth am I do to?'

He patted her affectionately on the shoulder. 'If you
would summon your servants and request some hot water,
my dear, we could both get washed and dressed. Then you
could go out and buy yourself new shoes and a new stole to
match the setting of the emeralds.'

Her frowns disappeared in a trice, to be replaced by
another happy smile. 'How well organised you are,
William,' she murmured. 'So decisive and masculine! What
a good thing we decided to get up so early.'

She gave him another enthusiastic kiss which he returned
with sardonic appreciation, and when she pulled herself
away from him, he saw that the sparkle had died out of her
eyes to be replaced by an entirely different kind of glow.

'You know, the purchase of my new shoes can easily

wait,' she said huskily. 'That is, it can wait if you have time to come back to bed with me.'

He was touched by the genuine warmth of her offer, but he merely grinned and caressed her lightly on the cheek. 'Don't try to flatter me, Annabelle. I know that I cannot hope to compete for your attention with the combined pleasures of an emerald necklace *and* a new pair of shoes.' His grin deepened. 'One or the other, perhaps, but not both.'

She looked up at him and for a moment there was no greed, no pleasure, no excitement in her eyes, simply a brief flash of sadness mingled with regret. 'If you would only give something of yourself, William, I believe that all of London would not hold sufficient emeralds to compete with what you could offer to a woman.'

There was a tiny pause. 'I am sure you mistake the matter,' he said coolly before his voice resumed its familiar bantering tone. 'I am flattered by your praise, of course, but I assure you, my sweet, that I gave you my all. I have no hidden reserves to bestow upon you or any other woman. Your own spectacular talents saw to that.'

She smiled as she turned away to pull the cord which would summon a servant, then touched the shimmering emeralds coiled round her neck. Her fingers hesitated for a fraction of a second over the bell-rope, then she tugged determinedly. William Moreton was the most exciting lover she could ever remember taking to her bed, but she was too wise a woman to lose her heart to a man who had no interest in caring for it.

'My husband's valet has remained in my employ,' she said. 'He will be happy to shave you, if you require his services.'

He thanked her courteously, but his thoughts had already leapt ahead to his forthcoming journey, and he scarcely noticed when Annabelle shrugged into a pale yellow négligé and went into her boudoir.

They did not meet again until he came to her private sitting-room to take his leave before returning to his hotel. His parting speeches were everything that a woman could hope for from her lover; the kisses he pressed against her delicate pink fingertips were everything that was graceful. She was left, glowing and content, to admire the elegant swirl of his cloak as he made his departure. She hoped that he would be back in London soon.

Captain Moreton's attention, however, was many miles away from Lady Annabelle. His thoughts had already winged north to Wellespont, where his mother and elder brother were undoubtedly awaiting his arrival. Wellespont, the home where he had grown to manhood. Wellespont, where he would have to run the gamut of his family's kindly curiosity.

Wellespont, where he would have to meet Diane.

CHAPTER
TWO

By THREE o'clock on Thursday afternoon, Diane had
worked herself into a state of anxiety unlike anything
she had achieved in the previous six and a half years of her
marriage. Her husband, obligingly pretending to be a
bear as he crawled over the nursery floor, finally could
tolerate her restless pacing no longer and propped himself up against a corner of the chimneypiece. He hauled
his two small sons on to his lap, cuffing William affectionately on the chin and tousling Robert's mop of dark
curls.

Lord Moreton turned his attention from his offspring
with some reluctance. At moments like these, although he
would never have admitted it, he was convinced that nobody in the world had ever before produced two such
delightful, intelligent children. His gaze softened as he
looked towards his wife.

'Diane, my love,' he said with forced lightness. 'Could
you please explain why you feel this sudden compulsion to
wear out a pathway on the nursery carpet? I don't believe
you have sat down once during the last two days.'

She blinked. 'What? I'm sorry, Edward, did you say
something to me?'

'Yes, my dear, but I dare say it wasn't important.' Lord
Moreton knew, of course, exactly what was troubling his
wife, and he wished there was some way he could alleviate
her worries. His brother's return, although eagerly
awaited, was undoubtedly fraught with problems for all of
them. And, Lord Moreton reflected, if Diane heard that
the Marques de Algarve Branca had arrived in London, her
worries would increase tenfold. He stood up, consigning
Robert to the care of his nurse and rescuing his pocket-
watch from William's inquisitive fingers.

'I believe my mother is waiting for us in the drawing-
room,' he said. 'Shall we join her? If my brother reached

Colchester last night, he should be arriving here at any moment.'

'Of course. I was about to suggest the same thing.' Diane hoped that her bright smile disguised the apprehension that was churning through her system.

Lord Moreton was not deceived by her attempt at cheerfulness. As soon as they left the nursery, he drew her into his arms, holding her cheek pressed protectively against his shoulder. 'Is it so very difficult to meet my brother again, Diane?' he asked softly.

She relaxed against him with a tiny sigh. 'Yes, it is. I cannot help but remember how dreadfully I deceived him. He was so young and trusting, and I deliberately took advantage of his trust for no other reason than to betray him.'

Lord Moreton gently stroked her hair. 'My love, I thought we had resolved all these feelings of guilt long ago. You paint far too black a picture of your own behaviour. It was your father and then your guardian who plotted to free Napoleon, not you. You were their victim, not their assistant. And it was I who coerced you into marriage and forced you to consummate our union. If I can manage to live with myself and what I have done to my brother, you surely have nothing for which to reproach yourself.'

She smiled softly. 'Ah, Edward, you always contrive to make me believe that perhaps I am not such a wicked creature after all. But I don't think I shall ever feel entirely free of guilt until your brother is as happily married as we are.'

Lord Moreton looked at her a touch quizzically, then his eyes darkened with laughter. 'Ah! I begin to suspect that I have been rather obtuse. Is Lady Catherine Richland's sudden appearance in our household connected with your desire to see my brother safely married off?'

'*Lady Catherine?*' There was no mistaking the absolute astonishment in Diane's voice. 'No, Edward! How could you possibly think such a thing? She is your mother's guest, not mine. To be perfectly honest, there have been several occasions over the past week when I have wished her at Jericho! It is hard to imagine anybody less likely to appeal to your brother than Lady Catherine. I know she is your mother's godchild and I should try to be charitable, but I swear I have never met such a pallid, lifeless young woman!'

'She is certainly very quiet.'

'*Quiet* is a miracle of understatement! When we are alone, she spends most of her time staring at the carpet. If I address her direct, the wretched girl gives every appearance of looking straight through me. If she actually responds, she rarely says more than "Yes, Lady Moreton," or—if I am exceptionally lucky—"Yes, indeed, Lady Moreton."'

Her husband grinned consolingly. 'It sounds very bad, my love, and you have all my sympathy, but I understand that Lady Catherine's mother died a couple of years ago and the Earl, her father, has recently remarried. I've heard that he is a morose man and, from one or two hints my mother has dropped, I suspect that Lady Catherine and her stepmother do not get on well. My mother probably feels an obligation to entertain the girl. After all, the late Lady Richland was one of her oldest friends.'

The resonant sound of the front door bell prevented Diane from making any response. She stiffened, unable to conceal her tension, then clutched Edward's hand tightly as they quickly descended the stairs. Her heart began to pound erratically against her ribs as the butler walked with his usual ponderous dignity across the marble vestibule.

The door was flung wide to reveal a tall, broad-shouldered man dressed in a multi-caped driving-coat. There was little light in the entrance so that his face was partially obscured, his eye-patch a black slash against the prevailing grey shadows, and the precise lines of his body muffled by the thick folds of his coat. And yet it was not merely the subdued lighting which distorted the once-familiar image. Diane had a sudden premonition that she would find little enough to recognise even if her brother-in-law moved into a blaze of brilliant sunlight. Instinctively she leaned a little closer to the support of her husband.

'Captain Moreton! You've arrived at last!' the butler exclaimed with evident pleasure. 'I hope you had a pleasant journey, sir.'

'Excellent, thank you. The roads were dry but not too dusty. You're looking well, Stanley.' Captain Moreton's words were conventional, his tone friendly, but Diane felt a shiver of astonishment ripple down her spine. She scarcely recognised the clipped, self-confident voice in which he spoke.

The butler accepted the Captain's coat and hat, handing them to one of his underlings. 'Thank you, sir. I haven't had a day's illness these two past winters, so I mustn't complain. You're looking very well yourself, sir, if I may say so.'

'I seem to thrive on long sea voyages. I evidently have a nervous system that benefits from a diet of salt pork and hard biscuit. And, fortunately, the rough weather never bothers me.'

'The Dowager Lady Moreton once told me the self-same thing, sir. Must run in the family.'

'Indeed it must. Where *is* my mother, Stanley?'

'Her ladyship is waiting for you in the drawing-room, sir, and I shall inform his lordship and Lady Moreton that you have arrived. They are in the nursery, I believe, with young Master William and Master Robert.'

'No,' Diane said. 'We are already downstairs.' She moved slowly out of the shadows at the foot of the stairs, the rustle of her skirts seeming loud in the silence of the hall. She held out both of her hands, hoping that no one would notice how badly they were shaking. This tall, cool, stranger was not the same young man who had sailed away six and a half years ago, she reflected. This new Captain Moreton projected a power that was almost intimidating. She swallowed over a knot of nerves that tightened her throat, and forced herself to smile. 'How good it is to see you again! Welcome home—it has been far too long.'

There was a moment of electric, quicksilver tension, then he bowed over her outstretched hands with a derisive flourish, brushing a formal kiss against her fingertips. It was only a few seconds before he straightened, running his gaze over her body with ironic appreciation.

'Diane, thank you for your kind words! I'm delighted to know that I'm still welcome at Wellespont.'

She flushed, sensing his sarcasm. 'Naturally you are welcome. It is your home.'

He smiled blandly. 'No, not my home, dear sister—not any more. Merely my birthplace.'

Edward strode forward and clapped his brother affectionately on the shoulder. 'Nevertheless, it is good to have you here with us again, William. In fact, it's wonderful.'

The Captain seized his brother's outstretched hand, his expression softening into a warm smile. 'Edward, you old reprobate! I need not ask how you are doing, because I can see it all. I swear I detect a slight paunch at the edge of your waistcoat! You look as if our fair Diane has you thoroughly domesticated and actually enjoying your captivity.'

'And you, my dear brother, look anything but domesticated. In fact, you look more than half wild! I think it's fortunate that you've finally condescended to return home from the jungle. Another few months, and we should undoubtedly have been forced to prevent you swinging from tree to tree as you came up the drive.'

The Captain grinned, laughter temporarily dissolving the remoteness of his hard features. 'Has my tanned skin thrust me totally outside the bounds of the civilised world, Edward?'

Lord Moreton looked appraisingly at his brother. 'I suspect that your tan is the least important of the changes that have occurred in you, William.'

The Captain smiled lightly. 'Good lord, Edward, you are beginning to sound as obscure and oracular as dear Mama. I remember now that I never could tolerate your deep philosophical reflections on an empty stomach, and I have been driving since ten o'clock this morning.'

'Oh, how thoughtless of me!' Diane exclaimed. 'Please go to the drawing-room, William. Your mother is waiting there to welcome you, and I will see to it that refreshments are sent in immediately.'

With a quick murmur of apology, she excused herself and hurried down the corridor towards the kitchens. Lord Moreton's eyes darkened with tenderness as he watched his wife's flurried departure, but he soon turned back to his brother, asking a friendly question about the state of the roads near Colchester as they crossed the hall and entered the drawing-room.

The Dowager Lady Moreton was seated by one of the french windows, spectacles perched on the end of her nose as she peered at the pages of a large, heavy book. A nondescript young female sat by her side, an equally heavy book resting precariously upon her thin lap. The door squeaked as it swung open, and the Dowager pushed her spectacles up on her forehead, slamming her book shut and thrusting it to one side.

She gave a little cry of pleasure, hastily disguised as a snort. 'Well, William, I'm honoured that you have finally decided to come and bid me good afternoon! I dare say it cannot be more than an hour since we heard your carriage arrive in the courtyard. Sit down and catch your breath, my dear boy, for I suspect you must be panting from your exertions. You probably ran straight from the stables to the drawing-room so as not to leave me on tenterhooks, waiting to see you again. Am I not right?'

William laughed, his expression truly relaxed for the first time since he had stepped through the front door at Wellespont.

'Dear Mama, it's scarcely ten minutes since I stepped through the front door! But if you wish to be angry, you should blame Edward. He insisted on keeping me talking in the hall, even though I was longing to see you. Not to mention the fact that I am near dead with hunger.'

'There is salt fish and cheese curds waiting for you in the kitchen,' the Dowager said slyly. She glanced down, trying unsuccessfully to hide the twinkle in her eyes. 'I made the cheese curds myself, to my own special recipe. I still keep my herd of goats, you know.'

The Captain laughed again, gathering her into his arms and kissing her soundly on both cheeks. 'You cannot frighten me with such culinary horror-stories any longer, Mama dearest. Since we were last together, I have learned to eat roasted snake meat and drink sour llama's milk. There was an occasion, a mere ten months ago, when black beans stewed with pork innards would have seemed a meal of indescribable luxury. So I'm afraid that salt fish and home-made cheese curds no longer hold any terrors!'

'I have no idea what a llama might be,' the Dowager said. 'And no idea why you would find it necessary to eat snake meat. My ignorance, of course, is owing to the fact that you saw no reason to write to me with any degree of frequency during the last three years. But then, I am only your mother, and naturally I should not expect you to write to me.'

'There are no mail services in the South American mountains, Mama. But I wrote whenever I was in a town, and as soon as I found a mail-carrier, I let you know that I had been lucky enough to make my fortune.' He touched her lightly on the cheek, his voice very gentle. 'If you really wish to know what a llama is, I shall tell you. It's a species of camel, used by the Indians in the mountains both for its wool and as a beast of burden.'

'Hmm. I rode a camel once, when I was in Arabia. They are dreadful bad-tempered creatures and smell revolting.' The Dowager's eyes sparkled with lively curiosity. 'Later, when you have rested, you must tell us *everything* you have done since we saw you last. I am sure you had a great many interesting experiences in South America.'

Lord Moreton and the Captain exchanged amused glances. 'Yes, well, that is quite true, Mama,' the Captain murmured. 'And I shall be delighted to give you an account of my—er—explorations.'

'At least your geographical ones.' The Dowager's voice was tart.

The Captain smiled, then held his mother at arm's length and examined her carefully. 'You are looking younger than ever, my dear, and monstrous elegant to boot. Can I flatter myself that you are rigged out so fashionably in my honour?'

The Dowager sniffed, but her eyes were suspiciously bright as she looked at her son. 'I'm like every other female in the world, William, I enjoy having an excuse to wear a new gown occasionally.'

She allowed her eyes to roam over the hard planes and angles of his face, noting the new, harsh lines that were etched sharply from his nose to his mouth. She felt a twinge of regret for the innocent young man who had gone for ever, lost somewhere on the island of St Helena. She retrieved a lace handkerchief from inside her sleeve and blew her nose firmly.

'Don't fish for compliments,' she said brusquely, covering her emotion. 'You know I never pay them. And you already know how I feel about having you home again.'

She moved out of the Captain's embrace, and appeared to notice her companion for the first time since her sons had entered the drawing-room. The dowdy young woman had remained seated by the window, her position unchanged all the time they were talking. The heavy book was still open in her lap, but there was no indication that she had actually read anything, or even turned one of the pages. The Dowager's eyes took on a speculative gleam as she looked at the young woman.

'Catherine, my dear, how rude you must think us all! You should have reminded me to make the necessary introductions.'

'It was more important for you to welcome your son, Lady Moreton, than to introduce him to visitors.'

Her low voice was so lacking in emotion that for a moment the Captain's interest was piqued. He would have thought it impossible to make any statement sound so flat and devoid of emphasis. One glance at the speaker, however, was more than enough to dispel his brief flare of curiosity. She was pale and thin, and her face – what he could see of it – was as lifeless as her voice. She was dressed in a fussy white gown that did nothing to flatter her pale complexion or her straw-coloured hair. He could not see the colour of her eyes because she kept her gaze fixed firmly on the floor. He groaned mentally. If there was one thing he had lost the patience to tolerate during his years in South America, it was virtuous virgins. And this young woman was obviously not only virtuous and virginal, but boring in the extreme. If ever a man wanted to freeze in his bed, he thought derisively, this woman would make the ideal companion.

The Dowager's voice interrupted the cynical train of his thoughts. 'William, I haven't introduced you to my godchild. Catherine, this is my younger son, Captain Moreton. William, this is my dear friend Lavinia Richland's daughter. My goddaughter, Lady Catherine Richland.'

'How do you do?' This time, Lady Catherine's voice was not only flat, it was little more than a whisper. She extended her hand and the Captain shook it as briefly as possible. Her fingers, he noticed, were icy cold and she did not lift her eyes higher than the middle of his waistcoat.

'How do you do?' Common politeness demanded that he should make some further remark, but he could think of almost nothing to say to such a stick of a girl. He searched his memory. The past seven years had demanded little in the way of idle drawing-room chatter. 'I hope you are enjoying your stay at Wellespont, Lady Catherine?'

'Yes, indeed. It is everything I imagined it would be.'

Her voice was as colourless as before, and there was no logical reason for him to think that her words concealed a secret world of bitter emotion. He looked at her sharply, but she merely returned to her seat by the window, allowing her shoulders to droop foward as she fixed her gaze once more on the red swirls of the Turkey carpet.

Whatever he might have said next was interrupted by the arrival of two servants carrying trays laden with food and drink. Diane followed in their wake, cradling a sleepy toddler in one arm and holding her elder son firmly with her other hand. Her eyes, as she glanced down at her children, were misty with tenderness.

Captain Moreton stared at his sister-in-law and his two nephews, feeling an almost intolerable wrench somewhere in the region of his heart. His tiny spark of interest in Lady Catherine died completely.

Young Robert was restored to instant alertness by the enticing smell of almond cakes, and he began to wriggle in his mother's arms. Diane put him down, and he smiled at her with angelic gratitude before waddling as fast as he could across the drawing-room floor. The Captain held his breath, but by some miracle, the toddler's chubby limbs managed to avoid precious ornaments, jutting side-tables and the bountiful trays of refreshments. He was physically more competent than his waddle suggested.

'Gwandmuvver, here I is!' he exclaimed as soon as he reached his objective. He climbed on to the Dowager's knees without a moment's hesitation, in no doubt as to his welcome. He curled happily against her corseted bosom, stuck his thumb in his mouth and surveyed the room with the arrogant satisfaction of a child who knows himself totally loved. After a moment, he removed his thumb and sighed.

'I hungry, Gwandmuvver,' he said wistfully. His huge blue eyes suggested the plight of a foundling who had not been fed properly for at least a twelvemonth.

The Dowager scowled. 'Children should never eat between meals,' she said sternly, her tone at its most severe. 'It is extremely bad for them.' A few seconds later, she surreptitiously slipped him a macaroon. William followed his younger brother across the room and was similarly rewarded.

Diane suppressed a smile, while Lord Moreton turned to his mother, his expression a helpless mixture of amusement and reproof.

'I would like to know, Mama, why my brother and sister and I were trained from infancy to bow to our elders and remain standing until we were told to sit, whereas Robert may clamber all over you and then be rewarded with a sweetmeat for his appalling behaviour.'

'He is still very small,' the Dowager said, as if that fact explained everything. 'Besides, it is *your* duty and Diane's to discipline him and William. I merely have the pleasure of loving them.'

Diane and Lord Moreton once again exchanged speaking glances; then he grasped his elder son by the hand and conducted him across the room to the chair where his brother was seated.

'William,' he said, unable to keep the love and pride from his voice, 'I would like to introduce your nephew to you. His name, as you know, is also William.'

The Captain held out his hand, and it was grasped by five stubby fingers, still sticky with macaroon. He felt an involuntary spurt of amusement at the inevitable affinity of dirt and small boys.

'How do you do?' his nephew said, bowing politely. Despite the sticky fingers, young William was obviously on his very best behaviour.

'How do you do?' the Captain replied. 'It's a great pleasure to meet you. We have had to wait far too long to make each other's acquaintance.'

'Are you my uncle? Mama promised my uncle would come today.'

'Yes, I am your Uncle William. You're very tall for a young man who is only five years old.'

'I shall soon be six.' Reluctant honesty compelled him to amend his statement. 'Well, in ten months' time I shall be six. My brother is only two. It's a long time until he'll be three, nearly a whole year. His name is Robert Edward Louis Moreton.'

'It sounds a fine name.'

'*My* name is William George Alain Henri Moreton. I am named George after my English grandfather, who is dead. I am named Alain Henri in honour of my French grandfather, who is also dead. And I am called William after Papa's brother. Are you Papa's brother as well as my uncle?'

'Yes, indeed I am. And I'm very honoured that you should be named after me, since I'm not even dead.'

Young William frowned, evidently intrigued by this new and interesting thought. 'But you have always been very far away. Perhaps that is almost the same thing as being dead?'

'Well, from my point of view, it's not at all the same thing. You see, although we have not met, I have actually been quite busy these past few years.'

'So have I. I have learned to tell the time, you know, and I have built a fort for my soldiers. Papa only helped me a little.'

'Perhaps you would show me your soldiers some time—I should like that very much. I was a soldier myself until quite recently.'

'I know you were. Mama says you were very brave, and Papa told me how you fought at Waterloo against Napoleon and you defeated him.'

'I did not defeat him entirely on my own, you understand. There were several thousand other soldiers on the battlefield helping me.'

'But you were the bravest—Papa said so. You rode your horse right through the French lines in order to rescue some of your men who were trapped by cannon-fire. That is how you were wounded, and Papa says it is a great honour to be named after a hero.'

A faint trace of colour darkened the tan along Captain Moreton's high cheekbones, and he was relieved when Diane broke into the tiny silence.

'Your uncle has been driving for most of the day, William. Would you like to offer him a cake and some macaroons while I pour the tea?'

Young William responded promptly to his mother's suggestion, and the Captain seated himself on the sofa next to his mother, gradually relaxing in the warmth of his family's welcome. He allowed the cheerful flow of chatter to ebb and flow around him, contributing little. In truth, he was tireder than he cared to admit, even to himself, and the weariness sprang from more than the natural exertions of two long days spent driving his travelling-chaise. His weariness seemed to have roots that grew deep into his soul.

It was not until much later, when he had temporarily taken leave of his family and withdrawn to his bedroom to prepare for dinner, that he gave thought to his mother's goddaughter. He could scarcely recall her presence at the tea-table. He wondered briefly if the girl was half-witted, then dismissed the speculation from his mind. Lady Catherine, half-witted or not, held no possible interest for him.

He tossed aside his shirt and summoned his valet. He normally shaved himself, but today he was content to drift off into a pleasant daydream while his servant shaved him. He thought about Lady Annabelle, who was neither thin nor silent, and had probably never in her life cast down her eyes when there was a man available for her to look at.

It was a very agreeable daydream.

CHAPTER
THREE

CATHERINE USUALLY had no difficulty in dressing herself for dinner without the aid of her maid, but tonight she found that her hands were shaking so much that it was impossible to pin up the fly-away clouds of her long, straight hair.

It was Captain Moreton's arrival that had overset her calm, she acknowledged silently, as she wrestled with steel pins and uncooperative pieces of hair-ribbon. She had been well aware that her position at Wellespont was morally unjustifiable even before the Captain's arrival. Now that she had actually seen him, the true sordidness of her situation had crystallised into a stark and unflattering reality. The choices in front of her, she reflected, were beginning to appear even more impossible than she had feared.

She had cherished the hope that Captain Moreton might be pompous, or foolish, or even monstrously self-centred, so that she would not mind deceiving him quite so much. But he had been none of those things. A tremor of apprehension snaked down her spine as she recalled the hard line of the Captain's mouth and the cynicism of his expression when he had looked at her—a cynicism rendered almost sinister by the dramatic slash of his black eye-patch. He was obviously not the sort of man to react kindly to trickery and deception, and she shuddered at the thought of how he would behave towards any woman who tried to trap him into marriage.

After her third unsuccessful attempt to scrape her hair back, she admitted defeat. Waist-length hair was not easily confined into a single, severe twist, and tonight her fingers lacked the skill necessary to achieve the desired effect. Reluctantly, she reached for the bell-pull and summoned her maid.

While she waited for Mary to arrive, she walked over to the window and stared out into the moon-dappled gardens, but she registered little of the silvery beauty spread out in front of her. Her thoughts drifted wearily as she tried to decide just when her life had wound itself into such an impossible tangle.

Death was responsible for many of her problems, and at some deep level of her subconscious, she recognised that her inability to reach even simple decisions was partially caused by the draining effect of too much sickroom nursing and too much grief. Even after two years, she had not recovered completely from the unexpected, lightning-quick, loss of her mother.

But sadness for her mother paled into insignificance when compared with the tormenting grief she still felt for the loss of her cousin Matthew. His death a year ago had left a raw wound in her heart and a gaping emptiness in her life that remained impossible to fill.

She and Matthew had grown up together, studying with the same tutors, holding each other's hands as they tumbled in and out of childish scrapes. Sometimes it seemed that she could not remember a single important occasion in her life when he had not been there. Her twentieth birthday in September had been the first one she ever celebrated without Matthew at her side. Quite apart from what they had come to mean to each other later in life, his untimely death from consumption had deprived her of her oldest and dearest friend.

Sorrow for what she had lost, however, was no longer Catherine's most pressing problem. The year before, her father had remarried. His new countess came from a large family, and had been selected chiefly for her potential as a breeder of Richland heirs. She had proved her value by becoming pregnant within weeks of her marriage, and her stock with the Earl had risen accordingly.

Never fond of his three daughters, who should all have been sons, the Earl no longer had any interest in them whatsoever, except that they should not disturb the happiness, tranquillity and mental equilibrium of his second wife. He wanted no miscarriage to delay the prompt production of his son and heir.

The new Countess of Richland, jealous by nature and already ambitious for her unborn child, delighted in her power to make life miserable for the three stepchildren consigned to her care. She was lazy and not very clever, so that her tyranny was exercised randomly and was therefore all the more difficult to bear.

Catherine would have left home and found a teaching position in a girls' boarding school if her younger sisters had not begged her to remain at Richland Towers. Margaret, at barely fourteen, was physically not very strong. Jane was seventeen, and although her constitution was robust, she depended on her sister for companionship and emotional support.

And yet, Catherine thought despairingly, her good intentions had caused nothing but trouble. Six weeks ago, the Earl had returned from a business meeting in Bristol and announced that the fabulously wealthy Captain Moreton had sailed into port from the Americas. The Countess's pale eyes had immediately gleamed with interest.

'Captain Moreton?' she queried sharply, looking straight at Catherine. 'Is he related to your godmother?'

'I believe so,' Catherine replied warily, already sensing a need for extra caution. 'Although Moreton is a common enough name.'

'Of course he's related,' the Earl said. 'He's her younger son. The elder boy married some foreigner, a Frenchwoman or the like. There's also a daughter in the family, married to Sir Alfred Chester. I think he's the Ambassador in Vienna at present. They're a very important family politically. Good breeding stock. The line goes back to the time of Richard II.'

The Countess leaned back in her armchair, modestly adjusting her lacy shawl over the bulge of her stomach. 'With her daughter so far away, the Dowager Lady Moreton must be lonely. How very nice it would be if she decided to invite Catherine to Wellespont for a visit. Your daughter has been cooped up with all of us far too long, my lord. Have you noticed how pale she is? The more I think about it, the more I am sure she needs a change of scenery. Suffolk would be just the place for her, and I'm sure

Captain Moreton would appreciate the company of a well-brought-up young English lady after so many years among the heathen in America.'

Catherine's stomach lurched sickeningly at her step-mother's words. She had no difficulty in understanding exactly what the Countess intended. A marriage between Lady Catherine and the fabulously wealthy Captain Moreton would suit her plans down to the ground. The Earl of Richland enjoyed a modest income from his estates, but there was no room in his present budget for the many luxuries which the Countess considered her due. Catherine had realised months ago that her stepmother had decided that profitable marriages for her husband's daughters would be the easiest and most obvious way to increase the Richland family fortune.

Unfortunately for the Countess's plans, the immediate neighbourhood did not provide an abundance of eligible young men. In any case Catherine, who was the acknowledged beauty of the family, was adamant in her refusal to consider any of them.

The Countess, however, did not easily acknowledge defeat. When a wealthy merchant from London bought up the local manor house, she was ecstatic. Mr Craddock was welcomed into the Richland household and encouraged to spend time with Jane. The countess's scheming quickly reached a triumphant conclusion. Anxious to buy himself into the aristocracy, impressed by Jane's obvious vitality and breeding potential, Mr Craddock had offered to marry her. His suit had been received with enthusiasm by the Earl, who, like his wife, cared only for the fact that Mr Craddock possessed an income in excess of ten thousand pounds a year. The fact that Jane actively disliked the man was considered a triviality by both of her parents. The fact that he was over fifty, whereas she had only recently celebrated her seventeenth birthday, was dismissed as irrelevant.

Catherine protested the match in vain, pleading with her father to reconsider his approval. Her appeals carried no weight at all when counter-balanced by the opposite pleas of the Countess.

It was in the midst of all this turmoil over Jane's betrothal that the invitation arrived from the Dowager Lady Moreton, inviting her godchild for an extended visit to Wellespont. The Countess reacted to the invitation with all the satisfaction of a cat taking its final lick at a large bowl of cream. She ushered her stepdaughter into her private boudoir and proposed a bargain. Jane would not be forced to marry Mr Craddock—if Catherine agreed to marry Captain Moreton.

Catherine's first reaction was simply disgust at the vulgarity of her stepmother's thought-processes. This was swiftly followed by a fierce anger that Jane's freedom could be bargained for in such a despicable fashion. She was relieved when she realised that there were no means whereby the Countess's scheme could be assured of success. She would not have to make any difficult decisions, and she would not have to weigh Jane's future happiness against her own, because of course the Captain would never offer to marry her.

She had long ago learned the uselessness of expressing moral repugnance to the Countess, so her tone of voice was quite mild when she pointed out her practical objections to the proposed bargain. 'Captain Moreton is nearly thirty years old, Lady Richland. He has successfully avoided matrimony all these years, and we have no reason to think he will propose to the first eligible female he encounters upon his return to Wellespont.'

'I agree,' the Countess said. 'And it is certainly true that he's not likely to tumble head over heels in love with you at first glance. Your looks have gone off shockingly these past few months. I swear there's not a lick of colour in your cheeks and I'm sick to death of seeing you in that dreary black: it's enough to depress anybody. But the fact is, of course, that I don't expect you to win a marriage proposal simply on the basis of your personal attractions. Even when you're in looks, I'll warrant there aren't many men who want to sit around discussing all those dreary Roman battles with you. And you have opinions on subjects no lady should ever discuss. I'll never forget the day you lectured the bishop about the condition of young females who were widowed while they were still *enceinte*. At the dinner-table, too! I was thoroughly mortified. Your mother over-educated you, my girl, and so I have told your father. Most men aren't like Matthew, you know.'

Catherine swallowed hard, forcing the tears back into her throat. 'I am very well aware of that,' she said quietly. She forced herself to speak calmly. 'Just how do you expect me to obtain an offer of marriage from the Captain, since we are agreed that my charm of person could never do the trick?'

'La, child, you remain so extraordinarily naïve! It's the simplest thing in the world. You and Captain Moreton will both be guests at Wellespont. There will be a hundred opportunities for you to be alone with him.'

'And so? I'm afraid, Lady Richland, that I do not per-ceive how being alone with the Captain will bring forth the desired proposal. We are agreed that he is unlikely to find my company agreeable, and you yourself have pointed out that my looks would no longer attract anybody.'

'Compromise him,' the Countess said briefly. 'Leave him no choice but to offer you marriage. The Dowager is your godmother. If you are found in a sufficiently incriminating situation, she will insist that he offers for you.'

Catherine drew in a harsh breath. 'You must know that I will not do it! I could never agree to such a scheme!'

The Countess smiled. '"Never" is a long time. When you've considered Jane's future more carefully, I think you'll be amazed at what you can persuade yourself to do. I shall grant you one week from the day of the Captain's arrival at Wellespont to get a proposal out of him, and two days for a message to reach us. If we hear nothing by then, your father and I shall announce your sister's betrothal to Mr Craddock. He wishes to marry her by the middle of June, you know. How impatient he is, to be sure!'

Catherine felt sick. She couldn't speak, and she couldn't move.

'That will be all, Catherine.' The Countess put her feet up on a stool and leaned back in her chair, closing her eyes. 'You may leave me now, since I am somewhat fatigued. Producing heirs is an exhausting business.' She paused for a moment, her lips curving into a smile, although her eyes remained closed. 'I understand Mr Craddock hopes for a very large family. He is counting on having five children before he is sixty, you know. Did Jane tell you? La, how busy she will be kept!'

Catherine ran out of the room, unable to deny the Countess her minor victory. She returned to her chamber and flung herself on the bed, her heart pounding with a mixture of defiance and despair. She knew that her stepmother's threats were not empty. The Countess wanted some of Captain Moreton's money in the Richland family coffers, and she did not care what methods she used to obtain it.

In the end, Catherine had accepted the invitation to Wellespont because there seemed to be no other option. Her stepmother insisted that she was to cast aside her mourning, and the local dressmaker, working frantically with a bevy of village girls, cobbled together a new spring wardrobe. Ironically, the new pastels were hardly more flattering than the old blacks. The styles had all been chosen by the Countess, whose taste ran to the ornate, and the fussy, ruffled gowns might have been expressly designed to emphasise Catherine's painful thinness and extreme pallor.

On the morning scheduled for her departure to Suffolk, Catherine stared resignedly into her mirror. She had difficulty in recognising the hollow-cheeked, pinched-featured face that stared back at her from an absurd pink bonnet that clashed with her yellow hair and merely made her complexion look sallow. Only two years ago she had been considered the most beautiful girl in the neighbourhood, perhaps in all of Wiltshire, and she started to laugh. As she caught sight of her maid, who was watching with anxious eyes, she swallowed her laughter before it could turn into hysterical tears.

'Are you all right, my lady?' Mary asked anxiously.

'Oh yes! Perfectly wonderful, in fact. I'm going on holiday, after all.'

She cast one final, self-mocking glance into the mirror before walking wearily towards her door. There was certainly no danger of Captain Moreton falling in love with her, she thought wryly. If her looks did not improve dramatically over the next few days, his family might have trouble in bringing him up to scratch, however compromising the situation in which she might trap him.

The journey from Wiltshire to Suffolk was long, and she had arrived at Wellespont almost at the end of her strength. More important, she felt virtually paralysed by mental indecision. If she tricked Captain Moreton into marriage, she would compromise every principle she had previously held dear. If she did not, her sister would be compelled to marry Mr Craddock, a man whom she justifiably loathed and feared.

Her heart ached for her younger sister. But how could she trick an innocent man into marriage? Perhaps her deception would not be so very wicked, she consoled herself. The Captain might not be getting such a bad bargain, after all. She would be a dutiful wife and try to make up to him for the wretched start to their married life. She reminded herself that many marriages did not begin as love matches, but they seemed to work out quite tolerably in the end. She would be content to stay quietly in the country, tending to Captain Moreton's household and bearing his children.

But, to bear his children, she would have to share his bed! She knew precisely what sharing a bed entailed, and even for Jane's sake, she was not sure that she could endure it when there was no love to cloak the harsh reality of the physical union.

The terrible choices whirled endlessly in her mind, never coming to resolution. With the Dowager she was able to relax just a little, taking refuge in their common interest in the Classical world, but with Lord and Lady Moreton, she found herself tongue-tied by the weight of her guilt.

Catherine sighed and pulled the window draperies closed. She wished—how passionately she wished!—that she had the financial resources to provide her sisters with a home away from her father's indifference and her stepmother's cruelty. If only Matthew had not been so generous, and so tragically careless, with their money—her money. Hurriedly, almost guiltily, she pushed the thought away.

She heard the sound of her maid scratching on the door panel, and told her to come in.

'You sent for me, my lady?'

'I need you to do my hair, Mary.'

'Oh yes, my lady, it will be a pleasure!' The elderly maid beamed happily and reached for the comb. 'I thought you were never going to take your hair out of that dreadful style, my lady.'

'I'm not,' Catherine said tersely. 'Please make sure that you pull my hair back tightly from my face and make the knot as flat as possible.'

'But you have such beautiful hair when I'm allowed to dress it properly! When you pull it back like this, you take all the colour and richness out of it.'

'Please do as you've been told,' Catherine said sharply, then bit her lip guiltily. Things had reached a pretty pass when she took out her frustrations on her servants. She drew in a deep breath.

'I'm sorry, Mary, but I don't wish to draw any sort of attention to myself. It's . . . er . . . This is an important family occasion, and I don't want to intrude on something which is personal to the Moreton family.'

'Yes, my lady,' Mary said.

It was no wonder that the maid looked at her so oddly, Catherine thought, but she could hardly explain her confused emotions even to herself, let alone to Mary. She had a muddled feeling that if she made herself appear unattractive, she somehow would not be quite as much to blame if the Captain ended up in a situation where he was forced to offer her marriage. With more than a touch of bitter humour, she reflected that, looking as she did now, nobody could accuse her of deliberately luring a man into indiscretion.

Catherine arrived downstairs to find the drawing-room still empty of company. She spotted a book left lying open on the window-seat and picked it up gratefully. When she was reading, she sometimes managed not to think about anything personal for several minutes together.

But tonight the silence of the room did not seem conducive to concentration. The words on the page danced before her eyes and the same old problems danced within her head. It was almost a relief to hear the sound of the door opening, but her relief turned to panic when she saw that it was Captain Moreton who had come into the room. Dear heaven, she wasn't ready for a tête-à-tête with the object of all her problems!

The tumble of thoughts and fears inside her was so great that she could conceal them only by keeping her face utterly blank. She schooled her features into a flat, tight mask and closed her eyes momentarily. When she opened them again, she hoped her expression was devoid of even a hint of feeling.

She heard the rapid stride of Captain Moreton's feet as he came further into the room. Out of the corner of her eye, she saw that he had left the double doors wide open in deference to the proprieties. Seven years in the jungle had not caused him to forget that unattached males and females were not supposed to find themselves alone. The footman stationed in the hall would have a clear view of everything that went on in the drawing-room.

She heard his footsteps halt in front of the fireplace, where a stack of birch logs burned brightly in the grate. Although it was well into May, summer was reluctant to arrive this year and the evenings were chilly. The leaping flames provided a welcome boost to the warmth of the drawing-room.

'Good evening, Lady Catherine. How are you? How pleasant it is to see such a large, cheerful-looking fire.'

Her guilty conscience made her acutely sensitive to other people's moods, and she heard the boredom in his voice even though he tried to conceal it. She felt an irrational spurt of resentment that he should have categorised her as a bore on so brief an acquaintance. What right did he have to dismiss her after a mere hour spent in her company?

Common sense, however, demanded that she should conquer her resentment. She still had five days to make up her mind whether to give in to her stepmother's immoral demands. As long as she made no move to attract the Captain, she somehow maintained to herself the illusion of freedom of choice. Smothering a sigh, she deliberately drained all trace of animation or vitality out of her voice. 'Good evening, Captain Moreton. How are you?' She sounded, she thought wryly, rather less lively than the average ninety-year-old reclining upon his death-bed.

The Captain was too courteous to allow the conversation to wither into total silence. 'I trust you are looking forward to dinner as much as I am,' he said with a heartiness that sounded only a little forced. 'Travelling always seems to whet my appetite, although it is supposed to have the opposite effect.'

'I have not been travelling today, Captain Moreton.'

With her eyes trained on the floor, she could not see him, of course, but she could almost feel him gritting his teeth.

'No, I realise you have not been travelling today, Lady Catherine. You arrived here last week, did you not?'

'Yes, last Wednesday, in fact.'

'I understand your home is in Wiltshire? Has the spring season there been as chilly as it has been here in Suffolk?'

'Yes, I believe it has. We had snow in the middle of March.'

'Did you, indeed? That is most unusual, isn't it? Wiltshire is noted for the mildness of its climate.'

'Yes, it is very mild in our region.'

'Well, that seems to take care of our discussion of the weather, your home county and your journey,' he said. 'Am I to introduce yet another topic of conversation, or might we consider it your turn?'

'You may introduce another topic if you wish, Captain Moreton. Or we could sit in silence if you prefer.'

She felt the sudden sharpness of his gaze fix itself upon her face, and she realised that she had carried the insipidity of her responses much too far. Even a shy young girl, fresh out of the schoolroom, had more conversation at her command than this.

'Oh no!' the Captain said. 'I am not at all in the mood for silence. Let me see now, what else could we try to talk about? I have it! You were reading when I came into the room. Shall we talk about literature? Do you recommend the book you were reading? What is it called?'

To her acute embarrassment, she found that she had no idea what the book she held in her hands was entitled. She had picked it up without glancing at the cover, and her thoughts had immediately spiralled off into their usual frantic inner debate. Flustered by the realisation, she spoke without stopping to think.

'I . . . er . . . I didn't notice the title. I had only just picked it up, and had not yet become very absorbed in it.'

Too late, she was aware how her confession must sound to him—by now, he probably considered her feeble-minded! Glancing up, she saw his mouth curl in derision.

'Good heavens, what a voracious reader you must be, Lady Catherine, to devour volumes without even pausing to glance at their titles or their authors!'

'Yes, I am a voracious reader.'

'No doubt you are an admirer of gothic adventures. I have heard that most young ladies are secret devotees of Mrs Radcliffe and Sir Walter Scott.'

She hated the mockery she could hear in his voice and, just for an instant, pride overcame all the other emotions warring within her. For some reason it seemed intolerable that the Captain should scorn her. It was even worse that his scorn should be so well deserved.

'I am not particularly enamoured of either writer,' she said coolly. 'Of the two, I prefer Sir Walter Scott. I enjoyed *Marmion* and parts of *Ivanhoe*. On the whole, however, my taste runs in somewhat different directions. The book I am at present reading—not this one, but the one that I have in my bedroom—is a treatise that deals with the Minoan influence on the culture of Mycenae. It also discusses the interesting possibility that the Mycenaeans spoke the original form of the Classical Greek language. Perhaps you know that scholars have not yet been able to decipher either the Minoan or the Mycenaean script—this would, of course, effectively settle the debate about the precise structure of their languages.'

She experienced a brief, exhilarating moment of triumph when she looked up and saw that she had finally managed to shock him into a state of total, disbelieving silence. But with disastrous or brilliant timing—Catherine wasn't quite sure which—the Dowager Lady Moreton chose this tense moment to walk into the drawing-room. She took her seat on a sofa near the fire, and looked shrewdly from her son's stunned features to Catherine's unusually flushed cheeks. Whatever her inner feelings, her smile as she greeted them both remained a model of blandness.

'How nice that the two of you have had some time alone together! I hope you have had the chance to become better acquainted?'

Neither the Captain nor Catherine managed much more than a brief nod, but the Dowager continued to look cheerful.

'I have often thought that the pair of you have a lot in common,' she said brightly. 'I am sure you will enjoy each other's company once you get to know one other.'

The Captain finally recovered his voice. 'Lady Catherine has just been telling me about her studies of the ancient Minoan culture,' he remarked drily. 'I must say that it strikes me as an even more fascinating topic than the rival merits of Sparta and Athens. That, if I recall correctly, Mama, is your own personal favourite as a topic for light conversation.'

The Dowager gave a little bark of laughter, and Catherine looked away, feeling a grim smile twist at her lips until she hastily concealed it. Captain Moreton had obviously decided that she was some horrible combination of dreary dowd and babbling blue-stocking. She wondered why the fact that he considered her utterly boring should prove so painful, but there was no time to pursue the thought.

Lord and Lady Moreton arrived full of apologies for their tardy appearance. Lady Moreton's aquamarine eyes glowed with brilliant colour, and her cheeks were flushed a rosy pink that owed nothing to artifice. Lord Moreton's gaze followed her with lazy appreciation.

It was all too obvious, Catherine thought, that her host and hostess were deeply in love, and she felt a pang of envy so piercing that it was physically painful. She glanced in the

Captain's direction and saw that he, too, was looking at Diane Moreton. There was a momentary anguish in his hard features that astonished her by its intensity. She turned away, and the loneliness of her situation suddenly overwhelmed her. Oh Matthew, she thought, why did you have to become so sick so soon? Why did you have to die when I need you so badly? She blinked away tears she was unwilling to shed, and stared into the middle distance, but her gaze was caught and held by the imperious stare of the Dowager.

'Come and sit next to me,' she said, patting the sofa cushion. 'So what do you think of my younger son?' she asked, quietly, as soon as Catherine was seated.

'He is . . . I am sure he is most agreeable. In looks, he is very like his brother, is he not?' She managed to sound convincingly casual when she added, 'They are both extremely handsome men.'

'Even though I am their mother, I can't help but agree with you! They are both good-looking, and at a distance they could almost be mistaken for twins.'

'Except for the Captain's eye-patch, of course.'

'Yes, except for the eye-patch.' For a moment the Dowager seemed lost in some memory, then her eyes lit up with a twinkle as she returned her thoughts to the present.

'They may look similar, but they are nothing alike in their characters. Edward spent many years abroad in the diplomatic service when he was a younger man, but basically he is a true English nobleman, with roots that lie deep in his native soil. He has no wish to visit America and learn how a taggle of yokels managed to defeat the might of the British army. He doesn't want to go to China and see a civilisation that my husband claimed was in some ways more advanced than our own. He doesn't much care what happens in Persia or India—or even in Europe, as long as it doesn't adversely affect the peace and prosperity of England.'

'He is very knowledgeable about foreign affairs, however.'

'Indeed he is, and his knowledge once made him cynical. But Diane has managed to melt most of the ice round his heart. Edward loves his wife and his children with a devo-

tion I would not have believed possible. I have decided that
there is nobody more sentimental than a reformed cynic.'

'Captain Moreton also appears . . . That is to say, do you
find your younger son equally cynical?'

'William has changed a great deal over the past few years.
He was an open-hearted young man when he returned to
England after Waterloo, full of friendliness and courage,
even though he was in great pain.'

'You must have been very proud of him?'

'Well, as a matter of fact, most of the time his brother and
I were in a state of advanced irritation! He had no understanding of women at all, you know, and he was forever on
the verge of offering for some female who was all beauty
and no brains. For a year or so, Edward was almost fully
occupied in disentangling his brother from unsuitable be-
trothals. It was as though all William's common sense was
buried in his sword-arm. There were times when we were
convinced he would get himself married off before he grew
up enough to find out what it was that he really wanted in a
wife.'

The Dowager stared into the fire, and then gave a little
snort of laughter. 'He was the sort of young man who felt
compelled to write terrible verses extolling the perfection
of his adored one's eyebrows.'

'He certainly no longer gives any impression of having a
romantic nature,' Catherine said with uncharacteristic tart-
ness. 'And he looks as if he understands women much too
well to waste time penning poems to their eyebrows.'

The Dowager glanced at her goddaughter's unusually
flushed cheeks, and smiled.

'Oh, now that he has finally grown up, I'm sure he
considers himself a devil of a cynic, and a bit of a rake into
the bargain. If he wrote a poem today, I'm sure it would be
only because he thought it a convenient method of seduction. He probably considers love an emotion felt only
by fools—and he, of course, is determined never to be
foolish.'

'A woman, surely, wants to feel loved by her suitor? I
imagine Captain Moreton is in danger of becoming quite
lonely.'

'That's as may be. You are young and still very innocent, Catherine, despite everything you have undergone.' The Dowager pulled herself up short and seemed to alter the thrust of her remarks.

'Speaking as an old woman who has observed the folly of human behaviour for a great many years, I have no doubt that most women find my son's current attitude well-nigh irresistible. To be a successful rake, you know, it is necessary to be attractive to women. Any female worth her salt naturally imagines that *she* will be the one woman capable of reforming him—the one woman capable of capturing his elusive heart.'

'I'm sure any sensible woman would know better than to imagine anything so unlikely.' To her dismay, Catherine realised that her voice sounded a great deal more caustic than she intended but, for some reason, the Dowager merely seemed amused.

'My son imagines that he spent seven years in the wilderness because his heart was broken,' she said coolly. 'In fact, he spent the last three years wandering round South America because he thrives on the challenge of conquering the unknown. He will need a very special sort of woman to be his wife. I have recently come to the conclusion that he will be just like his father. That means he will be quite likely to suggest a voyage into the back of beyond even when he is fifty and supposed to be relaxing in his carpet slippers.'

Lord Moreton chose this moment to interrupt their tête-à-tête. 'You are looking very well pleased with yourself, Mama. What scheme are you cooking up now?'

'I never scheme,' the Dowager said loftily. 'Scheming is invariably vulgar. I am merely enjoying Catherine's company. It's a rare treat for me to have somebody residing in this house who is sufficiently educated to understand all of my conversation.'

'I refuse to take offence at such an obvious insult, Mama.' Lord Moreton grinned cheerfully at his mother and extended both of his arms. 'Come, ladies! If you will do me the honour, I shall escort you into the dining-room.'

Catherine sprang to her feet with alacrity. For the first time since coming to Wellespont, she was looking forward to eating dinner. Anger with Captain Moreton, she decided, had given an unusually sharp edge to her appetite. She attacked her meal with an almost forgotten energy, feeling her irritation mount every time the Captain tossed one of his seemingly casual comments in her direction. She was all too aware of his subtle mockery, even if the other people round the table appeared to be entirely deceived by the superficial courtesy of his manner.

It was not until she was undressed and almost ready for bed that she stopped to ask herself precisely what the Captain had done or said that was so aggravating. A great many things, she decided, pulling her brush through her hair with considerable violence. His behaviour had been intolerable, even though she could not precisely list his offences.

By the time she climbed into bed, she had convinced herself that Captain Moreton deserved to meet a humiliating fate, preferably in the shape of a woman who would tame the mocking glint in his eye and humble his arrogant spirit. Unfortunately, however, her basic honesty of character could not be completely banished and she could not convince herself that he merited a fate quite as unpleasant as the one designed by her stepmother. He had done nothing to justify being trapped into a marriage he had not sought and did not want. Especially with a woman he appeared to despise.

At that final thought, Catherine's anger drained away as swiftly as it had come, leaving her wide awake and restless in the emptiness of her bed. She sighed, pummelling the non-existent lumps in her soft pillow. In the end, she sat up and lit a candle, dragging a book on to her knees.

It looked as if sleep – that solace of the innocent – was once again going to prove elusive.

CHAPTER
FOUR

IT WAS long after midnight before she fell asleep, but Catherine was not particularly surprised when she awoke early the next morning. Since coming to Wellespont, sleep had been a prize not easily attained. After about an hour of restless tossing, she got up and walked to the window. The sun had begun to tint the eastern quarter of the horizon with a clear, golden light. It was going to be a beautiful day, she thought, and the prospect of a brisk canter before breakfast suddenly seemed irresistible.

She washed in the jug of cold water left on her marble dressing-stand, splashing her face vigorously until she felt it tingle with vitality. With the ease of long practice, she pulled and pushed herself unaided into her riding-habit, adjusting the lace jabot of her shirt with a touch of impatience. Frills and furbelows would be a waste of time this morning. She bundled her hair carelessly into a twist on top of her head, not caring that several wisps straggled about her cheeks and neck. No one except stable-hands and servants would have to get up as early as this.

Her riding-habit, tailored out of leaf-green worsted wool, was almost three years old, and it no longer fitted very well since she had lost a great deal of weight. Nevertheless, its severe style flattered the tall, slender lines of her body a great deal more than the fussy dresses selected by her stepmother. Best of all, she felt comfortable wearing it.

Without pausing to glance in the mirror, she picked up the trailing skirt and tiptoed quickly down the main staircase, stopping in the kitchens to beg a couple of dried apples from the pantry-maid. As soon as she reached the freedom of the gardens, she drew in a deep breath of dew-sparkled air and ran along the path to the stables. It felt wonderful to be out of the house.

She was panting, her cheeks glowing with colour, when she finally reached the paddocks. One of the grooms was filling a bucket at the pump outside the stable and she asked him to saddle her favourite gelding.

He tugged at his forelock. 'I'll be on to it directly, Lady Catherine.'

Smiling her thanks, she turned in the direction of Midnight's stall. She had seen Midnight's foal only hours after it was born, and looked forward to learning how it was doing. She walked into the stable, whistling softly through her teeth, but drew up short, her cheerful, unladylike whistle coming to an abrupt halt when she realised that she was not alone. A tall, commanding figure was already standing in the mare's stall.

'Captain Moreton! What are you doing here?'

'I'm waiting for the grooms to saddle my horse, Lady Catherine.'

'You're going for a ride? *Now?*'

It was a foolish question, and she cursed herself for the way she always managed to sound so silly whenever she spoke to him. He inclined his head with a derisive courtesy that made her cheeks burn.

'That is usually why one asks a groom to saddle one's horse, Lady Catherine.'

'Yes, yes of course.' She swallowed hard. 'I've brought an apple for Midnight.'

'I'm sure she would enjoy it. Why not give it to her?'

'Yes, I will.' She walked into the stall, taking care not to brush against any part of his body, even though it was hard to avoid him in the narrow confines. She straightened out her palm so that the mare could take the titbit, then edged out as soon as she could.

Her scuttling progress must have looked remarkably similar to that of a wounded crab, she thought, wondering why she always appeared either awkward or feeble-minded when she was with the Captain. It was probably the effect of her guilty conscience, as she felt her mouth twist into a hard smile that was oddly at variance with the trembling softness of her lips. There seemed little doubt that Captain Moreton considered her monumentally unattractive—so unattractive that he would probably have to be discovered naked in her bed before he would agree to marry her.

And there was no way in the world that he was ever going to find himself in her bed! Quite apart from the fact that she would never invite him there, she was sure he would not accept an invitation. Her smile faded into bleakness. So much for her stepmother's brilliant plans. So much for the future happiness of her sister.

As she walked back to the main door of the stable, she wished that the groom would bring her horse and yet dreaded that she would inevitably have to ride with the Captain. What on earth were they going to talk about, when he so obviously disliked her? And did she have any right to try to alter his unfavourable impression?

'I have found, since my return, that I am usually the only one in the family who is up at this hour of the morning.'

It was almost a relief when Captain Moreton's voice broke into the silence. He had strolled out of the stable and propped himself comfortably against a wooden fence-post, moving so quietly that she had been unaware of his arrival.

'Are you always such an early riser, Lady Catherine?'

'In recent months I have been. I enjoy riding before breakfast, and so did my . . . that is to say, so do my younger sisters.'

'During the past few years, I have worked while the sun shone and slept as soon as it was dark. It has certainly made a change from the habits I acquired in fashionable London.'

'I have never been to London,' Catherine said. 'I suspect one is supposed to be scornful of the endless round of fashionable frivolity, but I confess that I should love to go there.'

'Did you not enjoy the usual Season when you came out?'

She turned away, biting her lip. 'No. There were several reasons . . . My mother died . . .'

'I'm sorry. But surely it's not too late to make up for lost time? You are no longer in mourning, so there is no reason why you should not enjoy everything that London has to offer.'

'I suppose it might be possible. But the Earl, my father, feels that in the circumstances . . .'

The grooms arrived at that moment, leading out two

frisky horses, and Catherine was saved the necessity of giving any more detailed reply.

She knew that the Captain was watching her closely while she mounted, and his attention was still fixed upon her when he directed their horses into a sedate trot down the path that led in the direction of the woods. For once, there was no trace of mockery in his voice as he chatted amiably about nothing in particular, and she was unexpectedly touched when she realised that he was quietly gauging the level of her riding skills. He had no intention of humiliating her by setting a bruising pace if she could not keep up with him. They skirted the small copse at a slow canter; then he recognised her ability to keep up with him and he allowed his mount to lengthen its stride into a modest gallop.

'Do you know the track to the Westhill lookout?' he called.

'Yes, I've ridden there two or three times before.'

He nodded, allowing his horse to increase his speed, and with a burst of sudden exhilaration, Catherine urged hers forward. She felt the wind buffet her face and snatch at her breath as she headed towards the open country at the edge of the horizon. Her heartbeat quickened with excitement.

She felt rather than saw the admiring glance the Captain shot in her direction, and suddenly it seemed as though the wearisome burden of grief was beginning to slip from her shoulders. Her stepmother had been right, she thought with a trace of astonishment. She *had* been cooped up in Richland Towers for too long. She *had* needed a change of scene. She *had* needed some outside influence to prevent her from brooding endlessly over Matthew's final illness. How angry the Countess would be if she knew her lies were not lies at all and that her stepdaughter was actually enjoying herself!

The thought struck Catherine as irresistibly funny, and she laughed out loud. When she flicked her whip lightly against her horse's withers, he rushed forward with an intoxicating surge of speed. Her laughter floated back behind her, carried away on the wind, but her cheeks, she suddenly realised, were wet with tears.

She heard the sound of the Captain's horse pounding fast

and hard behind her, and she urged her gelding to even greater speed, panic-stricken at the thought that her companion might notice. It would be intolerable if he knew that she wept. It would be even worse if he attempted to comfort her. She took the gelding over a low stone wall, permitting almost no interruption to the reckless speed of his gallop. Her hat flew from her head when they jumped across a narrow stream, and the pins tumbled out of her chignon, loosening her hair into a rippling cloud of wild silk that whipped across her cheeks then blew out behind her.

Only the realisation that her mount was beginning to shudder with the strain of maintaining his speed finally returned some sanity to her behaviour. Reluctantly she tightened the reins until the gelding slackened his pace and finally came to a complete halt just at the crest of a low, tree-shaded rise.

It was only a few seconds before Captain Moreton drew up his mount beside her. He held her riding-hat in one hand, and offered it to her in silence.

'Thank you.' She accepted it without meeting his gaze, acutely conscious of the barbaric disorder of her hair, of the beads of sweat gathering on her forehead, of the rapid rise and fall of her breasts as she struggled for breath. 'How did you find it?'

'It fell into a bush. I picked it up with my crop as I rode by.'

At the speeds they had been travelling, it must have been no mean feat of horsemanship. 'Well . . . Thank you.'

He shrugged. 'You ride superbly well.'

'Thank you,' she said again. She held the reins with one hand, using the other to tug ineffectually at her tangled mass of hair. His praise pleased her more than she wanted to admit, even to herself.

Captain Moreton sprang out of the saddle, looping his reins over the branch of a near-by tree.

'You had better let me help you to dismount. The wind will be behind us when we return, and you won't be able to see properly unless you tie your hair out of your eyes.'

She was grateful that he did not reproach her for the wildness of her ride, grateful that he did not question her reasons for behaving with such a complete lack of decorum. He held out his arms and she rested her hands on his shoulders. Beneath her fingers, she felt the ripple of solid muscles which could have been developed only by years of hard physical labour. He lifted her easily from her horse, his hands slipping round her waist to steady her as she slid to the ground.

'Thank you,' she said, wondering why her voice sounded so husky. 'You may . . . You may release me now. I am in no danger of falling.'

He released her at once, but it was unexpectedly difficult to catch her breath; the headlong gallop must have exhausted her more than she had thought. Her breathing became a fraction easier as soon as the Captain turned away to admire the view over the Wellespont estate. She walked a little distance away from him, and turning her back, began to twist her hair into a long, neat plait.

'Here,' he said, as soon as she had finished the braid. His voice was very near and she jumped a little, startled to discover that he was so close and that, after all, he must have been watching her.

Turning round, she saw that he was holding out a length of string.

'It isn't very elegant, I'm afraid, but it's all that I have. You will need something to tie the end of your plait.'

She reached out to accept his offering, and entirely against her will, her gaze lifted up until she met his eyes. At the quick rasp of his indrawn breath, she experienced a perverse moment of feminine triumph. It was suddenly good to know that whatever else had changed during the past two years, the effect of her eyes was still as dramatic as ever.

'You have green eyes,' Captain Moreton said. 'They are the colour of the brightest emeralds.' His voice was prosaic and emotionless, and it certainly did not sound as if he was paying a conventional compliment.

'So I have been told.' By some miracle she managed to keep her voice as expressionless as his. When she was younger, when she had been launched into the local Wilt-shire society, a dozen flirtatious swains had compared her eyes to emeralds, so she had no idea why the Captain's flat statement should make her knees shake and her heart beat suffocatingly fast.

She turned away from him once again and tied up her plait with the string, then attempted to coil the long braid round her head so that her riding-hat would fit on top. It was an impossible task, particularly since her fingers continued their inexplicable shaking. In the end she gave up and allowed the plait to hang down her back, leaving her hat perched precariously on the top of her head.

She smoothed a non-existent crease out of her jacket, brushed non-existent leaves from her skirt, and told herself that she wasn't going to look at the Captain again. Two seconds later her eyes had somehow swivelled in his direction.

He was smiling, with none of the mockery she had learned to dread lingering behind his smile.

'It is certainly a novel style,' he said, nodding towards her hat. 'But I cannot believe it will ever catch on.'

Smiling back at him, her eyes lit up with a faint, irrational happiness, but she was bewildered when she saw the sudden tightening of his mouth. Even before he turned away, she knew that the warmth had entirely faded from his expression.

'We have been gone far too long,' he said abruptly. 'The grooms will soon imagine there has been an accident and come in search of us. Allow me to help you back on to your mount, Lady Catherine.'

'Of course.' She was pleased to find that her coolness matched his own. She walked over to the gelding and he threw her into the saddle with the ease of a man accustomed to lifting far greater burdens than her light weight. He did not look at her again before he vaulted lightly into his own saddle.

He made no attempt to start up a conversation as they rode back towards the house, but she was determined not to allow the ride to proceed in silence. For some reason she could not bear the thought that Captain Moreton might consider her tedious company. She searched for a neutral topic that would not be likely to lead them on to dangerous conversational ground, and eventually settled on the subject of his years in South America.

'Would you tell me about your travels, Captain Moreton? I have often longed to journey outside England, and it would be a great pleasure for me to hear something about what you have seen. You must have observed much that is unique.'

'I travelled mostly in Spanish South America,' he said, 'although I have spent the last few months in Brazil, to the east. I am not sure what you would wish me to tell you about, Lady Catherine.'

'Tell me if the Spanish people who live in South America are the same as the Spaniards who live in Spain. Tell me if the Brazilian countryside looks like English countryside, or like Italy, or like the mountains of Switzerland. In fact, you may tell me almost anything and know that I shall be interested.'

'The scenery is nothing like any of the places you have mentioned. It is either more lush or more barren and it is nearly always more spectacular—more frightening, because it is as yet mostly untamed by man. The Spanish colonies I visited were a curious mixture of typically Spanish culture and vast wilderness, empty spaces greater than anything we Europeans can imagine until we have seen it for ourselves.'

'And what of the natives, the Indians? Do they live in tribes as they do in North America?'

'It depends. In Brazil, the Indians remain hidden in the jungles of the north. Further to the west, many of the Indians are little more than serfs, labouring in bondage to their Spanish overlords. Those Indians who still live free in the forests or the mountains are usually considered to be savages. They would undoubtedly prefer to kill any white man first and ask questions afterwards.'

'That is not surprising, perhaps, if they have seen their brothers and cousins carried off into virtual slavery.'

He looked at her in feigned amazement. 'That is a shocking statement, Lady Catherine. Your views would not be popular with most of the European colonists. When they slaughter a group of Indians, everyone agrees that their action is justifiable self-defence. When Indians wipe out a group of Europeans, however, it is naturally considered the vilest of murders.'

'I read an account once, written by a Frenchman who had joined a Spanish mission in Mexico. He wrote of magnificent temples built by the Indians for their worship of the sun, but he described their religion as cruel and brutal.'

'Yes, it probably was. But the Indians did not all share the same religion, you know. Explorers have discovered traces of several vanished civilisations, and there is convincing evidence that it was only the Aztecs who practised human sacrifice. There are rumours of whole cities, not built by the Aztecs, buried beneath the creeping foliage of the jungle, or lost high on the slopes of unclimbable mountains.'

'It is difficult to imagine how a city could become lost,' Catherine said. 'The buildings of ancient Rome and ancient Athens may have crumbled, but we still know exactly where they stood, and the walls of many buildings survive even to this day.'

'You would find it easier to understand if you had seen the incredible rate of growth that takes place in the rainforests. If the inhabitants of a city abandoned their homes for even a dozen years or so, by the time they tried to return, they might well find that the routes back were completely obliterated by the growth of the natural vegetation.'

'Are there no Europeans interested in leading expeditions into the jungle? Only think how exciting it would be to discover a whole city lost beneath a tangle of leaves!'

'There are more things to contend with in the jungle than an over-abundance of leaves, Lady Catherine.' The Captain's voice was annoyingly patronising. 'There are snakes, and poisonous plants of every description. There are insects whose bites will drive you insane with irritation, or they may be lethal. There are unfriendly Indians, impenetrable creepers, and impassable gorges. There is intolerable heat and incessant humidity. Exploring the jungle is not quite as easy as planning an afternoon's excursion to one of Suffolk's local beauty-spots.'

'I meant only that the rewards of such an expedition would be very great. Naturally, I did not mean to imply that it would be simple.'

'I'm sure you did not.' She was not looking at him, but she heard the laughter creep back into his voice.

'Besides, most of the European population do not have time to waste in mounting anything as boring as an expedition. They are all fully occupied in planning their next revolution.'

'I would not have thought that that would preclude other interests,' she retorted stiffly. 'One presumably plans a revolution only once, and it is either successful or it is not.'

'Ah, that is where you are mistaken, Lady Catherine. To the colonists living in South America, plotting revolution against Spain and, to a lesser extent Portugal, is a fascinating part of everyday life. They pursue their goal of freedom from the mother country with great enthusiasm for a month or so, then an important saint's day comes along and they forget about it for a week or so while they celebrate the fiesta. Eventually some silly new order will arrive from Madrid or Lisbon—and the orders sent out from both those cities are invariably silly—and they will remember that they are furious with their king and his government. They will then call a meeting of all their friends and set about developing a wonderful new scheme for winning their freedom. One day, someone will come along and force them to plan so that they achieve their objective. I have no idea what the governing class will then do to entertain itself.'

'It will invent opposing factions,' Catherine said promptly. 'Then they can have revolutions against each other.'

He threw back his head and laughed heartily. 'Of course! Why did I not think of that?'

'Because you think like a man. Masculine logic is invaluable in certain situations, but limiting in others. A woman's mind does not necessarily work within the same bounds as a man's.'

'No,' he said, and she detected a definite note of

bitterness in his voice. 'That is certainly true. And it is a lesson that most young men take too long to learn.'

'What about young women?' she asked, unable to restrain her curiosity, even though she suspected it would not be wise to probe into his opinions about women. 'Do they not have to learn the same lesson about the opposite sex?'

'I think not. Women, I have concluded, are born with the power to deceive the gullible males who surround them. It is a fortunate man who can armour himself against the wiles of the female sex.'

'From the tone of your voice, I conclude that you consider yourself fully armoured?'

The look he turned upon her was devastating in its combination of weariness and cynicism. 'Oh yes, Lady Catherine, I have definitely learned my lesson! It required a certain degree of ruthlessness on the part of my instructor, because I was a thick-witted young man. But I pride myself upon the fact that, although I was rather slow, I finally learned my lesson very well.'

'I think that you do not much enjoy the company of women, Captain Moreton.'

'On the contrary, I enjoy everything it is within their power to offer! But I do not torment myself with expecting what is not within their natures to give. The feminine definitions of honour and loyalty and truthfulness are very different from their male counterparts.'

She drew in a quick breath. 'You do have an unflattering view of women, Captain!'

He smiled without mirth. 'Not at all. Believe me, my lady, I am a devoted admirer of the charms of your sex.'

They rounded a final bend in the path as he spoke, and the house came immediately into sight. Their discussion halted as they cantered up to the stable, where a groom was already waiting to receive their horses.

Captain Moreton sprang quickly from the saddle, offering his assistance to Catherine without words. She accepted his offer in equal silence, and it was only as the groom led the horses out of sight that he spoke.

'If you should happen to wake up early tomorrow

morning, Lady Catherine, I should enjoy the pleasure of your company for another ride.'

She did not allow herself to think of the implications of his invitation, and was careful not to think of the implications of her reply.

'Thank you. If I should happen to waken early, I shall look forward to joining you.'

They walked up to the house without saying anything further. But they both knew that, the next morning, she would be there and he would be waiting.

CHAPTER
FIVE

CATHERINE WAS up even earlier than usual the next morning, but when she arrived at the stables, Captain Moreton was already waiting for her. She nodded to him as they exchanged greetings, a sudden excitement flaring deep inside her.

'I have asked the grooms to saddle Blaze for you,' he said. 'I thought it would save time for us.'

'Thank you. He and I usually deal well together.' She did not ask why the Captain had been so certain that she would come, and a small silence fell between them.

The clatter of hoofs on the paved stable-yard announced the arrival of their horses. One of the grooms led Blaze to the block, and the Captain, with impersonal courtesy, helped her to mount. He vaulted unaided on to his own horse, and by mutual consent they set off along the well-trodden path they had followed the previous day.

They guided the horses round the small copse that marked the western boundary of the park, cantering slowly as they moved out of the gardens and on to the gently rolling farmland of the estate. Flocks of sheep grazed in the distance and the early morning sun was warm on Catherine's back. As they rode across the fields, the terrain became rougher, demanding more skill from the riders, and sheer physical pleasure soon overcame all her other feelings. She gave a tiny sigh of utter content, and smiled at the Captain.

'Wellespont is magnificent at this time of the year, isn't it?' she said.

'Yes, but I find it beautiful at almost any season. It is the range of colour that I love so much. The delicate green of early spring when the leaves look like a soft haze against the horizon. The yellow and blue of wild flowers in the early summer. In autumn the beeches seem on fire in the sunlight. And in winter, if it happens to snow heavily, there is a magic moment early in the morning when time stands still and there is nothing left in the world but white hills and silence.'

'And yet you have chosen to remain out of England for a very long time, Captain Moreton.'

It was a moment before he answered her, then he laughed lightly. 'Ah, I'm afraid you have caught me out, Lady Catherine. The truth is that after a few months of cosy comfort in England, the urge to travel to wilder places invariably overwhelms me.'

'The wildflowers, perhaps, are all the more appealing because you often see them only in memory.'

He glanced at her, his expression startled. 'Perhaps.'

'Will you tell me something about your experiences on St Helena? Your nephews have already regaled me with several exciting stories, and I would like to hear a first-hand account. According to young William, you personally defeated at least half a dozen dastardly French plots to rescue Napoleon.'

'The truth of the situation is far otherwise.' The Captain's expression was guarded and his voice unexpectedly tight. 'Most of the plots to rescue the Emperor were ill conceived, badly executed and easily discovered. It was my brother who foiled the only scheme that came anywhere close to achieving its objective.'

'I didn't know that Lord Moreton had been involved in guarding Napoleon Bonaparte.'

'My brother was not officially involved, Lady Catherine. His interest was of a . . . more personal nature.'

'It all sounds very mysterious,' she said, sensing his tension but unable to resist asking another question. 'Were you already on St Helena when this plot was discovered? If so, you were probably able to help your brother.'

'You are mistaken, I'm afraid. Far from helping Edward, my absurd antics almost guaranteed Napoleon's escape. The conspirators, in fact, counted upon my weaknesses in formulating their plan.'

She could hear the bitterness in his voice, and wondered at the cause. She knew how highly he had been praised for his outstanding conduct as commander of the troops on St

Helena, and found it hard to accept that he had really been as foolish as he claimed. But, although she was curious, she had no desire to probe into areas of his life that he wished to keep secret. She valued her own privacy too much to intrude into other people's, so she instinctively switched the direction of the conversation.

'It's difficult to believe that it is more than a year since Napoleon died,' she said. 'He came to power at such an early age that it sometimes seemed as if he would threaten the peace of Europe for ever.'

'Yes, that's true. And it's especially hard for me to accept his death, since I knew him personally. Despite his ill-health, he always seemed vital and full of energy. He was only a small man, you know, and not particularly handsome. And yet, when one was in his presence, he dominated the room by sheer force of his personality. He was one of those rare men who had no need to speak in order to command attention. His silence was almost as riveting as his conversation. We British officers were always required to wait in a small ante-room when he received us at Longwood, and one could feel the vibrations of his presence as soon as he stepped through the door from his private quarters.'

'You sound, Captain, as if you were deeply impressed by your prisoner.'

'To a certain extent, I was. He was misguided in his military aims, and his conquests devastated many parts of Europe. Nevertheless, I believe future generations will consider him a great man. He took over the government of France when the country hovered at the very brink of disaster, and he managed to impose order and a measure of justice for the ordinary citizen. France might well have destroyed herself had it not been for Napoleon.'

'Did you have much opportunity to speak with him while you were on the island?'

'Not as much as I would have liked. The Governor, Sir Hudson Lowe, did not encourage visits between the French and the English.' The Captain suddenly grinned. 'I think he suspected Napoleon of possessing supernatural powers. He was convinced that if any of us spoke to our prisoner more than two or three times, he would somehow convert us all into Napoleonic supporters.'

'One must sympathise a little with the Governor. You have already confessed how impressed you were after only a few meetings, and I have heard that his manner could persuade the most unlikely people into championing his cause.'

'Yes. His success in winning the support of the French nobility is remarkable, and almost inexplicable in logical terms. However, I personally was never in any danger of forgetting that, in pursuit of his own grandiose vision, he loosed twenty years of brutal war upon the peoples of Europe.'

'We should not forget that he also gave many European peasants their first taste of civil justice and the rule of law,' she replied. 'Emperors and kings do not always need to wage war in order to be unjust to their subjects.'

'Be careful, Lady Catherine!' The Captain smiled at her with teasing warmth. 'Yesterday you defended the cause of the captive South American Indians. Today you defend the cause of the monstrous Bonaparte. I am almost afraid to think whom you will defend tomorrow!'

Her answering smile was rueful. 'Probably somebody entirely unsuitable! The Irish rebels, perhaps, or the Lancashire loom-breakers. I'm afraid, Captain, that I have never been good at drawing-room conversation. My mother shared her love of Classical studies with all three of her daughters and encouraged us to think for ourselves. I sometimes feel that she bequeathed us a burdensome legacy. Ladies of fashion are not supposed to think. Their sensibilities are considered too delicate to sustain rational thought for more than a few seconds at a time.'

His gaze was gently mocking as he looked at her. 'You shouldn't despair, Lady Catherine! Even the best of educations is not an insuperable handicap to the determined young lady. You need only the polish of a London Season to set you to rights. I guarantee that after a few weeks in town you will be able to shudder at the mere mention of Napoleon's name. You will know how to look suitably bewildered if anybody mentions his Code of Law, and you will look adorably vague if a gentleman is crass enough to mention the savages of South America in your presence. You will know that a Greek is somebody who cheats at cards, not a citizen of an ancient civilisation. And you will never exercise your own judgment except on important occasions, such as when you are purchasing a new bonnet. It is amazing, you know, how a London Season adds gloss to the dreariest of blue-stockings or the most gauche of country bumpkins.'

She laughed, her green eyes lighting up in appreciation of his dry humour. 'I'm not likely to have a London Season, Captain Moreton, so I shall have to take your word as to its beneficial effects. And you must console yourself with the thought that although you are condemned to spend the morning with a wearisome country bumpkin, at least I am able to ride!'

She spurred her horse into a gallop. 'I shall race you to the thicket at the crest of the rise! And the loser must agree to pay some dreadful penalty chosen by the winner!'

Her voice floated back over her shoulder as Blaze responded willingly to her skilful urging. A low hedge separated one field from the next and she took the gelding over it, exhilarated by his easy movement beneath her. When she arrived at the top of the small hill she was panting, flushed and triumphant. She wheeled her mount, and saw the Captain draw rein. His expression was enigmatic as he gazed down at her, and inexplicably she felt her flush deepen. Her teasing claim of victory died unspoken in her throat, and her surroundings faded away until the world seemed to contain nothing save herself and her companion.

'That was well done,' he said, after a silence that seemed to last for ever. 'You ride magnificently, my lady.'

'But you could have beaten me if you had wished to do so.' She realised the truth even as she spoke the words.

'Perhaps, but not easily.' When she did not reply, he swung his horse round, moving into the shade of the oak trees. 'I confess that I am curious to discover my penalty, Lady Catherine. What is it to be? Must I slay dragons? Or capture gorgons? More terrible yet, must I eat a whole portion of Mama's special recipe cheese curds?'

She pulled her crop through her gloved fingers. 'Nothing as dreadful as that, I think. Merely that some time this week you must tell me the story of how you discovered emeralds in the middle of the South American jungle.'

His mouth quirked. 'That is a heavy penalty indeed. So far, by dint of looking mysterious and avoiding direct questions, I have managed to convey the impression that my discovery required great skill and feats of outrageous daring. The true story reveals that I was merely extremely lucky.'

'You could always lie just a little,' she said. 'I promise not to look too hard for inconsistencies in your tale.'

'It is a tempting thought,' he said. 'Yes, I think I shall spend the hour before I fall asleep tonight concocting a story that casts me in a suitably heroic light.'

She had the strangest impression that the words they spoke had little to do with the conversation they were actually conducting. It was an uncomfortable impression that left her heart pounding and her skin hot. She was relieved when he flicked his mount lightly with his riding-crop and moved ahead of her.

'Shall we walk the horses so that they don't take a chill?' he asked.

'Yes, of course. We should do that at once.' She tucked a stray wisp of hair firmly under her hat, and the hammering of her heart gradually slowed to a more normal pace. She swung her gelding into step alongside the Captain's, and they headed in the direction of the stables.

They did not hurry on the return journey. Their conversation roamed over a variety of subjects, touching lightly on one topic before leaping to the next. It was late, later than Catherine had imagined it could be, when they finally drew their horses to a halt outside the stables.

Captain Moreton helped her to dismount.

'If you come a little earlier again tomorrow morning, my lady, we could ride as far as Moreton Grove. It is a long ride but a pleasant one, and in a direction you may not yet have explored.'

She had arrived at the stables at seven o'clock that morning and they had ridden for two and a half hours. Any earlier start and any longer ride was pushing the bounds of propriety to their limits and beyond.

She stroked Blaze on his chestnut muzzle, staring at the white star above his nose as though she had never seen it before. 'A ride to Moreton Grove would be very agreeable,' she said, inexplicably. 'I shall look forward to it if the weather holds fine.'

'It will be fine, I can guarantee it. Tom, our shepherd, told me yesterday that we are going to have a full week of sunshine, and his predictions are never wrong.'

A renewed tightness in her throat made her swallow hard. 'Then I shall be here early tomorrow morning, Captain Moreton.'

'I shall be waiting,' he said softly. 'You had better hurry back to the house, my lady, otherwise you will miss breakfast.'

'You are not returning to the house?'

'I shall stay here to supervise the care of the horses. Until this evening, Lady Catherine.'

The Dowager was eating coddled eggs served with unsweetened curds of goat's milk when Catherine came downstairs to breakfast. She politely declined her godmother's offer of a similar meal, even managing to avoid wrinkling her nose at the prospect. When she had finished her coffee and toast, the Dowager suggested that the two of them should spend the remainder of the morning translating a volume of epic Greek verse, and Catherine willingly agreed.

Except on those rare occasions when she could be persuaded to go on calls or receive visitors, the Dowager always retired to the comfort of her own rooms during the afternoon. Catherine, finding herself at a loose end, decided to follow her godmother's example. She went up and lay on the chaise-longue, intending to read, but months of near exhaustion caught up with her and she did not wake until her maid came in to dress her for dinner.

'The rest has done you good,' Mary said, as soon as she entered the bedroom. 'You have colour in your cheeks, my lady.'

'It's probably sunburn. I was riding this morning and the sun was strong for the first time since I arrived here. If I'm not careful, I shall become freckled.'

'You never get freckles,' Mary said. 'You have a perfect complexion if you would only wear something that shows it to advantage.'

Catherine's mouth twisted into an unladylike grimace, but she did not reply, and the maid sighed. Sometimes she wondered if her mistress was ever going to return to the lively, cheerful young girl she had been only two years earlier. 'Which dress are you going to wear tonight, my lady?' she asked. 'You wore the white silk last night, and the silver gauze over white satin the night before.'

'I don't know, Mary. All my clothes displease me so much that I can hardly bear to put any of them on.'

The maid looked at her sharply, then walked over to the wardrobe and rustled through the hideous collection of evening gowns that the Countess of Richland had provided for her stepdaughter. Reluctantly, she held up a pale pink robe with a soft peach-coloured petticoat. The fabric was pretty, but the dress was trimmed with ungainly ruffles round the hem, and the neckline was liberally adorned with satin ruching and artificial silk rosebuds. Even so, it was less decorated than most of the others in Catherine's wardrobe.

'You haven't worn this one before, my lady, and the shade would be flattering to you now that you have some colour in your cheeks. And the sleeves are really quite pretty.'

'What you can see of them under all those satin frills!' Catherine viewed the dress with equal dislike. 'Is there time to take off those flowers? Maybe it would look a bit better if the neckline were plain.' She smiled wryly. 'But, really, it could hardly look worse!'

Mary's gloomy expression lightened. She was all enthusiasm as she hurried away to the sewing-room, returning in less than half an hour with the dress shorn of all its rosebuds and most of its satin ribbons.

She helped her mistress into the dress, then stood back to examine the effect. 'Well, it's a definite improvement. The flounces round the hem don't look nearly so exaggerated now that they are the only decoration. But you are too thin, my lady. There is no disguising the fact that your bones practically stick through your flesh.'

'Better to see my bones than to have my shoulders buried in a wreath of artificial roses,' Catherine remarked drily. 'This dress used to look as if I'd got my head caught at the top of a rose-bush.' She glanced at the small ormulu clock on the mantelpiece. 'You had better do my hair, Mary. We have no time for second thoughts.'

For once she made no protest when the maid arranged her hair in a soft style that revealed a subtle sheen of darker gold in among the pale flaxen strands. Mary gave a little murmur of contentment when her work was complete. 'You look more like your old self, my lady, indeed you do. And that Captain Moreton is such a handsome man.'

The sudden dark rush of colour in Catherine's cheeks owed nothing to sunburn. 'I'm late, Mary. Would you please hand me my shawl?'

Mary eyed her mistress's burning cheeks with considerable satisfaction. 'Certainly, my lady,' she said, her voice at its most prim.

Catherine was the last person to enter the drawing-room, and the quiet hum of conversation died away as she walked in, murmuring an apology. Although she had told herself not to pay any particular attention to Captain Moreton, she noticed him at once. He was standing slightly apart from the rest of his family, looking out of one of the windows. He turned as she entered the room, and for an instant their gazes locked. Neither of them spoke.

'Lady Catherine!' Diane Moreton exclaimed. 'It is wonderful to see you looking so very well,' she added, warmth replacing astonishment in her voice. 'I think our bracing Suffolk air must agree with you.'

'I think it must.' Catherine pulled her gaze away from Captain Moreton, and smiled slightly as she glanced towards the Dowager. 'Although perhaps I am merely reaping the benefits of an unexpected change in my diet. My godmother and I were so busy disputing a point of translation at luncheon today that I drank two glasses of goat's milk before I noticed what I was doing.'

Lord Moreton laughed. 'It must have been a *fascinating* dispute, Lady Catherine!'

She smiled shyly. 'Certainly. Although my godmother is so knowledgeable that she is capable of making a discarded laundry-list seem like fascinating reading.'

The butler announced dinner at that moment, and Edward offered one arm to his wife and the other to the Dowager. Catherine stood, and found Captain Moreton waiting at her side.

'Allow me to escort you, Lady Catherine,' he said.

It was one of the few direct remarks he addressed to her during the course of the evening, but the Dowager was at her most forthcoming, and kept up an endless stream of dry banter with both of her sons. With the exercise of almost superhuman will, Catherine forced all thought of her step-mother's ultimatum out of her mind and concentrated on listening to the general conversation. For the first time since her arrival at Wellespont, she managed to respond coherently to direct questions and even tossed two or three unsolicited remarks into the conversation pool. She noticed that Diane Moreton's eyes were often turned in her direction, pleasure and surprise about equally mingled in her expression. Catherine reflected with a touch of wryness that after appearing virtually an imbecile for two weeks, her perfectly ordinary conversation must, by contrast, seem positively sparkling.

When the three ladies retired to the drawing-room, the Dowager complained of a slight headache and asked to be excused.

Once they were alone, Diane smiled brightly at her guest, and launched determinedly into conversation.

'I do hope you are enjoying your stay here at Wellespont, Lady Catherine,' she said. 'I know that my mother-in-law relishes your company.'

'Wellespont is beautiful and the Dowager is a charming, witty companion. You and Lord Moreton have been the most gracious of hosts. It would be difficult for any guest not to enjoy herself, Lady Moreton.'

Diane blushed slightly. 'You are too kind. In fact, I believe Edward and I have not been as attentive as we should have been. When you first arrived, I think we were overly preoccupied with the arrival of my brother-in-law. It had been almost seven years since we last saw him, you know.'

'Yes, the Dowager explained to me that he had been on active duty on St Helena, and your sons regaled me with a marvellous collection of tales about his travels in South America. I was informed that he had ridden on an elephant and killed a tiger with his bare hands, as well as achieving such lesser feats as defeating an entire army of marauding Indian tribesmen. I'm afraid young William was extremely offended when I pointed out that there are no elephants or tigers in South America. It was several days before he would condescend to talk to me again.'

Diane laughed ruefully. 'My children have exceptionally vivid imaginations, I'm afraid. I hope young William hasn't been bothering you with his chatter?'

'Not at all. We met in Midnight's stall, waiting to see if her foal had arrived. Both your sons are delightful children and wonderful company. You and Lord Moreton must be gratified to see how sturdy they are, and how lively their intelligence.'

Diane's cheeks turned pink with pleasure. 'I think this is where I am supposed to make modest disclaimers, but I'm afraid that I cannot. My husband and I are both equally entranced by our offspring and amazed that we managed to produce such handsome young men.'

'They both look very much like their father, do they not?'

'Yes, and I am quite jealous! We are hoping that if we have a daughter this time, she will be obliging enough to bear at least some faint resemblance to me!'

Catherine looked up, smiling. 'You and Lord Moreton are expecting another child, my lady?' As she spoke, she was aware of the sound of footsteps, heralding the arrival of the two gentlemen.

There was a fractional hesitation before Diane responded, then she returned Catherine's smile, her expression suddenly radiant. 'Yes,' she said, her gaze turning instinctively towards her husband. 'Edward and I hope that our third child will arrive in October.'

Some tiny, almost imperceptible movement caused Catherine to turn in Captain Moreton's direction. A flash of—torment?—flickered briefly across his face before he wiped his features clean of any expression and walked quickly across the room to shake his brother's hand with hearty affection.

'Congratulations, Edward! You and Diane are fortunate indeed to become parents so easily.'

For an instant, Lord Moreton's gaze seemed troubled as it rested on his brother, then he smiled, his eyes crinkling with laughter as he grasped his hand. 'I have given strict instructions that this time Diane is to produce a daughter for us both to spoil. Do you think there is any chance that she may obey me?'

'Obedience is perhaps not my sister-in-law's most notable characteristic,' the Captain said lightly. 'But you can always hope that this time will prove an exception to the general rule.'

He crossed to where Diane was seated and took her hand, raising it to his lips in an elegant gesture of homage. 'My felicitations, dear sister,' he said. 'May your new child be as healthy as your two sons, as honourable as Edward —and as beautiful as you.'

'Thank you, William.' Diane's voice was little more than a whisper and Catherine, now that she was no longer totally submerged in her own problems, was aware of the undercurrents swirling dangerously. She realised that her hostess was at a loss for words, and that even Lord Moreton was not entirely comfortable. However, it was such a long time since she had deliberately put herself into the centre of any conversation that she was amazed when she heard herself speak.

'My stepmother, the Countess of Richland, is expecting the birth of her first child quite shortly. But unlike you, Lady Moreton, she hopes very much for a son. It is frustrating, is it not, that we cannot choose the gender of our offspring? Imagine how the history of our country would have been changed if King Henry VIII, for example, had been blessed with several sons.' Almost without pausing for breath, she continued, 'My youngest sister wrote to me that the flower gardens at Richland Towers were devastated by a severe hailstorm last week. We were lucky to have avoided the storm here in Suffolk, were we not?'

Diane cast Catherine a look of undisguised gratitude, and for the remainder of the evening the conversation remained on the safe topics of the weather, the summer planting and the repair of the Norman church tower in the village of Wellespont. When the tea-tray was brought in, Catherine drank her cup quickly, then excused herself on the grounds of being exceptionally tired. Despite her long afternoon nap, she was telling nothing but the truth. After months of being unable to sleep, she felt suddenly as if she could sleep for ever.

Once she was in bed, however, her sleepiness disappeared. The menacing image of her stepmother, successfully banished for almost twenty-four hours, returned to haunt her. Each day that passed brought her closer to the moment of decision: some time very soon she would have to choose either her sister's happiness or her own honour.

Her stepmother had claimed that it would be simple for Catherine to compromise the Captain. All too clearly, she now saw that her stepmother had been correct. It was amazingly easy to picture herself in some lonely spot with only Captain Moreton for company. Her horse had cast a shoe, perhaps . . . or they had ridden too far and a summer storm had overtaken them . . . She had a vivid mental picture of a grassy bank, far from Wellespont, protected by the overhang of a great oak. Dust drew its cloak around them as they waited for the storm to pass overhead. The evening air was chilly, and the Captain gathered her into his arms to protect her from the lash of the rain. His head lowered towards hers, the firm line of his mouth only inches away from her lips . . .

She jerked upright, horrified by the trend of her thoughts, and shocked by the unladylike clarity of her mental images. No virtuous woman *ever* yearned to be kissed. Even with Matthew, whom she had cared for so deeply, the passion had been exclusively on his side, a duty she had tolerated only because she loved him. Which was, of course, exactly as it should be.

Catherine rolled over and buried her face in the softness of the pillow. Her last thought, just before sleep claimed her, was that tomorrow she and Captain Moreton would spend at least four hours together. Alone.

CHAPTER
SIX

MORETON GROVE was one of the prettiest villages Catherine had ever seen. Sturdy cottages, their front steps flanked by bright flowers, were built haphazardly along four small roads that radiated out from an old stone market cross. The ruins of a medieval abbey dominated the northern end of the village, its soaring arches graceful in the early summer sunshine.

Catherine and the Captain, followed by a cluster of noisy children, led their horses through the abandoned abbey grounds, admiring the delicate tracery of ancient stonework and the perfect proportions of the vaulted ceilings. Catherine gasped with pleasure as she rounded one of the cloisters and came upon a huge stained-glass window that had somehow survived both the normal hazards of time and the calculated attacks of Cromwell's soldiers.

'I'm so glad you suggested coming here!' she said. The sun filtered through the red and purple glass, turning the ground beneath them into a shimmering rainbow of colour. 'It has been a perfect morning.'

The Captain looked at her intently before turning somewhat abruptly away. 'It has been my pleasure,' he said. 'Shall we go and find ourselves something to drink?'

The local innkeeper was able to provide them with newly-baked wheat bread and mugs of cool cider before they set out on their return journey. Catherine rode easily, unable to remember another occasion during the past year when she had felt so relaxed. 'I hope you haven't forgotten that you owe me a forfeit,' she said teasingly as they cantered the horses along a flat stretch of road about five miles from Wellespont. 'Remember that you promised to tell me how you discovered emeralds in the wilds of South America.'

'They were hidden in a cave deep in the thickest part of the rain-forest,' he said promptly. 'At least a hundred brave men had already sacrificed their lives searching for the lost path through the jungle when I came into possession of a secret map that pointed the way.'

She laughed, her green eyes sparkling. 'And just how did you happen to acquire this invaluable map, sir?'

'It was given me by a dying Indian tribesman, whose life I had nobly, but unsuccessfully, attempted to save. Naturally, the most important directions were marked on the parchment with his own blood.'

'I can tell that you were very busy last night before you fell asleep. I am sure that even young William would find this tale a little hard to swallow!'

'Then you would be quite wrong,' he said, turning to look at her. A hint of tenderness around his mouth belied the severity of his tone. 'In fact, I am indebted to my nephew for some of the most exciting details. The blood on the secret map, for example, was entirely his invention. Am I to be allowed to continue, Lady Catherine?'

'Please do. The view from the road holds little of interest for the next couple of miles, so I am delighted to be entertained.'

He continued to spin his tale of heroic nonsense, claiming feats of such outrageous derring-do that she soon found herself chuckling with a carefree warmth that, since Matthew's death, she had thought lost to her for ever.

'Now please tell me the real story,' she said when he had finished speaking. 'I am greatly interested in hearing about your travels, even if to you they sound dull. Remember that you have travelled widely, Captain Moreton, whereas I have rarely journeyed more than fifty miles from my home.'

'Even for somebody who has travelled so little, the truth of my discovery is extremely dull, but I shall give you the details if you wish for them.'

'Yes, please.'

'During my stay in South America, I became fascinated by the traces of a vanished civilisation that I found all round me. When I was in the province of La Plata, I decided to indulge myself by spending a few weeks searching for an ancient temple of the Sun God. It was reputed to be of great antiquity and considerable size, although no Europeans had actually seen it. I ventured into the high plateau, accompanied by ten competent Indian guides, but somehow we lost our way. In our efforts to return to civilisation, we eventually followed a path that seemed to me to lead higher and deeper into the mountains. The guides, however, insisted that it would eventually lead us back to the city. Since I had no idea where I was, it seemed only prudent to follow their advice. We eventually came upon the ruins of an ancient trading-post, and the entrance to the mine shaft was right there in front of our noses. Somewhat creeper-covered, it's true, but otherwise unguarded.'

'I confess I am somewhat disappointed. Were there no jungle predators or head-hunting tribal chiefs to be conquered?'

'Not a single one, I'm afraid. We discovered a dozen huge polished onyx boxes at the mouth of the shaft, each one stuffed full of emeralds. The truth is that I did not even have to dig for my fortune—it was lying on the ground, waiting to be picked up.'

'The Indians weren't superstitous about removing the emeralds from the site?'

'Not at all. They greatly admired the onyx boxes, but they placed no particular value on the jewels, and there was nothing to indicate that the site had ever been sacred ground. Besides, few of the natives have any active memory of their ancient religion; they are all converted to Christianity now.'

'Did you eventually discover the temple?'

'No, never. My guides were very worried that I might not pay them, since they had failed to find what they had promised. When we got back, I bought them each a few acres of good farmland and they considered themselves the luckiest of men. Four of them were unmarried, and they instantly became highly desirable bachelors. They were able to wed the plumpest of that season's eligible young maidens.'

'The *plumpest*?'

'Yes. In that part of the world, the menfolk measure a woman's worth in very practical terms. Slender Indian girls have a hard time catching a husband unless their dowry is unusually ample.'

Catherine laughed a little wryly. 'I suppose I must be grateful that I am not a South American Indian! There would certainly be no hope for me unless my father were the tribal chieftain!'

At that moment a dog barked loudly in the distance, and a partridge shot out of the hedgerow immediately ahead of them, flying within inches of Blaze's head. Startled by the noise and the flapping movement of the wings, the gelding reared in fright. Normally, Catherine would have had no difficulty in maintaining her balance, but her attention had been on the Captain, not on her riding, and the unexpected movement unseated her. She slithered down the side of the horse in an ignominious tangle of legs and skirt, landing at the side of the road in a pile of bracken.

Captain Moreton grabbed Blaze's reins, needing all his strength to prevent the skittering horse from stepping backwards on to Catherine's limp body. He murmured a soft, frantic command to him to remain still, then flung himself to the ground, tossing the reins of both horses over a sturdy branch of hawthorn.

He knelt beside Catherine and took one of her hands, stroking his other one gently across her face.

'Lady Catherine, can you hear me? Will you please tell me where you are hurt?'

Her eyelids fluttered, but the breath had been knocked out of her lungs and it hurt too much for her to speak. She closed her eyes, allowing herself to drift away into a comfortable, grey darkness.

She was dimly aware of Captain Moreton leaning over her, lifting her head and cradling it in the crook of his arm. Very carefully, his fingers smoothed a strand of hair out of her eyes and then, after a momentary hesitation, she felt him unfasten the buttons that closed the high neckline of her riding-habit. He did not undo many buttons before he pushed the lapels apart, reaching inside her collar to touch the pulse beating at the base of her throat. His fingers were warm and strong against her skin, and she experienced an inexplicable desire to press her lips against the hard curve of his palm. His hand moved slowly to cup her chin, and she stirred, knowing that she ought to move away but unable to summon the necessary energy. Her body seemed to sink deeper into a blissful languor the longer the Captain held her, and she could not for the life of her remember why it was imperative to open her eyes. Something to do with propriety, she thought vaguely. Nothing that was worth worrying about when it felt so good to lie in his arms.

'Catherine, for God's sake, will you answer me?' His voice shook with a new urgency. 'Can you tell me where you feel pain? I cannot move you until I know where you are injured. For heaven's sake, try to speak!'

His harsh, rapid words penetrated the warm cocoon that enveloped her. With considerable effort she forced her eyes open and found herself staring directly up at him. Dazed by the fall, and still too breathless to speak, she reached out instinctively, her fingers brushing against the black silk of his eye-patch in a hesitant caress.

Immediately his body became still and his face totally expressionless. After a minute, he disengaged his arm from beneath her head, allowing her to rest on a cushion of bracken.

'It is good to see that you have regained consciousness, Lady Catherine,' he said with extreme formality. 'Are you now able to tell me precisely where you are injured?'

Acutely embarrassed, she allowed her hand to fall back to her side, suppressing the extraordinary urge to continue stroking her fingers down the rigid line of his jaw. She seemed to be trembling inside, and her skin burned with a fierce, dry heat. Shock, she told herself with the tiny part of her brain that still functioned rationally: she was feeling the typical after-effects of shock.

'When you are able to speak,' the Captain said coolly, 'it would be helpful if you could indicate where you have been hurt.'

She finally succeeded in forcing some air into her protesting lungs. 'I am only winded.'

'That is good news. Nevertheless, you should sit up slowly, since I think you were unconscious for a little while. Allow me to assist you, my lady.'

The polite formality of his words was perfectly matched by the impersonal courtesy of his touch. His arm tightened round her waist, efficiently easing her into a sitting position.

'You had better lean against my shoulder, Lady Catherine.' He did not look at her as he spoke. 'Are you certain that you have no injuries? Your ankles, perhaps, or your wrists?'

Common sense was returning with each breath that she drew. She moved her ankles in a cautious semicircle and ran her hands swiftly down her sides, feeling for any particular soreness.

'I shall be bruised, but I don't think there is any other damage,' she said, forcing a smile. 'It will certainly teach me to keep my attention on what I am doing. If my sisters knew that I had fallen simply because my horse reared, they would never let me live down the humiliation!'

'Then we shall not tell them,' he said. He rose to his feet and extended his hands towards her. 'May I help you to stand, Lady Catherine?'

She held out her hands and he grasped her firmly, pulling her to her feet. She had overestimated her strength, however, and swayed slightly as he made to release her. At once his arms went to her waist, rock-steady in the support they offered.

'Th-thank you,' she said, as the strange breathlessness returned. 'I shall be all right now. It was only a momentary dizziness.'

'Are you sure?' He looked down at her with a hint of some unreadable emotion in his gaze. 'This is not the time for false courage, you know.'

'Thank you again, Captain Moreton, but I am feeling perfectly recovered.'

It was not true. Her heart hammered in a fashion she had never before experienced, and her head started to swim every time she looked up at him. His own features, she noticed, appeared pale and distinctly strained, and his mouth was drawn into a taut, hard line.

He released her and walked somewhat abruptly towards the tethered horses. 'You may wish to fasten the buttons on your riding-habit, Lady Catherine. I was compelled to undo

some of them when you fell.' She blushed hotly, but he gave
her no chance to speak. 'Fortunately, we are only a mile or
so from Wellespont. If you feel fit enough to ride, I think it
would be best for you to return to the house as soon as
possible.'

'If you will lift me into the saddle, Captain, you will see
that I am completely recovered. I confess that I have at least
half a dozen earlier falls to my credit, and I learned long ago
to fall in a way that causes a minimum of damage to
everything except my pride.'

The Captain kept their pace to no more than a fast walk
for the remainder of the ride home. Once or twice she
caught his gaze fixed upon her, presumably assessing the
state of her health, but he did not harass her with enquiries
as to how she felt.

He helped her to dismount at the stables, then escorted
her back to the house, summoning her maid as soon as they
reached the hall. They took formal leave of each other
when the servant arrived, and Catherine wondered wryly if
he was as relieved to be rid of her as he seemed.

After a hot bath, Mary soothed scented embrocation on
her mistress's sore limbs, urging her to recuperate by
spending the rest of the day sleeping. Catherine, however,
refused to be tucked up in her bed. She had no desire to lie
for hours staring at the ceiling while her thoughts rampaged
free. There were far too many subjects that she did not wish
to think about.

'Oh, my lady, I almost forgot,' Mary said as she closed
the buttons on her mistress's muslin day dress. 'There is a
letter come for you from Richland Towers. It is on your
dressing-table.'

'Thank you.' Catherine picked up the heavy letter as she
dismissed the maid.

The letter was from Jane, and she decided to go downstairs to read it. As she had expected, the conservatory was
deserted, and she sank into a chair, breaking the crested
seal with eager fingers. The letter, however, brought her
little joy, and she read it with a heart that became heavier as
she skimmed each line. Jane recounted only the trivial
doings of a normal country household, but Catherine had

no difficulty in reading between the lines and she could see that her sister was sick with dread at the approaching announcement of her betrothal to Mr Craddock. The letter was all the more affecting because her sister strove so hard to sound cheerful.

Catherine crumpled the closely-written sheet into a tight ball and walked restlessly towards the window, staring at the smooth expanses of lawn without really seeing them. For two days she had managed to forget the invidious nature of her position at Wellespont, but now the choice between her sister's happiness or her own honour lodged itself in her mind with stark, fearful simplicity.

An image of the lecherous eyes and snuff-stained nostrils of Mr Craddock was replaced by a vivid mental picture of Captain Moreton smiling at her as they rode that morning. For no reason she could understand, tears began to trickle down her cheeks in a relentless stream.

She rested her forehead against the cool pane of the window, attempting to stanch the flow with her tiny hand-kerchief. Then she was mortified to hear the rustle of silk behind her, and realised that someone else was in the room. Her body stiffened as she forced down the last of her sobs. She turned to find Lady Moreton standing in the doorway.

'I am sorry to have intruded,' Diane said quietly. 'I came into the conservatory almost an hour ago because the light is so good and I wanted to complete a piece of embroidery, but I must have dozed off for a moment. When I am with child, I always seem to be sleepy, and I nod off in the most inconvenient places. I didn't hear you come in, Lady Catherine, or I would have spoken to you.' Her gaze was compassionate. 'I trust your letter did not contain bad news from home,' she said softly.

'Not at all. On the contrary, my sister Jane reports that everybody is well and that they are all relishing the warm weather. Summer took so long to arrive this year that we are all doubly glad it has finally come.'

'If the news from your home is so good, I trust your —unhappiness—was not caused by anything that has happened at Wellespont.'

Catherine drew in a deep breath. 'I took a slight tumble

from my horse this morning, Lady Moreton, and I must be more shaken than I had thought. I assure you that everyone here has been all kindness.'

Diane gave no sign of suspecting that her guest's tears might have been produced by something more cataclysmic than a fall from a horse. 'I had not heard of your fall,' she said. 'Would you like me to send for a physician, Lady Catherine? There is an excellent doctor in the village of Moreton Grove.'

'No, thank you. I am truly not hurt.' She forced herself to smile. 'In fact, the Captain and I rode to Moreton Grove only this morning. The ruined abbey is magnificent.'

'Yes, it is.' Diane looked at her guest with sudden, piercing scrutiny. 'Did you enjoy the time you spent with my brother-in-law, Lady Catherine? He has a reputation as a somewhat bruising rider, but he is an entertaining companion, is he not?'

'Very entertaining.'

'He has visited some fascinating parts of the world. He accompanied his parents to the Ottoman Empire when he was still a boy, and then fought in all of Wellington's later campaigns. He is always determined to downplay his own bravery, but in fact he received the Duke's personal commendation for his conduct on the battlefield at Waterloo.'

'I didn't know that, although your sons have told me a dozen stories about his bravery. The Captain has talked to me a little about his tour of duty on St Helena, but we have not discussed his earlier career.'

'My brother-in-law rarely speaks about his military experiences. Do you know that he has never revealed to anyone how he injured his eye? For some reason, the final battle at Waterloo is not a subject that he finds easy to discuss, even with his family.'

Because his memories are so terrible, Catherine wanted to say. Because he does not wish to burden the people he loves with the nightmare images that are probably burned into his soul. She was shocked by her own intuitive understanding of the Captain's motives, and avoided Diane Moreton's gaze by turning back towards the window. 'It is fortunate that the Captain was on leave when you became engaged to Lord Moreton,' she remarked politely, chiefly for the sake of something to say. 'It is always pleasant to meet one's future in-laws before the wedding ceremony.'

There was a tiny pause. 'I think, Lady Catherine, that you cannot be aware that I was betrothed to Captain Moreton before I met my husband,' Diane said. 'I first met Lord Moreton on the very night that I agreed to marry his brother.'

Catherine's astonishment was so great that she forgot to be discreet. 'You were once engaged to the Captain? But you and Lord Moreton appear so blissfully happy together! I had imagined you destined for each other from the first time you met.'

'I think perhaps that we were, and our reluctance to admit the truth caused everyone a great deal of trouble. Sometimes, Lady Catherine, it is very difficult to acknowledge the emotions that we feel most deeply. And for men, I think it is perhaps even more difficult than for women.'

'Forgive me the question, Lady Moreton, but was there not the most terrible scandal when you became engaged to one brother and then married the other?'

Diane smiled faintly. 'I dare say there was, but people's memories are short, and the Dowager was on our side. As you can imagine, she is a formidable champion.'

Catherine smiled in return. 'Yes, I can well believe that even the greatest stickler might quail a little under the weight of my godmother's piercing gaze!'

'Now that you know something of the circumstances surrounding my marriage to Edward, I'm sure you will understand why we all awaited the Captain's return with such eagerness. His absence abroad lasted too long to please any of his family. Now he needs only to find the right wife, and then I am sure he will be happy to settle down on his estate at Long Acres.'

'No,' Catherine said, speaking without pausing to think. 'A wife who required him to stay at home would merely stifle him. He would give up his travels if she asked it, of course, because he is a kind man and his wife's wishes would be important to him. But the right woman for Captain Moreton will not want him to settle down into a false domesticity. She will want to travel with him and share in his adventures.'

Diane glanced up, her expression startled. 'My brother-in-law no longer has the reputation of being *kind*, Lady Catherine. Cynical or harsh are the words most often used to describe him.'

To Catherine's considerable relief, the announcement of luncheon precluded the need for her to make any direct response. As soon as it was over, she retired to her room and mulled over the significance of Diane's revelation. Captain Moreton, she realised, was hopelessly in love with his sister-in-law, and had been for over seven years. If he ever married, therefore, it would not be for love. How could it be, since his heart was given irrevocably to his brother's wife?

A flicker of hope flared deep inside Catherine's soul. Perhaps, in the circumstances, she would not be acting too wickedly if she compromised the Captain. Like most men, he probably wanted a son to inherit his estates, and in order to have a legitimate heir, he needed a wife. Since any marriage he made was destined to be loveless, surely it would not much matter which woman became his bride and how he acquired her?

And she would be such a suitable wife for him, Catherine reflected. She would bear his children willingly and make no demands upon his time or his affections. In fact, she would be so dutiful and obedient that he would never have cause to regret the dubious beginnings to their marriage.

A sudden squall of rain beat against the windows, but she ignored the sounds, feeling unexpectedly pleased by the train of her thoughts. Perhaps, after all, she could save Jane without totally compromising her own honour.

By the time evening arrived, she had almost convinced herself that she would be doing the Captain a favour if she married him.

Almost.

CHAPTER
SEVEN

FOR MOST of the next day, Catherine's feelings hovered somewhere between feverish optimism and black despair. Only during the hours that she rode with Captain Moreton was she able to put all thought of the future out of her mind and simply enjoy the present.

Lord and Lady Moreton had arranged a dinner party for some of their neighbours that evening to celebrate the Captain's return, and Catherine was glad of the distraction. She summoned her maid to help her to dress, relieved to have something to think about other than the relentless approach of her moment of decision.

Mary was smiling as she came into the bedroom, a froth of leaf-green silk draped over her arm. She shook out the gauzy folds and triumphantly held up a shimmering evening dress.

'What do you think of it, my lady? Isn't it just the perfect dress for you to wear tonight?'

Catherine reached out to stroke the soft folds. 'Where did you get it from, Mary?' she asked, unable to keep a quiver of pleasure out of her voice. She held the dress up against herself, smiling as she saw how the delicate colour flattered her complexion and highlighted the vivid green of her eyes.

'It is one of your own gowns, my lady. I simply removed the orange ribbons and the yellow floral trim, then re-designed the neckline and altered the style of the sleeves a little. It wasn't more than a few hours' work, not with Lady Moreton's maid to help me.'

With scarcely a pause in the flow of her chatter, Mary indicated that her mistress should sit at the dressing-table. 'Virginie, her ladyship's maid is called, which is just the nonsensical sort of name I don't hold with. But she was very obliging, even though she's French. It was a pleasure to sit upstairs with her and chat. She speaks English as well as you or I, my lady. You would know she's a foreigner only because she waves her hands every time she tries to tell you something.'

Even after twenty years, Catherine had never quite resigned herself to the fact that Mary considered everybody born south of Dover or north of the Mersey as a dangerous heathen, and she attempted to remonstrate.

'Lady Moreton's maid was born in London,' she explained patiently. 'It is only her parents who were French. Lady Moreton told me that they escaped to England during Robespierre's Reign of Terror.'

'Well, you don't expect foreigners to sound just like us when they talk, even if they were born here. Once a foreigner always a foreigner, that's what I say.' Mary's tone of voice brooked no argument as she gave a final pat to her mistress's upswept hair. 'You need earrings, my lady. It's a pity you don't have any emeralds, but I suppose your mother's pearls will do quite nicely.'

She selected two slender loops of pearls from her mistress's small jewel-box and waited patiently while Catherine put them on. She then carefully slipped the refurbished evening gown over her and fastened the row of tiny silk-covered buttons. She gave the skirt a few twitches until, satisfied that everthing was as perfect as she could make it, she stood back to admire her handiwork.

'You look wonderful, my lady.' Her sigh was gusty in its heartfelt approval. 'I haven't seen you look so beautiful in over a twelvemonth—not since poor Mr Richland died.'

A shadow crossed Catherine's features, and the maid dropped her gaze. 'I'm sorry, my lady, maybe I shouldn't have mentioned his name. But he is gone, and you have to accept that fact sooner or later.'

Catherine drew in a trembling breath. 'Perhaps you are right.' She hesitated for a moment, then added, 'Matthew was in such great pain at the end that sometimes I could hardly bear to be in the same room with him. His death was a release for him, I do realise that.'

'And a release for you too, my lady. You exhausted yourself in nursing him. But it's over now. He wouldn't have wished you to grieve for ever.'

Catherine could not reply, but her maid's down-to-earth advice remained with her as she descended the great oaken staircase. Captain Moreton was already in the drawing-room, talking to his brother, but their conversation stopped as she walked into the room. For the space of a single heartbeat, she saw a look of interest in the Captain's gaze, then his features returned to their normal expression of faint cynicism, mingled with boredom.

'Lady Catherine'—he inclined his head towards her —'you look more beautiful every evening. Does she not, Edward?' The cool mockery in his voice made the flattering words sound less than complimentary.

'She certainly does,' Lord Moreton said with a warm smile. He glanced at his brother, a hint of secret amusement in his eyes. 'Our golden-haired English beauties must make a delightful change for you, William, after so many years among those dark-eyed Spanish señoritas.'

The Captain's gaze flicked briefly over Catherine's hair, then switched back with seeming indifference to his brother. 'As you suggest, Edward, the ladies of of South America are usually very dark.'

Then Diane Moreton and the Dowager entered the drawing-room together, followed swiftly by the first of the invited guests, the Bishop of St Edmunds and his wife. The Bishop was a congenial man of less than middle-age; his wife a young, attractive matron who was clearly a good friend to Diane.

The visitors had hardly settled into their chairs when the butler announced the arrival of Sir Arthur Jefferson. Sir Arthur was an elderly widower, a long-time acquaintance of the Dowager and her late husband. As soon as the introductions were complete, he seated himself happily beside his old friend and began an earnest, low-voiced conversation.

The local squire, accompanied by his son and daughter, were the last of the guests to arrive. Mr Archibald Carruthers was a genial man, whose booming voice and red cheeks formed an incongruous contrast to his lanky height and almost gaunt body. He talked a great deal and gave no indication that he ever stopped to think before he opened his mouth.

His son seemed on first acquaintance to have no outstanding features at all, being of medium height, medium colouring and modest demeanour, but Miss Pamela Carruthers, the squire's beloved only daughter, amply compensated for her brother's apparent mediocrity. Her luxuriant hair was piled on top of her head in an artless confection of curls and ribbands that, Catherine calculated, must have taken her maid a minimum of two hours to arrange. Her slightly-pouting lips gleamed with moist, cherry-red invitation, and her honey-coloured eyes took one swift glance round the room and latched with unerring instinct on the only eligible bachelor.

'Captain Moreton,' she said huskily, her eyes peeping up at him with enchanting confusion as Diane performed the introduction. 'I was so thrilled when Lady Moreton invited me to this dinner, and Papa said that I might come. I have been longing to meet you for positively *ages*. I was only ten at the time of Waterloo, you see, and I have never met a real hero before. You will have to tell me *all* about the battles you fought!'

Catherine thought she saw a flicker of resignation cross the Captain's features, but he took Pamela's hand and smiled so charmingly that she decided she must have been mistaken.

'I am certainly delighted to have such an attractive new audience, Miss Carruthers. My dreary stories have long since become so tedious to my family that I am no longer allowed to bore them by further repetitions.'

The girl's long eyelashes fluttered. 'I could never grow bored listening to you, Captain Moreton,' she said. 'You were so brave, and you sacrificed so much to keep England safe from that dreadful man . . . that monster . . .'

'That monster?' the Captain queried. 'Ah, you must mean the Emperor Napoleon, of course.'

She shuddered with pretty exaggeration. 'Oh heavens, Captain Moreton, I can hardly bear even to hear you say his name.'

The Captain's gaze slipped towards Catherine and, quite

involuntarily, she smiled. A gleam of answering amusement appeared in his eye, then the smile abruptly faded and he turned back towards his companion.

'Let me tell you what happened the night before the start of the battle,' Catherine heard him say. 'Did you know, Miss Carruthers, that Wellington's staff officers were all invited to a reception at the Duchess of Richmond's house in Brussels when word came that Napoleon had stolen a march on us and advanced twenty miles into Belgian territory? We junior subalterns dashed off to the battlefield still dressed in our ball clothes, but the Duke himself stayed dancing almost until suppertime so that the townspeople would not panic.'

Mr Archibald Carruthers seated himself next to Catherine, beaming indulgently as he watched his daughter flutter her fan and gasp at the Captain's stories.

'My little girl is almost as beautiful as her dear departed mother,' the squire said, glancing up complacently as Pamela's silvery laugh drifted across the room.

'I believe you have been a widower for some years, Mr Carruthers?'

'I fear so. My dearest Adeline left us all many years ago, but we still mourn her loss.'

'I am sure you must. Your daughter is certainly very beautiful.'

'And she is accomplished. She paints the prettiest watercolours you would ever want to see, and she plays the pianoforte better than her teacher.' As an obvious afterthought, he added, 'Do you play, my lady?'

'Not at all. Unfortunately, I have very few of the traditional accomplishments. My mother was once subjected to hearing me play the harp, and after that she immediately released my teacher and me from our weekly hour of torment. The poor lady shed tears of relief when she realised that she would no longer have to instruct me.'

'I have never before met a young lady who could not play any musical instrument,' the squire remarked compassionately. 'But perhaps you sing, Lady Catherine?'

'Only when I am absolutely certain that there is nobody within earshot! My youngest sister tells me that even when I am in good voice, I sound like a crow suffering from acute indigestion.'

The squire remarked that his little Pamela sang like an angel, and that her mother had sung like an angel, too. His rapturous description of her remaining accomplishments —which were apparently endless—was interrupted only by the announcement of dinner. Catherine found herself seated between the Bishop and young Mr Carruthers. Regrettably, the table arrangements afforded her an unimpeded view of the luscious Pamela and her attentive dinner companion, Captain Moreton. Catherine was dismayed to find that her thoughts about the talented Miss Carruthers were less than charitable.

She repressed a sigh and exchanged polite comments with the Bishop, spooned her soup without tasting any of it, then listened determinedly to Mr Carruthers, speaking affectionately of his brothers. She struggled to give the appearance of attention, while all the time a strange emotion was beginning to stir deep inside her. She glanced up before she could stop herself and saw that Captain Moreton's head was bent close to Pamela's. He seemed deeply interested in whatever she was saying.

Catherine had been about to begin on her spiced, preserved pear when her throat suddenly rejected the thought of swallowing. It dawned on her that what she was feeling was acute, searing jealousy: jealousy, moreover, of a girl only a few months out of the schoolroom. She put down the spoonful of pear and stared at her plate as if her life depended on it. How could she possibly be jealous? Why should she care if Captain Moreton was intrigued by Miss Pamela Carruthers?

The answer came all too swiftly. Because she wanted the Captain to be interested in *her*, not in some gushing, overripe schoolgirl. Because she wanted the Captain to tell her that she looked beautiful in her leaf-green gown. Because she wanted to be the only recipient of those rare smiles that lit up his entire face, smoothing out the harsh lines and obliterating the cynical tautness of his mouth.

Catherine was ashamed and bewildered by the intensity of her own feelings. She redoubled her efforts to be an entertaining dinner companion, commenting on the rapid growth of towns such as Manchester when the Bishop discussed the need for more ministers of religion in areas where factories were being built, and agreeing politely when Mr Carruthers deplored the threat of violent rebellion in south-western Ireland. She studiously avoided looking across the table, and so could not know how many times the Captain's gaze was turned in her direction.

The gentlemen did not linger over their port at the end of the meal, and Pamela had scarcely seated herself at the pianoforte when they all trooped in. She got up quickly, blushing with becoming modesty, but the Captain went to her and said, 'Oh no! You must not get up, Miss Carruthers. Your father has promised us that you will sing, so please don't deprive us of our treat. I shall turn the pages of the music for you.'

Pamela did not need any further persuasion. She promptly sat down again, rippled surprisingly competent fingers over the keys, then broke into the lilting melody of a popular Italian ballad. Her voice, while not quite as celestial as the squire had promised, was pure and sweet and true. Her Italian, however, was mangled, and Catherine was chagrined to discover how much pleasure each mispronounced word gave her. Never before had she known herself to be so petty.

Pamela's performance ended in a burst of well-merited applause and several sincere requests for an encore. As she once again modestly blushed and disclaimed, something she was clearly skilled at doing, Lord Moreton suggested that Miss Carruthers and his brother should sing a duet.

'Oh no! I haven't sung for at least seven years,' the Captain protested laughingly.

'Then now is surely the time to start again. Please, Captain Moreton, do let us perform a duet!' Pamela's breathy little voice rose into a final plea. 'I would *so* much like to sing with you, Captain.'

The pause before he responded was infinitesimal. 'Your request is naturally irresistible, Miss Carruthers.' He gave a slight shrug of his shoulders then sat down on the seat next to her. His pleasant baritone was soon added to her soprano in a skilful rendition of 'The Lass of Richmond Hill'.

The sight of Pamela's white hands on the keys next to the Captain's darkly-tanned ones inexplicably reminded Catherine that the next day would be the last occasion she had to ride with him before the expiry of the week's grace granted by her stepmother. Unless she compromised the Captain tomorrow, it would be too late to save her sister from marriage to Mr Craddock.

Catherine felt faintly sick, and under cover of the applause that greeted the end of the duet, she slipped out of the drawing-room and made her way down the long corridor which led to Lord Moreton's library. A detailed map of the Wellespont estate hung on the wall opposite the fireplace, and she stood in front of it, forcing herself to scan the contours analytically.

She searched for land flat enough to permit an all-out gallop, and wild enough to make a stumble believable. She knew that, to stage an accident convincing enough to deceive the Captain, she would run the risk of hurting herself seriously, but she had no means of avoiding that particular hazard. Most of the Wellespont land was divided into small farms, which meant that help would be too close at hand to suit her purpose. She searched the eastern boundary of the estate, looking for a stretch of country that was isolated enough to prevent help arriving too quickly. There was no point in doing herself an injury, she thought with grim humour, unless she was certain of achieving her objective.

Until the Dowager spoke, she had no awareness of anybody entering the room. 'You do not enjoy the musical entertainment?' she asked quietly.

Catherine jumped and whirled round, guilt at what she was planning making her cheeks turn scarlet. 'Oh, God-mama, you startled me. Of course I enjoyed the singing. Miss Carruthers has a lovely voice. I—er—I simply found the room a little too warm.'

'Well, in that case you have come to the right place. This room isn't just cool, it's positively chilly. May I ask what you were finding of such fascinating interest in that out-of-date map of Wellespont?'

'Out-of-date? You mean this map is no longer accurate?'

'It was drawn up in my husband's time, and there have been several changes since then. Edward has made innumerable improvements, you know. He is a much more efficient landowner than my husband ever was.'

'I see.'

'You look worried, Catherine,' the Dowager said gently.

'Oh no, not at all, Godmama. I was—um—I was looking at the map of Lord Moreton's estate merely out of casual interest. I—er—I hadn't realised Wellespont was so large.'

'Yes, it is very large.' The Dowager's gaze was far too shrewd to be comfortable as it skimmed over Catherine's burning cheeks. 'And what do you think of William's singing? He and Miss Carruthers make interesting partners, do they not?'

'Very interesting,' Catherine said in a small voice. She drew in a deep breath. 'Shouldn't we return to the drawing-room, Godmama? It will appear discourteous if we are absent for too long.'

'I don't think our company will be missed for a few more minutes. Shall we sit here for a little while?'

Catherine sat on the edge of a leather chair placed to one side of the empty fire place, while her godmother relaxed comfortably in its pair. The Dowager broke the small silence.

'My dear, will you grant me the privilege of a very old friend and tell me if everything is as it should be at home?'

For a few seconds Catherine played with the idea of confiding the truth about her situation, but she rejected the idea almost at once. The Dowager had the power to circumvent any scheme to compromise Captain Moreton, but she had no authority to prevent Jane's forced betrothal to Mr Craddock. If she told her godmother the truth, she would in fact be condemning her sister to a lifetime of guaranteed misery.

Catherine swallowed hard and forced a smile. 'Everything at home is splendid, Godmama. My sisters are both very well, and my father looks forward eagerly to the birth of his heir . . .'

'And your stepmother, the Countess?'

Catherine stared hard at the empty grate. 'The Countess is well and active, despite her condition. She is a most efficient mistress of Richland Towers.'

'I am glad to hear you say so. Catherine, if you ever feel the need to consult someone about a personal problem, I shall be happy to give you my advice. You have always been very dear to me, child, and it grieved me to see how Matthew's death had turned you from a beautiful, eager young girl into a sad, withdrawn woman. It has been wonderful these past few days to see a sparkle return to your eyes and a lilt to your voice.'

'I think this holiday has helped me to see Matthew's death in better perspective,' Catherine replied honestly. 'It has been good to know that I am among people who do not automatically link me in their thoughts with Matthew.'

'Yes, here you are simply Lady Catherine Richland, not *poor dear Lady Catherine*. Well, enough of this sad subject. I believe you have ridden every morning this week with my son. How do you enjoy his company?'

Catherine carefully rearranged the folds of her gauzy overskirt before replying. 'He is an excellent rider and most interesting to talk to,' she said finally.

The Dowager gave a bark of laughter. 'He's always had an excellent seat on a horse, of course, but his conversation used to put one to sleep after the first five minutes. He was one of those romantic young men who were all dash and eagerness and no common sense.'

'He has certainly changed,' Catherine said drily.

The Dowager gave a rueful smile. 'Yes, he has indeed. You know, before he left for St Helena I used to spend all my time worrying in case he married. Since his return, I spend all my time worrying in case he does not. I worry so much over useless things where my sons are concerned that I am rapidly reaching the conclusion that motherhood has permanently damaged my powers of rational behaviour.'

'Your powers seem quite unimpaired to me, Godmama.'

The Dowager smiled, but a trace of anxiety lingered in her eyes. 'William needs the anchor of a happy family life to keep him from behaving recklessly. Some couples who are not particularly in love can marry and make each other tolerably happy. But unless William loves his wife, I think he will make both her and himself utterly miserable. I dread the consequences if he marries the wrong woman.'

Catherine gulped, wondering what excuse she could invent for the guilty, flame-red heat of her cheeks. 'The Captain has only just returned to England,' she said. 'There is a lot of time for him to find the right woman. In London this Season, perhaps . . .'

'He needs a wife who is educated, intelligent and as physically courageous as he is. Do you really believe he is likely to find such a woman simpering at Almack's?'

'Men and women find their soulmates in the most unlikely places,' Catherine said, doing her best not to squirm on the edge of her chair. She knew her godmother was hinting that Catherine would make Captain Moreton a suitable bride. But if she knew the truth, Catherine thought wretchedly, her approval would be withdrawn instantly.

Lord Moreton chose that moment to put his head round the half-open library door. 'We have been looking everywhere for you two,' he said. 'What Greek tragedies have you been setting to rights while we discussed the pleasures of a London Season?'

'Catherine and I have not mentioned Greece once today, Edward. We frequently have better things to discuss with each other than events which were settled quite satisfactorily over two thousand years ago.'

Lord Moreton looked astonished, as well he might, since his mother usually insisted that nothing of great interest had happened in the world since the Roman legions seized power from the Greek city states in 146 BC.

The Dowager did not wait for him to speak. She drew herself to the full extent of her modest height and swept regally past him in the direction of the drawing-room, leaving Catherine and Lord Moreton with nothing much to do save glance at each other in silent amusement, before following meekly in her wake.

CHAPTER
EIGHT

THE BISHOP of St Edmunds and his wife lived at some distance from Wellespont so, although the evening was fine and the moon high, the guests did not linger very long. Catherine said good night to Lord and Lady Moreton along with the other visitors, relieved to escape to her room before the Dowager could initiate any more heart-to-heart conversations.

Once in her room, she allowed her maid to take down her hair, fidgeting at the dressing-table while Mary completed the hundred brushstrokes she considered necessary. But when it came time for the maid to remove her evening gown, Catherine realised she was nowhere near ready for bed. Her guilty conscience and restive body would never let her sleep. She jumped up from her seat, dismissing Mary with a polite word of thanks and no attempt at any explanation.

She paced across the polished floor of her room, picking up a book, then putting it down again without even glancing at the title. There was no longer any possibility of avoiding the issue that confronted her. The moment she dreaded had finally arrived. Tonight she would have to decide whether to compromise Captain Moreton or sacrifice her sister to Mr Craddock. She thrust her hand against her mouth, forcing down a strange gasp that hovered somewhere between laughter and frantic tears. Her stomach churned with the sickness of indecision until she felt physically nauseated.

The day had been unusually hot, just as the previous week had been unseasonably chilly, and the night was still too warm to be comfortable. She imagined the coolness of the garden and longed to be outside where she might, for a moment or so, feel free of the pressures facing her inside Wellespont.

Without giving herself time for reflection, she grabbed a

lacy shawl from her cupboard and crept light-footed from her room. She was halfway down the stairs, when she saw her godmother emerge from the library.

The Dowager smiled and held up a slender volume. 'I have just taken Wordsworth's *Intimations of Immortality* from Edward's poetry shelf,' she said. 'I find that his descriptions of nature make pleasant reading on a warm summer night. What about you, my dear? Are you, too, coming downstairs in search of something to read?'

Catherine hesitated, trying to make up her mind how to reply. She was heartily sick of telling lies and yet, over the past week, she had constantly found herself in situations where it was impossible to tell the truth. Young ladies were not supposed to wander around the gardens after dark, and even though the Dowager was hardly a stickler for convention, she would have no choice but to recommend that Catherine return to her room.

The hours of the night stretched endlessly ahead of her, and Catherine knew that she could not tolerate confinement to her bedroom at this precise moment. With a flash of unusual bitterness she wondered why she cavilled at telling the Dowager a small lie tonight, when tomorrow she was planning to involve the entire Moreton family in a scheme that would make all her previous deceptions seem trivial.

'It is always enjoyable to read before falling asleep,' Catherine said, avoiding her godmother's eyes. 'I . . . er . . . I dare say I shall follow in your footsteps and find some poetry to read. Yes, I think that is just what I should like to do.'

The Dowager's gaze became speculative, but she added nothing more than a polite good night as she watched Catherine enter the library.

Catherine shut the library door and slumped against it, holding her breath as she listened to the Dowager's firm footsteps fade into the distance of the upstairs hall. After five minutes of silence, she peeped out of the room, expelling a deep sigh of relief when she saw that the corridors were empty. The servants, like their masters, had obviously gone to bed.

She slipped wraith-like along the hall and into the servants' quarters, confident that she would find one of the kitchen doors unbarred. Yes, the door leading into the herb garden was unlocked and she stepped into the freshness of the night, savouring the spicy smell of thyme, sage and mint. The weight of her depression was lifting very slightly.

The moon, which had been waxing since her arrival at Wellespont, was now almost full and the gardens were awash in cool, silver light. It was easy to find her way along the neatly-trimmed paths, and for no particular reason, she wandered in the direction of the rose arbour which nestled in a sheltered corner of the grounds.

The dark silhouette of the arbour finally took shape ahead of her. It was too early in the year for the roses to be in bloom, although the white trellises were already covered by leafy, climbing branches, and the bushes were laden with tight buds. As she let herself in through the low wrought-iron gate, she noticed that the air was scented with a pungent tang, sharper and more penetrating than roses even when they were in full blossom. She sniffed a couple of times, but the smell was completely unfamiliar to her and she soon abandoned her attempts to identify it. She latched the gate quietly behind her and walked up the narrow gravel path that led to a sundial, erected on a marble dais at the centre of the arbour.

The shiny brass face of the sundial revealed nothing at this hour of the night, but she stepped up on to the platform surrounding it, lifting the weight of her hair away from her neck. She was no longer too hot, she was no longer confined to her room, but her dilemma seemed not one whit easier to resolve than it had been before she left the house. Had she really thought that communing with the stars would resolve the problem of whether she was going to stage a riding accident tomorrow?

A faint rustling in the corner of the garden attracted her attention and she glanced up, expecting to see a rabbit disappearing beneath the hedge. Instead she found herself staring straight at a stone bench. Seated on the bench was Captain Moreton.

Her heart seemed to stop beating, before racing forward

again faster than before. Neither of them said a word, and
her body grew rigid with nervous tension. Her fingers
tightened round the sundial pointer until the metal cut into
her palms.

The Captain finally spoke. 'Good evening, Lady
Catherine.' He stood up, sweeping her an overly polite
bow. He threw down the cigarillo he had been smoking,
crushing it carefully underfoot. 'You must excuse me,' he
said coolly. 'I have been indulging one of the vices I picked
up in South America. I thought I had chosen somewhere far
enough away from the house to avoid offending anyone.'

'I have never smelled tobacco smoke before,' she admitted. 'It never occurred to me that somebody else might be in
the arbour.'

'It is a strange coincidence, is it not, that we should both
choose this small garden for our nocturnal wanderings?'

'Very strange,' she said, ignoring the note of mockery
that laced his words. 'Although I chose it because it always
seems so peaceful. Perhaps you chose it for the same
reason . . .'

Her voice trailed away into silence. In truth, discovering
the Captain here in the rose garden was a coincidence
disconcerting enough to leave her tongue-tied. She was all
too aware of the ironic fact that their presence in the rose
garden at this time of night was scandalous in the extreme.
The riding accident she had planned was nowhere near as
compromising.

Catherine pushed nervously at her flowing hair, and
struggled against the impulse to laugh hysterically. It was
bad enough that they should be alone in such a secluded
spot, but the impropriety of her appearance made their
situation even worse. She wondered wryly why Fate always
seemed to have such a perverse sense of humour. In her
wildest imaginings she could not have invented a more
perfect setting for winning an enforced proposal of marriage from the Captain. The rigid dictates of the social code
were such that the fact neither of them had planned to meet
in the garden was completely irrelevant to their situation.

And at that moment, at the precise instant when
she realised that her goal was actually within her grasp,

Catherine knew that she could never go through with her stepmother's scheme. She did not want to entrap Captain Moreton into marriage and she liked him far too well to compromise him. Whatever the difficulties, however impossible it seemed at this moment, she would find some other method to save Jane from the loathsome Mr Craddock.

'It is late to be taking a stroll, Lady Catherine,' Captain Moreton said as he walked slowly towards her. His voice was expressionless, but his gaze seemed to be fixed upon the moon-whitened fairness of her hair.

'It was too warm to sleep easily,' she said. 'D-Did you not find it so?' She clutched her shawl more tightly to her, as if a layer of gossamer-thin wool might somehow help to prevent her heart pounding like a barrage of exploding cannon.

'Yes, it is hot tonight,' he agreed. 'Are you sure you need to wrap your shawl quite so tightly about you?'

'Th-there is quite a breeze in this part of the garden.'

He didn't bother to conceal his amusement. 'Strange, I have not yet felt it at all.'

He halted on the opposite side of the sundial but then, to her alarm, he walked round the dais and leaned close to her as he examined the flat, gleaming face of the clock with every appearance of consuming interest.

'The moon is so bright that you almost expect to be able to tell the time,' he said conversationally.

The velvet sleeve of his evening jacket brushed against her shawl. She wondered if he could feel that she was trembling. She wondered why he did not go away and save himself from the possibly disastrous consequences of being discovered here. She drew in a deep, shaky breath, knowing she ought to say something. What had he asked her? It was no use; she had already forgotten.

'Well, I think I should return to the house, Captain Moreton.' Her voice was little more than a high-pitched squeak, and she cleared her throat nervously. 'I expect you would like to light another cigarillo and smoke it in peace.'

'You are all consideration, Lady Catherine.'

The mockery in his gaze made her shrivel inside, but she

drew herself up proudly before she spoke. 'Good night,
Captain Moreton.'

In her eagerness to escape, she forgot that the sundial
was erected on a high platform. She stepped backwards,
away from the Captain and out into space. Her ankle
twisted sickeningly beneath her, and she would have fallen
heavily if he had not leaned forward to catch her, successfully breaking the impact of her fall.

For a few crucial seconds she was too shocked to move.
His hands had become entangled in her long hair and he
removed them very slowly. Then his arms tightened convulsively round her waist, and she felt a responsive tightening
deep inside her own body. For a while, she forgot to
breathe.

They stared at each other across a tiny space that seemed
infinitely wide and yet dangerously easy to bridge. She
wanted to save the situation by making some light-hearted
remark about how clumsy she seemed to be whenever they
were together. She wanted to move herself briskly out of his
embrace and thank him politely for his assistance. She
wanted to stop shaking. Unfortunately, she seemed in-
capable of accomplishing any of those simple tasks. He held
her clasped within the circle of his arms and she stared
silently into the enigmatic darkness of his face, waiting with
trembling anticipation as he brushed his thumb gently
across her mouth, then bent his head to kiss her.

She closed her eyes, aware that her lips softened as his
mouth slowly caressed hers. Her hand, trapped between
their two bodies, curled tightly against his stiff shirt-front as
he wound his fingers in the silken thickness of her hair. The
pearl studs that closed the front of his shirt pressed against
her breasts, and she was aware of a sudden, shocking desire
to part his shirt and learn how it would feel to have his bare
skin beneath her fingertips.

She grew hot with embarrassment when she realised
what she was thinking. Nothing in her life thus far had prepared her for the intensity of her reaction to the Captain's
kiss, and she was too bewildered to understand her own
feelings. Her body floated; her mind was a weightless void.

His arm slipped down to her waist, drawing her more

tightly against his body, and his other hand clasped the nape
of her neck, holding her head still as he gently—expertly
—forced her lips apart. She had no idea what he was trying
to do, no idea why he would want her to open her mouth,
but a sharp arrow of sensation ripped through her body as
she felt his breath mingle with her own. The midnight
darkness around them seemed to shimmer, mirroring the
trembling deep inside her.

The touch of his tongue against her teeth temporarily
jerked Catherine back to reality. She was shocked to the
core of her being at the incredible, immoral, intimacy of
their embrace. She knew that any true lady would faint in
these circumstances, not find herself tingling with a strange,
new pleasure. Matthew had rarely done more than kiss her
affectionately on the cheek, and they had both considered
such a gesture more than sufficient to demonstrate the
depths of their love.

As soon as she remembered her cousin, a modicum of
sanity returned, and she wrenched her head away.

'No,' she said frantically. 'Captain Moreton, you must
not! Indeed, you must not.'

'On the contrary, my lady. I think that I must.'

His mouth descended again, closing unerringly over her
parted lips. As his kiss deepened, as his arms crushed her
tighter to his body, a flame of pure pleasure twisted through
her. Her body went limp and her mouth opened invitingly
beneath his. Suddenly, she wanted to feel his tongue
touching hers. She wanted to feel the curious, liquid heat
uncoiling in the pit of her stomach. Her hands reached up of
their own accord and twined in his hair, her fingertips
caressing the nape of his neck.

'I am sure, William, that you have some excellent explanation for what I am seeing. I am waiting with some
anxiety to hear it.'

The Dowager's clipped words broke into Catherine's
consciousness with the brutal impact of a bucket of icy
water poured over her head. With a small gasp of horror,
she sprang away from the Captain, fumbling with the wild
cascade of her hair as she tried to bundle it into some sort of
order.

After one frenzied glance towards her godmother, she gave up her attempt to achieve the impossible. She simply stood still and prayed that a ravine would open at her feet, or a lion spring out from behind the rose bushes, or a lightning-bolt strike her dead. Anything, she prayed, so that she would not have to turn around and look again into the Dowager's reproachful eyes.

The Captain moved to the opposite side of the sundial, positioning himself so that Catherine could see only his profile and the black slash of his eye-patch.

'Lady Catherine stumbled,' he said in his usual cool way. 'I simply caught her.'

'Indeed you did catch her. Forcefully, according to my observation.'

Catherine prayed once again for a large hole to appear at her feet but, in view of her state of sin, she was not surprised when her plea for deliverance remained unanswered. Her throat was so dry that she was amazed when she managed to speak.

'I c-couldn't sleep, Godmama, so I came to the rose arbour for some fresh air.'

'At *midnight*?'

'I didn't realise that it was so late and, in any case, I did not plan to stay once I discovered that C-Captain Moreton was here. I was just leaving, when I stumbled. You can see for yourself that the pedestal to this sundial is awkwardly designed. I would have twisted my ankle quite badly if he . . . if the Captain had not chivalrously stepped forward to catch me.'

The Dowager paid no attention to this feeble attempt at an explanation which, Catherine decided glumly, was only to be expected, since it totally failed to explain why she had been locked in Captain Moreton's embrace, kissing him passionately.

'Knowing that you were not yet in bed,' the Dowager said, 'I went to your room, hoping to discuss a point of translation with you. When I found that you were neither in your bedroom nor in the library, I became worried and summoned your maid. She informed me that the butler, two kitchen-maids and the boot-boy had all seen you walking towards the rose garden. At least half a dozen servants knew that William was already there, smoking one of his cigarillos. Mary did not hesitate to apprise me of these facts.'

'And so, Mama?' the Captain enquired softly. 'Is the servants' remarkable information network supposed to be of special interest to us for some reason?'

The Dowager's expression became a shade more grim. 'By six o'clock tomorrow morning there will not be a servant in Wellespont who does not know that the two of you were out here alone together. By noon, I estimate that the entire village of Wellespont will have the story, and by mid-afternoon it will have reached the Bishop's household. By that time, with its inevitable embellishments, I do not doubt that you will be reputed to have conducted an orgy of epic proportions in the middle of the Wellespont rose garden.'

'Oh no!' Catherine reached tentatively behind her, glad to feel the solid support of the marble sundial beneath her fingers. 'I am very sorry, Godmama,' she whispered. 'I did not intend to cause you such unpleasantness, truly I did not. Perhaps the Bishop will . . .'

'It is already too late for apologies and regrets,' the Dowager interrupted ruthlessly. 'The damage has been done. I am sure, William, that I do not have to make any further specific reference to the distressing scene that greeted me when I arrived here. Even if I had not witnessed something so—unexpected—I am confident that you already know your duty.'

The Captain inclined his head with ironic courtesy. 'Indeed, Mama, no one of your sons could ever forget that he was brought up to be a gentleman.'

Almost before Catherine had time to realise his intentions, he turned and swept her a low, mocking bow.

'Lady Catherine,' he said. 'Will you do me the great honour of becoming my wife?'

CHAPTER
NINE

FOR A FEW blissful seconds after the Captain had made his proposal, Catherine's heart raced with excitement. Everything is going to work out, she thought ecstatically. I did not deliberately compromise him, and still he is prepared to marry me! Caught up in the exhilarating rush of joy, she did not stop to define to herself precisely why his proposal made her so happy.

She glanced at him, too shy to meet his gaze head on, but what she saw in his face caused her moment of happiness to die as swiftly as it had been born. There had been occasions in the past when she considered his expression cold and cynical, but she had never before seen such bitter anger as was now etched deep into his features.

His derisive gaze clashed with hers. 'My lady, pray do not keep me in suspense,' he said. 'I long to know if you will do me the supreme honour of becoming my wife.'

He could not know how much his biting sarcasm hurt her. She clasped her hands tightly in front of her, burying them in the folds of her shawl so that he could not see how they shook. She raised her chin high and faced him squarely.

'You are too good,' she said with a cool irony that miraculously matched his own. 'I appreciate your generous attempt to redeem my tattered reputation, but there is no reason for us to be tied to a marriage neither one of us wants. I believe my godmother exaggerates the seriousness of the situation.'

'I do no such thing,' the Dowager said quietly. 'On the contrary, child, I think you do not yet understand precisely what you risk.'

Catherine, relieved to have an excuse to turn her back on the Captain, swung around to face her godmother. 'I have no intention of trying to make my entrance into London's fashionable society, Godmama. Furthermore, it is not as if I were a sixteen-year-old fresh from the schoolroom. I am a married woman, and my reputation surely is less vulnerable than that of a young girl on the verge of making her début.'

Her words fell into a pool of silence, interrupted only by the hiss of Captain Moreton's indrawn breath.

'You are *married*?' he said, not attempting to disguise the astonishment and the cold fury of his question. 'In God's name, did it never occur to you to mention that fact? Did it not occur to you that I might have some interest in knowing that I rode each morning with another man's wife?'

The Dowager cast one swift, speculative look in the direction of her son, then relapsed into silence, staring into the middle distance as if she had become thoroughly uninterested in the drama being enacted beneath her nose.

Catherine saw that she would receive no assistance from her godmother. 'You have misunderstood, Captain Moreton.' She twisted her hands into an even tighter knot beneath her shawl. 'I was married three years ago, but I am now a widow. My husband died last year after a long illness.'

'I am sorry to hear it.' The Captain sounded curt rather than sorrowful. 'But I'm afraid I still do not understand. How can you be called Lady Catherine *Richland* if you are widowed? *Richland* is your maiden name: the name of your father.'

'If you would stop to think for a minute, William, you would realise that there is no particular mystery.' The Dowager had clearly been paying more attention to the proceedings than her expression indicated, although it was still impossible to judge what she thought about them.

'Catherine was married to Matthew Richland, who was a distant cousin. They shared one of the same great-great-grandfathers, and therefore they also happened to share the same last name. Matthew was orphaned as a baby and was brought up by the Earl and former Countess of Richland. He requested permission to marry Catherine on her seventeenth birthday. The Earl gave his consent, and they were married three months later.'

'I see,' the Captain said. He half-turned towards Catherine. 'And yet, my lady, I still do not understand why you did not mention to me that you were a widow.'

'My affection for my husband was very great,' she said, and the icy hauteur of her manner effectively masked the fierce pain she was feeling. 'His suffering at the end of his life was—difficult—to watch. His death and my widow-hood are therefore subjects that I find painful to discuss. My godmother knew very well that I was a widow, and no deliberate effort was made to conceal my status. If you feel that you have been deceived, I can only beg your pardon.'

The Dowager gave one of her familiar little snorts. 'It seems to me that you are both losing track of what we ought to be discussing. If you would both step down from your high horses long enough to think about what actually happens in the real world, you would understand that Catherine's widowed state only makes your present situation more precarious.'

'Please explain precisely what you mean, Mama.'

'It is true that Catherine's widowhood allows her greater freedom than that accorded to very young débutantes. Her status also makes her more vulnerable to malicious gossip rather than less. The world is always eager to believe the worst about the morals of a young and beautiful widow.'

'But who is going to gossip?' Catherine asked, aware even as she posed the question of the total absurdity of her situation. Here she was, fighting desperately against a marriage which, for Jane's sake, she ought to be doing everything in her power to promote.

'The entire fashionable world will gossip, child.'

'How will they ever hear the story? Surely nobody from Wellespont is likely to feed information to the London rumour-mills?'

'These things can never be successfully concealed,' the Dowager said with uncharacteristic vagueness. 'I might add, Catherine, that you are my godchild and a guest in my elder son's house. I have a double obligation to see that no damage is done to your reputation while you are in my care.' There was a certain ascerbity in her voice as she added, 'I cannot see why you are protesting so vigorously, Catherine. Judging by the extraordinary situation in which I discovered you and my son, I am forced to conclude that the idea of marriage cannot be totally repugnant to either of you.'

Catherine was silenced by sheer embarrassment, knowing there was nothing she could say. The Dowager had found her exchanging the sort of embrace with Captain Moreton that only married couples were permitted to share. And, judging by her experience with Matthew, even most married couples probably never indulged in the intimacies she had permitted to the Captain.

'Do I take it, Lady Catherine, that your silence indicates a willingness to accept my humble suit?' Captain Moreton asked, the mockery in his voice more pronounced than ever.

The corner of her shawl was almost unravelled where she had twisted it into so many different knots.

'Yes,' she whispered, staring at her shoes. 'I am delighted to accept your generous offer of marriage, Captain Moreton.'

He took her hand and raised it to his lips, although they did not touch so much as a fingertip. 'My dear Lady Catherine, you have made me the happiest of men.'

Her heart squeezed a fraction tighter under the lash of his unconcealed sarcasm, but she would not give him the satisfaction of revealing how successfully he had wounded her. With no thought of the Dowager, wanting only to return to the sanctuary of her bedroom, she pulled her hand from his light grasp, and ran blindly along the path towards the wrought-iron garden gate.

'Catherine! Wait!'

The stern command of her godmother halted her flight. She waited for the Dowager to join her; then, blushing and stammering, she once again made her apologies.

For the first time since that awful moment when she had discovered them locked in each other's arms, the Dowager's smile seemed warm and understanding. 'Don't worry, Catherine. I understand that it's been a difficult evening for you. Everything will work out for the best, you will see.'

'Perhaps,' Catherine responded bleakly. 'I am sorry, Godmama, for all the distress my thoughtless behaviour

must have caused you. I know I should never have come
into the garden alone at this hour of the night.'

'Oh well, we shall talk of that some other time. Not now.'

The accumulated strains of the past few weeks seemed to
descend simultaneously on to Catherine's shoulders, forming a single heavy burden. She was suddenly weary to the
point of absolute physical exhaustion. Every step that she
took towards Wellespont required a greater effort than the
one before, and it required all her willpower to remain
upright when they finally entered the house.

Mary was waiting for them in the hall. Through a haze of
fatigue, Catherine realised that the Dowager was giving
instructions to the maid.

'Take good care of her, Mary. She is exhausted. I think
she cannot have been sleeping well in recent weeks?'

'Not for months, my lady. Scarcely a night that she's slept
right through. And that on top of nursing her husband for
the best part of a year.'

'Ah well, I believe all that will shortly take a great change
for the better. Good night, Mary.'

'Good night, my lady.'

Catherine felt Mary's arm beneath her elbow, supporting
her as they walked up the stairs. They arrived at the door of
her room, and it had never before looked so welcome.

She was aware of the maid speaking to her as she
undressed for bed. It was possible that she even gave the
occasional reply. At last, Mary pulled back the covers and
smoothed out the sheet. Catherine sank on to the soft
mattress, placed her head on the pillow, and slept.

Captain Moreton's gaze was reflective as he watched his
mother and his new fiancée walk sedately along the path
towards Wellespont. Catherine looked weary, he thought.
Her footsteps were dragging, and twice she almost stumbled. Perhaps he should run and catch them up and offer his
arm for her to lean on . . .

Deliberately he turned his back on the retreating couple.
He pulled a cigarillo from its silver case, and rolled it
thoughtfully between his fingers. He knew his mother well
and usually had no difficulty in understanding her motives.

On this occasion, however, he could not decide what had prompted her insistence upon an immediate betrothal. Was it possible that she thought Catherine would make a good wife for him and was simply using the present situation to force the issue? With a slight shrug, he dismissed the idea as unlikely. His mother was not in the habit of coercing her children into any particular course of action.

On the other hand, her adherence to the rules governing aristocratic social behaviour was haphazard at best, and it was rare for her to suggest doing anything simply because convention demanded it. But he supposed that in this particular instance her sense of propriety might have been genuinely outraged. The kiss she had seen him exchange with Catherine was not easy to dismiss as a trivial breach of a rigid code of behaviour. His mother must have recognised that it had been the passionate embrace of two people destined shortly to become lovers. He had not meant to kiss Catherine like that, of course, but her green eyes had been tantalising him for days. And she had felt so soft in his arms, so incredibly yielding and yet so touchingly innocent.

He muttered a short, brutal expletive that he had learned from his soldiers, and cut off the foolish recollections. His mouth twisted into a harsh smile. Innocent, indeed! The woman had been married for two years before she was widowed, which meant that she probably had a repertoire of bedroom tricks that would put Lady Annabelle to shame. Surely to God he had learned by now that the more innocent a woman looked, the more devious her true nature was likely to be! Diane de Verette had taught him everything he ever needed to know about the perfidy of beautiful women. Catherine, even if she became his wife, was never going to be allowed close enough to his heart to inflict even the most minor of scars.

He walked back to the stone bench and found his tinder-box in the corner where he had left it. He lit up his cigarillo, watching the smoke drift away on the night breeze. In many ways, this incident could be considered a blessing, since it saved him from the tiresome process of going to London and making himself pleasant to a succession of rapid débutantes.

He glanced at his pocket-watch and saw that it was almost two in the morning. Definitely time to be thinking of bed, although he had little expectation of sleeping for more than three or four hours. He started to stroll towards the house.

Catherine was probably already asleep, he thought. He pictured her curled up in bed, the incredible cascade of her silvery hair splayed out across the pillow. He wondered how her naked body would feel, held close to his own. She was slender, but her small breasts had thrust against his shirt front with exquisite provocation. He was surprised to discover how much he wanted to see her lying beside him in his bedroom at Long Acres.

He gave a quick, irritated shrug when he realised that his rambling thoughts had once again led him straight back to Catherine. There was no reason for her to occupy his thoughts to such a ridiculous extent, no reason for him to feel this strangely intense physical desire. She was a convenience, nothing more. A substitute for Diane de Verette, the true love of his life, whom he could never marry.

As he walked slowly towards Wellespont, he attempted to put the events of the night into rational perspective. He needed a wife. Chance and his own reckless behaviour had decreed that Catherine should become that wife. Her character and feelings were really of little significance. He wanted an efficient mistress of his household and a kind mother for his children. Catherine, in common with half the other women whom he knew in the world, filled the bill with tolerable exactness. Her most endearing characteristic, he thought with a sudden flash of dry humour, was that she rarely seemed to ask personal questions, and she almost never spoke unless she had something specific to say.

Had he not decided at Lady Annabelle's, only a few days earlier, that lack of curiosity and the gift of silence were the two qualities he most desired in a wife? He gave a small, somewhat grim laugh. In future he would have to take more care about what he wished for, since it seemed that Fate was determined to exercise her sense of humour at his expense—and grant him his wishes.

He threw away his cigarillo and walked into the house,

taking the stairs to his bedroom two at a time. For the first time since he had landed in England, he slept as soon as his head touched the pillow.

The members of the Wellespont household did not usually meet until luncheon at the earliest, but the following morning found all five adult members gathered together in the breakfast-room.

The Dowager sipped her heated goat's milk and beamed happily around the table. 'What a very pleasant surprise to find us all here together so early in the day,' she said. She saw no reason to point out that they were all present simply because she had sent notes to their bedrooms requesting their attendance. 'I have a most gratifying announcement to make.'

'Let me guess,' Lord Moreton said dryly. 'Your chief nanny-goat is about to become a grandmother, thus ensuring our supply of cheese curds for several years into the future.'

'I think, on the whole, my news is even better than that,' said the Dowager, a faint twinkle in her eye. She glanced quickly at Catherine, who had not raised her eyes from her plate since the moment when the Captain walked into the room, and then at her younger son, who was spreading strawberry conserve on his bread with every appearance of total concentration. She smothered a sigh. In most families, it seemed to her, the task of finding the right mate did not require quite so much preliminary drama.

'Come, Mama,' Edward said laughingly. 'We are holding our breath in anticipation of your announcement.'

The Dowager rose to her feet and spoke with unexpected formality. 'I am delighted to inform you that last night my goddaughter, Catherine, agreed to marry my younger son, William. Naturally, we must wait to consult with the Earl of Richland before any formal announcements can be made, but I hope the ceremony will be arranged to take place very shortly.'

She sat down again, tactfully ignoring the fact that one of the footmen had just spilled a pitcher of water and Diane had choked on her hot chocolate. Lord Moreton, perhaps to cover his wife's confusion, instantly stood up and walked over to Catherine's chair. He bent down and kissed her lightly on both cheeks.

'Lady Catherine, please accept my warm felicitations. It is a pleasure and privilege to welcome you as a member of our family. William is certainly a lucky man to have found you.'

Catherine's gaze lifted for one moment, then fell back to her plate. 'You are very kind,' she whispered.

If Lord Moreton found this response less than ecstatic, he gave no sign of it. He crossed to his brother's chair, thumped him soundly on the shoulder, then shook his hand.

'Congratulations, William. I am very happy to see you have made such a wise choice. Speaking as an old hand at the business of matrimony, I can heartily recommend the married state.'

'Thank you. Lady Catherine and I can only hope to emulate the happiness you and Diane have found together.'

Edward returned to his seat, and Diane, having recovered from her fit of coughing, offered the newly-betrothed couple her hearty good wishes. Together with the Dowager and her husband, she was soon involved in a complex discussion of how news of the engagement could best be sent to Wiltshire, and whether the wedding ceremony would be better held in London or somewhere in the country.

Captain Moreton made no effort to listen to the chatter of his family, even though it pertained so closely to his own affairs. Glad that everybody's attention seemed firmly fixed elsewhere, he looked searchingly at Catherine, surprised at the interest he felt in assessing her state of mind. He wished very much to know how she had reacted to the public announcement of their betrothal.

It did not require close scrutiny to see that she looked anything but happy. All the colour her complexion had gained over the past few days had drained away, leaving her as white-cheeked as she had been on the occasion of their first meeting. Her soft and pretty hair-style had been replaced by the same tight, ugly knot she had originally worn, and her gaze seemed once again to be glued permanently to the carpet. Search as he might, he could find no indication that somewhere inside this pallid exterior lived the warm, passionate woman he had held in his arms the night before. He wondered how somebody who had already been married and who had displayed such a sensual reaction to his touch could possibly appear so frigid.

Even as he watched, she reached out to pick up her cup of chocolate, and he saw that her fingers were shaking so much that she had to cradle the rim with two hands before she could raise the cup to her lips. He felt a flare of unfamiliar sympathy tighten the muscles of his throat. He wanted to put his arm around her thin shoulders and ask what was troubling her. He wanted to assure her that once they were married everything would be all right.

His sympathy was short-lived and almost immediately replaced by anger. He had never expected Catherine to love him, but until this moment it had not occurred to him that she might be a reluctant bride.

For reasons that were not clear to him, the thought of her possible reluctance irritated him beyond bearing. Why the devil was she sitting at the table shaking? She had just brought off an engagement to one of the richest men in England. Should she not consider this her moment of triumph? A small, hard knot tied itself in his stomach. Maybe Catherine found the sight of his eye-patch so repellent that even his money could not compensate for her revulsion. In that case, what would she feel if he ever removed the patch and she saw the livid scar that slashed along the underside of his eyebrow?

He thrust this new uneasiness out of his mind. He would find a local jeweller to make up one of his largest emeralds into an engagement ring. He had no doubt that a gaudy enough stone would help Catherine to overcome any repugnance she felt at the prospect of marriage to a half-blind ex-soldier. A few large emeralds could always outweigh the disadvantages of a scarred face.

He came back to earth to find everyone at the table, with the exception of his fiancée, looking at him expectantly. His mother had obviously asked him a question.

'I beg your pardon, Mama. I'm afraid I did not hear what you said.'

'I would like to know if you will escort Catherine and me into Wiltshire so that the Earl of Richland can give his immediate approval to the match. If you agree that this is the most sensible plan, we can send one of the servants ahead of us today with the message that we shall be arriving shortly. We can then follow at our leisure.'

'I shall be happy to escort you, if that is your wish, Mama. How about you, Lady Catherine? Does the prospect of an early return to Richland Towers meet with your approval?'

'Yes, of course, Captain Moreton, if that is what is most convenient for my godmother and for you.'

The Dowager soon arranged for them to leave for Wiltshire at eight the next morning. Almost before he knew how it had happened, Captain Moreton found himself agreeing that the wedding ceremony would take place in the very near future, perhaps as soon as the banns could be called. The Countess of Richland's imminent confinement was cited as the chief reason for this unusual haste in establishing a firm date.

He made no protest at his mother's unusual burst of organisation, chiefly because he was secretly rather pleased that the wedding would take place so soon. He discovered within himself a surprising desire to show Catherine his home at Long Acres. He remembered that the London Season was about to start and thought that it might be rather pleasant to take her to town for their honeymoon. She had never seen the capital city, and he would undoubtedly find it amusing to see the familiar sights from her fresh viewpoint.

His thoughts wandered off at an agreeable tangent, only returning to the Wellespont breakfast-room when he heard Diane apologising for the fact that, because of her pregnancy, she would not be able to attend the wedding.

Suddenly Captain Moreton recalled that the last time his family had sat at this table discussing a wedding, the ceremony under discussion had been intended to unite him with Diane de Verette. He felt a faint twinge of regret for what might have been, realising even as he did so that the regret was almost as much for the naïve, idealistic young man he had once been, as for the love affair that had never come to anything. He looked across the table at his sister-in-law, appreciating her beauty, but this was the first occasion that he felt no frisson of frustrated longing.

'The health of your unborn child must come first, Diane,' he said quietly. 'I would not like to face Edward if anything happened to prevent the safe arrival of his baby daughter.'

'Don't worry, my love, I shall watch the proceedings very closely so that I can bring you back a full report,' Lord Moreton said, smiling at his wife. 'I even promise to note what all the ladies are wearing, so I beg, Lady Catherine, that you will take pity on my masculine ignorance and ask your attendants to wear something extremely simple to describe!'

Catherine, the Captain noticed, produced her first smile of the day for his brother. 'If you remind me, my lord, I shall write out a description myself, and then you will be able to dazzle Lady Moreton with the precision of your observations.'

The discussion ended in a ripple of laughter and a flurry of last-minute instructions. Catherine and the Dowager left the room to begin their packing before Captain Moreton had any opportunity to pursue a private conversation with his bride-to-be. Diane, ignoring her husband's suggestion that she should rest, hurried up the stairs behind the other two ladies.

'I have at least a thousand questions I must ask Lady Catherine,' she said, turning to her husband with an enchanting smile. 'Only think, I shall soon have two sisters to compare notes with! I must write and tell Juliana the news today! She will be so cross that she is in Vienna. I wonder where Catherine plans to buy the material for her wedding gown? Do you think she will have time to send to London?'

'It is certainly a question of burning importance,' Lord Moreton remarked, but he spoke only to his wife's rapidly retreating back. He turned and glanced sympathetically at his brother.

'You are lucky, William, that your betrothal looks like being of short duration,' he said. 'You may as well resign yourself to seeing very little of Lady Catherine between now and the day the wedding ceremony finally takes place.'

The Captain shrugged. 'There will be plenty of time for personal discussions once we are married.' He quickly changed the subject. 'May I ask one of your grooms to carry a message to Richland Towers, Edward? We don't want to descend upon the Earl and Countess without giving them adequate warning.'

Lord Moreton understood that his brother was not yet ready to confide any details about his unexpected betrothal. As a man whose own path to marital bliss had been decidedly bumpy, he knew this to be one of those occasions when it was wise not to press for confidences.

'Certainly,' he said. 'Let's find a groom and you can give him the message yourself.' He fell into step beside his brother as they strolled out into the garden. 'William, I have been meaning to speak to you about a letter I received recently from the Foreign Secretary. He wrote to let me know that the Marques de Algarve Branca had been accredited to the London staff of the Portuguese Ambassador.'

'Yes. Canning and I spent some time discussing that fact when I was in London. I assume the Foreign Secretary's letter made clear to you that the old Marques is dead. It is the son of the man we knew who is now resident in London.'

'I'm not sure that I find your information reassuring. The British Government, working on evidence we supplied, was responsible for the permanent exile of the former Marques de Algarve Branca. Why would his son choose to come to England? In the circumstances, it cannot be a country for which he cherishes warm and sentimental feelings.'

'Canning tells me that the new Marques is a hardworking young man who simply wants to restore the tarnished reputation of his family by a period of loyal service to the Portuguese crown. He did not choose to come to England. He was sent here by King John's government.'

'Do you believe such a story?'

The Captain raised his shoulders in a slight shrug. 'Probably not. A desire for government service is hardly typical of any Portuguese nobleman, let alone one who has suffered at the hands of the current régime. On the whole, the Portuguese show only marginal loyalty towards the Royal Family, which is not surprising considering that the King and his entire court fled for Brazil at the first sign of real trouble from Napoleon. As you know, there are so many cliques and factions at Court that it isn't easy to divine anybody's motives for doing anything. Everybody in the Embassy, from the Ambassador down, probably has dubious motives for accepting his assignment. The Marques, like other Portuguese aristocrats, must have learned years ago to put his family's interests above the interests of his government.'

'In the circumstances, is it melodramatic of me to suppose that the Marques has come to London with vengeance on his mind?'

'Yes, I think it is.'

'And yet, William, I am unhappy at the coincidence of your return from overseas and the Marques's sudden arrival from Portugal. I cannot forget that you and I between us caused the ruination of his father's schemes to free Napoleon from captivity on St Helena.'

The Captain's smile was bitter. 'You exaggerate my contribution to the affair, Edward. Left to my own devices, I would have done nothing save gaze adoringly into Diane's eyes.'

'Even if that is true, which is nonsense, the Marques de Algarve Branca doesn't know it. Remember that I was masquerading under your name when I met his father. It is *Captain Moreton* whom the Marques believes he has cause to hate. He is scarcely aware of my existence.'

'The list of enemies I have acquired during the past seven years is a long one, Edward. I shall add the Marques's name to it and then forget about him. Even if his intentions are as black as you fear, I cannot see how he could harm us. After all, we are upon our home ground and he is a stranger here. He couldn't come within twenty miles of Wellespont or Long Acres without our servants informing us of the fact.'

'You are probably right.' Lord Moreton grinned wryly. 'I accepted some years ago that matrimony and fatherhood have had a disastrous effect upon my common sense. I am delighted to think that you will shortly discover for yourself the devastating effect of love and marriage upon one's powers of rational assessment.'

'No doubt. I do not see any grooms around, do you? Perhaps they are eating?'

With secret amusement, Lord Moreton understood that the subject of his brother's forthcoming marriage remained strictly forbidden. He smothered a small smile as they walked round to the back of the stables, arguing amiably about the best route for the messenger to take to Richland Towers. As if, Lord Moreton reflected ruefully, there were nothing in the world more pressing for them to discuss. Curiosity, he could remember his governess telling him, was a vulgar, undesirable attribute found only in the lower orders of society. Lord Moreton hoped his old teacher, dead these many years, had acquired no angelic power to read minds. If she had, she would find her former pupil's head stuffed full of the most intense curiosity as to precisely what had happened the night before between his brother and the enigmatic Lady Catherine. Lord Moreton hoped that one day, not too far into the future, William would unbend sufficiently to tell him. In the meantime, he would have to content himself by discussing the affair at length with Diane.

CHAPTER
TEN

CATHERINE AND the Dowager, together with their maids, set off from Wellespont early the next morning in Lord Moreton's brand-new travelling carriage. Captain Moreton, taking advantage of the fine weather, chose to ride alongside, thus leaving more room for the ladies. In comparison to some of the rides he had endured in South America, the journey from Suffolk into Wiltshire should have seemed like little more than a pleasure trip.

He found, however, that frustration rather than pleasure was his dominant emotion during the journey, and his frustration mounted as they approached the market town of Chippenham and skirted its boundaries. They were less than two hours from their destination, and still he and Catherine had not exchanged a personal word since the moment she accepted his proposal.

They arrived at Richland Towers just as dusk was falling. The carriage had scarcely drawn to a halt when two young girls ran down the steps, the ribbons of their white muslin dresses streaming out behind them. They curtsied prettily to the Dowager, then greeted Catherine with warm hugs and several kisses, before turning to introduce themselves to Captain Moreton.

'Welcome to Richland Towers,' Jane said shyly, her somewhat plump features lighting up with a sweet smile. 'I am Jane, and this is our youngest sister, Margaret. My father is waiting to greet you inside the house, but my stepmother bids me to convey her apologies. She is resting now, and will join us all for dinner.'

They entered the house and found the Earl standing in the centre of the oak-panelled hall, his favourite hunting-dogs at his feet. He was an imposing figure of a man, blond and tall, like all three of his daughters. Unlike his children, however, his welcoming smile was full of self-importance rather than genuine friendliness. He greeted the Dowager, whom he considered undesirably eccentric, with cold civility. He greeted the Captain, whom he considered splendidly wealthy, with gushing enthusiasm. He greeted Catherine, whom he usually did not think about at all, with a cold kiss on her forehead and an enquiry about her journey which, the Captain noticed, he did not wait to have answered.

'No doubt you will be in a hurry to get to your rooms and refresh yourselves,' he said. 'Jane, have you followed your stepmama's directions about the housing of our guests?'

'Yes, Papa. Everything is arranged as she requested. The Dowager Lady Moreton is to have the Rose Bedroom, and I will take her there. Captain Moreton is to have the King Charles suite. Catherine will be able to show him where it is.'

'Very good. Well, we shall meet again at dinner, which will be at seven o'clock tonight. And I shall look forward to conferring with you in my bookroom once the meal is over, Captain Moreton.'

The Captain inclined his head in acknowledgment, and the party moved *en masse* up the stairs. The Rose Room was almost immediately at the head of the staircase, and when Jane and Margaret tactfully chose to follow the Dowager into her room, Catherine and Captain Moreton found themselves alone for the first time in four days.

'This is to be your room,' she said, indicating a sturdy oak door almost at the end of the corridor. 'It is reputed to be here that King Charles I slept for an entire week during the autumn of 1632. The bed is the original tester built in honour of the King's visit.' A fugitive smile curved her lips and then was gone. 'Fortunately, I can reassure you that the mattress and pillows have been renewed quite recently.'

'Good news indeed,' he murmured. He put his hand beneath her chin and tilted her face up to his inspection.

'You look tired, Lady Catherine. I trust it is not the prospect of marriage to me that takes all the colour from your cheeks and etches such lines of weariness about your mouth.'

'No,' she said, and he could see the effort it cost her to mask the faint tremor in her voice. 'I am just a little tired from the journey. A cup of hot tea and some warm water to wash in will revive me completely.'

'Lady Catherine . . .' He hesitated, not quite sure how to phrase his next sentence. He was not accustomed to seeking confidences from the women who passed through his life. 'If something was troubling you and I could help, would you do me the honour of confiding in me?'

For an instant he could have sworn he saw tears glimmer at the corner of her eyes, then she smiled at him with such radiance that he wondered if the tears had been no more than a trick of the light.

'You are too kind to me, Captain Moreton,' she said. 'When we are married and I run to you every time the cook has a fit of temperament, you will regret that generous offer!'

'I think not. Somehow, I feel sure that you are more than capable of handling any outburst the cook may inflict on you.' He paused a moment. 'Catherine . . .'

'Yes?'

'It is nothing. I only wanted to know if you would ride with me tomorrow morning.'

'With great pleasure, William. But we shall have to set out early if we are to avoid my sisters.'

She blushed like a schoolgirl when she realised what she had just said, and his blood ran hot with his need to embrace her. Her cheeks were so enchantingly flushed, her mouth was so invitingly close . . .

'Catherine . . .' he murmured again, barely conscious of saying her name.

She said nothing, and for a long moment they looked wordlessly at each other, then he reached out and brushed a stray lock of hair out of her eyes. She did not move away and, almost against his will, he ran his forefinger over the sensual curve of her bottom lip. At his touch, she closed her eyes and swayed towards him. Unbearably conscious of her warm, slender body so close to his own, he struggled to resist the temptation to take her into his arms and crush her against his body. He reminded himself that honourable men did not kiss their fiancées in the upstairs hall of their ancestral home. Honourable men, in fact, did not kiss their fiancées at all, except lightly on the cheek.

His attempt at self-denial lasted at least ten seconds; then, with a small groan, he put his arms round her and pulled her close against his heart. Fortunately, the thick folds of her travelling-habit disguised the extent of his arousal. Nevertheless, she opened her eyes immediately and he saw that they were hazy with a mixture of desire and panic.

'Captain Moreton, we must not . . . You should not embrace me so . . . It is not proper . . . A footman might come . . .'

'The servants are all busy downstairs at this hour.' He put one of his hands at the nape of her neck, gently forcing her head up so that she was constrained to look at him.

'A moment ago you called me William,' he said softly. 'I have discovered an irresistible urge to hear you call me so again.'

'But we are not married . . . It is surely not right . . . We have only known each other such a little while.'

'True.' He smiled softly. 'But I am a demanding man, my lady, and if you refuse to call me by my given name, I regret that I shall have to use stern measure to force your co-operation.'

'And what, pray, might those measures be, Captain Moreton?'

'Very unpleasant ones,' he said softly, looking at her lips. 'I warn you now that I plan to be a demanding husband. Either you call me by my given name, or I shall be compelled to kiss you into an appropriate state of obedience.'

Her eyes sparkled with shy laughter, lighting their green depths with dark, emerald fire. 'I can see that my cause is hopeless, and so I surrender. Please, *William*, I beg that you will not kiss me. It is not proper, and my godmama would not approve.'

Her laughter proved to be his final undoing. 'Ah, Catherine,' he said, with a sigh of frustration. 'You are so beautiful that a saint could not resist you. And, God knows, I am no saint.'

He bent his head and captured her lips in a long, passionate kiss. She did not immediately respond but neither did she reject him and, almost without thought, he deepened the embrace, thrusting his tongue into her mouth with an aching, savage hunger. When he felt the first tremble of her response, he knew that he had to move away or else abandon all hope of resisting the demands of the desire that clawed at him.

With a considerable effort of will, he lifted his head and loosened the grip of his arms. Drawing a deep breath, he stepped back from her, leaving a decorous gap between them.

'Catherine, I apologise. My behaviour was totally inappropriate and I can only beg your pardon and promise you that such an action will never be repeated.'

She did not look at him. 'Never again?' she asked in a small voice.

'I give you my word, Catherine. Never.'

She appeared totally preoccupied with plucking a piece of lint from her travelling-cape. 'I am sorry to hear that,' she said finally, her voice huskier than he had ever heard it. 'I had rather enjoyed the experience and I hoped that when we were married we might try it at least once more.'

The tiny, elusive smile was curving her mouth again and he almost swept her back into his arms on the spot. Only some lingering remnant of common sense kept him away from her.

'I am beginning to think that there is a great deal to be said in favour of marriage by special licence,' he said hoarsely. 'I trust that you father is on friendly terms with the local bishop?'

'They once shared the same Latin tutor, I believe.'

'Then I think that I may ride into Salisbury tomorrow and lay my case before him. Do you think that he will consider an urgent desire to kiss my bride as adequate ecclesiastical grounds for our immediate marriage?'

'I cannot help thinking that my stepmother's wish to attend the ceremony before she is confined would be more likely to sway the bishop in our favour.'

His smile was unwillingly tender as he watched her move down the corridor towards her room. 'Remember, we have an appointment to ride tomorrow morning.'

'Seven o'clock,' she repeated softly. 'I haven't forgotten. I shall be there, William.'

Captain Moreton was talking to his prospective parents-in-law, and trying hard not to dislike them cordially, when Catherine entered the drawing-room that evening, arm-in-arm with her two sisters.

She wore a gown of green satin that was a flattering contrast to the creamy pallor of her complexion and a perfect match for the vividness of her eyes. Unlike the clothes he had seen her wear previously, this dress was almost shocking in the stark simplicity of its cut, and she wore no jewellery save a pair of very large diamond earrings. Her fair hair was swept high on her head in a style that emphasised the perfect oval of her face and the slender length of her neck. Every time she moved, the earrings swayed against her cheek, and he had to fight back an insane impulse to walk across the room and press his lips to the place where the diamonds touched her skin.

He watched, hypnotised, as she murmured a polite word of greeting to her parents and then another, warmer greeting, to his mother. Finally she turned to him, her eyes peeping mischievously through impossibly thick lashes.

'Good evening, Captain Moreton. I trust you have recovered somewhat from the fatigue of your journey? You seemed—very tired—when I left you in the corridor earlier this evening.'

He swallowed hard. 'It was not as tiring as some journeys I have taken, Lady Catherine. And my rooms here are very comfortable. The servants have been most anxious to make me welcome.'

'I'm glad you find them so helpful,' she said. 'Many of them have been with us for a long time, since the early days of my parents' marriage.'

One of the diamond earrings nestled against her cheek in the precise spot where he ached to kiss her and he stared into her eyes, suddenly unable to shape even the most commonplace reply. He was saved from making a complete buffoon of himself only by the intervention of his mother.

The Dowager chose that moment to address some question to Catherine, thus affording him a couple of minutes to collect his wits. It was a long time since he had felt that particular sense of enchantment, he thought. In fact, he had never experienced even a twinge of it since the painful days when he had discovered the truth about Diane de Verette.

The brief, intrusive flash of memory was all he needed to break the spell Catherine had cast over him. Under no circumstances, he reminded himself, was he ever going to walk himself back into the toils of any woman, however bewitching he found her brilliant green eyes. Catherine was to be the mistress of his household and the mother of his children. She would never hold any place in his heart.

He waited until his mother finished speaking, then excused himself with a cool nod and went over to talk again to the Earl and Countess of Richland. He thought for a moment that Catherine looked hurt at his defection, but he soon convinced himself that he was mistaken. Seven years of hard experience had taught him that beautiful women could be wounded in their pride, but rarely in their other emotions.

Dinner was served with a paralysing display of pomp and ceremony in a dining-room that looked as if it had survived unchanged since the days of the medieval Great Hall. Now, in early summer, it was pleasantly cool. In winter he imagined that it must often be freezing. Catherine, seated across the table from him, was only dimly visible behind an arrangement of silver candelabra and enormous waving ferns. His mother, ensconced in the position of honour next to the Earl, was at least fifteen feet away from him.

While the footmen were setting out the dishes for the elaborate second course, the Countess of Richland turned to him with what he had come to consider her most poisonous smile.

'We certainly did not expect our little Catherine to make such a rapid conquest of your heart, Captain Moreton. We thought her far too wrapped up in grief for her poor dead husband to notice even such an eligible bachelor as yourself.'

'I think, perhaps, that it was I who noticed Lady

Catherine rather than the other way about, my lady.'

The Countess did not look pleased with this piece of information. She sniffed. 'It is generous of you to say so. Our dear little Catherine was used to be considered the beauty of the county, you know, but the Earl and I were concerned that her looks had permanently gone off these past few months. And then—I can confide this to you, Captain, because you are already almost one of the family —the truth is that when I am not around to advise her, the poor little thing has no taste in clothes. Absolutely none.'

The Countess emitted a flirtatious trill of laughter. 'It will be your role to advise her from now on, Captain Moreton, and I will confess—since you are so soon to become a member of the family—that you have taken on a burdensome duty.'

Her voice was tinged with acid as she glanced down the table towards her stepdaughter. 'I can assure you, Captain, that I had absolutely *nothing* to do with the selection of that bizarre gown she has chosen to wear tonight.'

'That I can well imagine, Lady Richland. It does not seem in the least in your style.' His eyes rested fleetingly on the tumble of silver and gold-embroidered lace that frothed around her shoulders, then he raised his wineglass and smiled at her blandly when he returned it to the table. 'Personally, I find that my fiancée looks particularly beautiful this evening.'

Catherine, who had heard every word of her stepmother's conversation, glanced round the waving fern-fronds and sent him a smile of such radiant gratitude that he felt his heart react with a violent lurch. Before he had time to reflect, his mouth softened into an answering smile.

When the interminable meal finally drew to its close, the Earl took Captain Moreton into his study. He poured them both a generous measure of cognac and listened eagerly while the Captain asked for permission to marry Catherine.

The Earl gave his consent with gratifying swiftness. He was a pompous man and a poor judge of character, but he had been fond of his first wife in his own limited way and, although far from a loving father, had more affection for her children than he knew how to express. He was genuinely pleased that his eldest daughter was going to have a second chance at marital happiness at so little cost to himself, and he clapped Captain Moreton warmly on the shoulder.

'You must know, sir, that I am delighted to accept your offer. Catherine has spent more than a year in deep mourning for her husband, which is only right and proper, of course. But she is too young to bury her heart in Matthew's grave, and I am sure she will make you a good wife. Her head's stuffed full of all sorts of intellectual nonsense which you will wish to ignore, but her mother was the same and I never paid any heed to her. Catherine's a pretty enough young woman when she's properly outfitted, and she's an excellent mistress of a household. I believe she will eventually make you a hostess you can be proud of.'

'I am sure she will, my lord.'

'She is strong, too,' the Earl continued. 'For all she is pale and thin, she has never had a day's real illness in her life. No need to worry that she may not produce you an heir. Matthew was taken sick only weeks after they were married. He is the reason that her first marriage was childless, you can take my word for it. Nothing to do with her, I can assure you.'

Captain Moreton found himself strangely repelled by this frank discussion of Catherine's breeding potential. 'I am not marrying your daughter only to produce heirs,' he said, his words clipped.

'No, no, of course not,' the Earl said, a touch impatiently. The Captain did not look like a sentimental type, but the Earl did not want to listen to any protestations of undying love, an emotion he found singularly inappropriate to the practical institution of matrimony.

'However, when all's said and done, healthy sons are what marriage is all about.'

Since he had decided only a few days previously that his sole purpose in marrying would be to produce legitimate heirs, Captain Moreton could hardly disagree, but the realisation that he and the Earl were in total agreement did not please him. He took a large swallow of his brandy, and decided to change the subject.

'We should discuss the financial arrangements, my lord,' he said curtly. 'I should like to have the general terms agreed as soon as possible, so that our lawyers can set to work to draw up the contracts. My mother has suggested that the wedding ceremony should take place as soon as possible . . .'

'Of course, of course.' For the first time, the Earl looked a little uncomfortable. 'The fact is, my good man, that I did not do quite the job I should have done in protecting Catherine's inheritance when she married her cousin. I knew Matthew to be a good and honourable man, so I consigned her fortune entirely into his charge. It was only right and proper that I should do so, of course, since she was only seventeen and obviously could not be trusted to take care of her own property. However, to cut a long story short, he ran through the lot. She is as close to penniless as makes no odds, Captain Moreton. I make her an allowance, naturally, but she has no capital.'

The Captain felt a surge of emotion that he was surprised to identify as sympathy for Catherine, coupled with anger at the Earl of Richland's self-righteousness and Matthew's incompetence.

'How did the late Mr Richland manage to dissipate several thousand pounds while languishing on a sick-bed?' he asked, an unfamiliar bite in his voice.

'Not as you might suppose, Captain Moreton. Matthew Richland lived a life devoted to good works. He wasted Catherine's fortune on inadequate schemes to support the shiftless and the idle. Benefiting the deserving poor, he called it.'

'I see. Well, it is too late to regret decisions taken several years ago. Perhaps, in the circumstances, it is fortunate that my income is more than adequate to provide everything that my future wife might need. I shall be happy to make a settlement upon Lady Catherine effective on the date of our marriage. Does thirty thousand pounds seem adequate?'

The Earl swallowed a gasp and decided, not for the first time, that Captain Moreton was truly a son-in-law after his own heart. He grasped him by the hand and shook it vigorously several times. 'Another cognac?' he offered, sitting down at his desk and drawing paper and pen towards him. 'Shall we just get the broad outline of your wishes down in writing, Captain Moreton? Then we can send off the details to our lawyers first thing in the morning.'

With a touch of resignation, the Captain pulled a chair closer to the desk. He began to recite the names of his bankers and to list the distribution of his assets. The Earl wrote eagerly, his eyes growing rounder as the huge sums mounted.

'My daughter is a very fortunate woman,' the Earl said. 'Very fortunate indeed.'

'I am gratified that you approve of my suit,' the Captain said.

His irony was entirely lost on the Earl.

'What father would not?' he asked simply. 'Indeed, what woman would not think herself incredibly lucky to have received your proposal?'

The Captain did not answer. He leaned back in his chair and sighed: there was still a great deal of writing left to be done. Did Catherine think she was incredibly lucky to have received his offer of marriage, he wondered.

He was surprised at how much he wanted to know the answer to his own question.

CHAPTER
ELEVEN

CAPTAIN MORETON thoroughly enjoyed his ride the next morning. His conversation with Catherine roamed easily over many different subjects, and it was late when they returned to the stables. The head groom was waiting for them, his expression openly accusing.

'Well, my lady, it be almost the middle of the morning.' Disapproval was rich in his voice. 'I were afeared Star had thrown the Captain.'

Catherine laughed. 'George, you know very well that you were not frightened of any such thing. You saw for yourself how well the Captain rides, and you knew that we would not be back much before ten.'

Captain Moreton acknowledged the head groom's fulminating presence with a cheerful smile. 'Don't worry, George. I thoroughly enjoyed the ride, although Star is a little placid for my taste. Next time I should prefer to ride something with a bit more spirit.' He turned back to Catherine without giving George any chance to reply.

'Are you ready to return to the house, my lady?'

'Yes, quite ready, thank you.'

She was giggling by the time they left the stable yard. 'Poor George! How could you inflict such a crushing blow to his pride? Star is his prize animal. To hear him referred to as "a little placid" will destroy his happiness for the rest of the day.'

'When a former cavalry officer has his horsemanship questioned, he is liable to seek revenge. But I can see that I shall have my work cut out if I want to convince your servants that I am a suitable husband for you.'

'Don't despair! I promise to put in a good word for you whenever the opportunity arises.'

They had arrived at a side entrance to the house. Captain Moreton held open the door for her, making some teasing remark, and she was laughing quietly as they entered the house. He thought as they walked along the narrow hall that he had never seen her look more beautiful. Her eyes sparkled with warmth, her lips were soft and full, and her cheeks glowed with colour. He was gratified to think that, to look so content, she must have enjoyed their morning ride as much as he had.

The Countess of Richland met them as they passed through the baize-covered door leading into the main wing of the house. She looked sharply at Catherine, and her plump, florid features settled into a smile that barely concealed her anger. When she had conceived the brilliant idea of coercing her stepdaughter into marriage with Captain Moreton, she had never dreamed that her two victims might find themselves well pleased with the arrangement. She was seriously displeased by her own miscalculation.

'Dear child, I am so pleased to see you,' she said gushingly. 'I have been wanting to talk to you this age. And how are you this morning, Captain Moreton?'

'Well, thank you, Lady Richland.'

The Countess's smile tightened. 'Good. But we must not keep you from your breakfast, Captain. Catherine, will you please step into the morning-room? There are some family matters which I need to discuss with you.'

Captain Moreton ignored the Countess's tapping foot and frowning brows. He took Catherine's hand and pressed the tip of her gloved fingers to his lips. 'I look forward to seeing you at luncheon, my dear. I thoroughly enjoyed our ride.'

Her smile was shy, but radiant. 'I, too, enjoyed every minute of our time together, William.'

The Countess cleared her throat angrily and Captain Moreton relinquished Catherine's hand, watching her as she followed her stepmother into the morning-room. He was half-way to the breakfast-room, humming contentedly under his breath, before he discovered that he held her riding-crop.

He had no compunction about intruding upon the Countess's discussion of 'family matters', since he was sure Catherine would be delighted by the interruption. He turned on his heel and walked lightly towards the morning-room. The door was not completely closed, but he froze with his hand raised ready to knock when he heard the low, passionate tones of Catherine's voice.

'But you cannot do that! You *promised* me that if I married Captain Moreton, Jane would be safe. You cannot go back on your bargain now!'

'My dear girl, I haven't the faintest idea what you are talking about. For your own good, I encouraged you to visit your godmother in Wellespont. I pointed out to you that Captain Moreton would be there, and that you should do your best to attract his attention. He is a fabulously wealthy man, and you are as close to penniless as makes no odds. It is an ideal match for you. What has all this to do with your sister?'

'Everything!' Catherine's voice was harder than the Captain had ever imagined it could be. 'You did not suggest that I should *bring myself to Captain Moreton's attention*. As soon as you found out the size of his fortune, you ordered me to trap him into marriage. You ordered me to compromise him. Well, I have performed my part of the bargain, and now I expect you to perform yours.'

'Are you telling me, Catherine, that Captain Moreton did not offer his proposal of marriage willingly? I am deeply shocked to think that there might have been some element of coercion on your part.' The mockery in the Countess's voice deepened into outright sarcasm. 'Surely no daughter of the Earl of Richland would ever allow herself or her virtue to be compromised. I think I must have misunderstood you.'

Captain Moreton heard the hiss of Catherine's indrawn breath and the rustle of her skirts as she moved across the room. 'You know very well what ultimatum you laid in front of me before I left for Wellespont, Lady Richland, and I don't understand what you are hoping to achieve by this pretended loss of memory. You must know that even when the Captain and I are married, I shall have no direct access to his money. I can do nothing more than I have already done to compensate you for the loss of Mr Craddock's fortune. If I had any money of my own, I would give it to you. What can you possibly hope to achieve by threatening to renege on our bargain?'

Captain Moreton did not wait to hear Lady Richland's reply. His hand, which had been suspended motionless over the panel of the door, finally fell back to his side. Anger thrummed in his ears with such overpowering force that he could not have heard what was being said even if he had listened. Unable to remain still for another second, he turned on his heel and stormed out of the house.

He felt a burning need for rough physical exercise, so he strode in the direction of the stables, roundly cursing his own folly. He could scarcely believe that, for the second time in his life, he had been on the brink of falling in love with a woman whose only purpose in pretending affection had been to deceive him.

'Can I help you, Cap'n?' George asked, when he arrived at the stables.

'Saddle a horse for me,' he commanded. 'And make sure that it isn't a slug.'

He paced up and down the yard while he waited, using Catherine's crop to slash the heads off several offending nettles. Seven years had obviously taught him very little, he thought furiously. Once again a beautiful woman had managed to beguile him into making a fool of himself. Like Diane de Verette, Catherine had seemed different from the crowd, more beautiful in her own cool way, more sensitive and infinitely more intelligent.

And indeed she had been different, he reflected bitterly. The trivial greed of the rest of her sex was nothing in comparison to what Catherine had aimed for. Most women could be satisfied with a few murmured words of passion and the gift of a trinket or two. She had aimed for nothing less than marriage and his entire fortune!

The groom led out a chestnut gelding, and the Captain mounted him with a brief word of thanks. Even in the full flare of his rage, he could not vent his wrath upon the servants. He took the horse out of the yard at a brisk trot, spurring him into a gallop as soon as he was outside the boundaries of the park.

How clever Catherine had been! First she had intrigued him by her silence, and by the subtle aura of secret sorrow she had managed to project. Then, as soon as his interest was piqued, she had skilfully drawn him further into her toils with a dazzling display of intellectual attainment and enticing shyness. Not to mention her skilful manipulation of his physical desires, the Captain reminded himself cynically. Unlike Lady Annabelle, she had learned the value of restraint and the benefits to be derived from pretending virtue. She had learned that the promise of passion was invariably a great deal more exciting than the sexual act itself. Her impersonation of a modest, physically unawakened young woman was so brilliant in its execution that she had somehow convinced him that she was an innocent child, hovering on the verge of sexual awareness. All this, despite the fact that he knew she was a widow!

He put his horse at a five-foot fence, jumping it with several inches to spare. Lady Catherine, he thought bitterly, had definitely missed her calling. She would have made a first-rate addition to the Drury Lane stage.

He had not consciously guided the gelding in any particular direction, so he was somewhat startled when he found himself at precisely the spot where Catherine had taken him earlier that morning. He drew rein, but did not dismount, and stared broodingly at the sparkling spray of the spring water.

She had felt so soft and yielding when he held her in his arms the day before, so unutterably *right*. Her mouth had trembled beneath his as if she had never before experienced the piercing excitement of sexual arousal. How many times had she played that particular trick on some unsuspecting man, he wondered? With a bitter smile, he concluded that half the county of Wiltshire might well have enjoyed her favours for all he knew to the contrary. Once they were married, if he wanted to be sure that the children she produced were truly his own, he had better lock her up in one of the towers at Long Acres and throw away the key.

The horse tossed his head angrily, and the Captain realised that he had unconsciously jabbed at the reins. The thought of Catherine confined to her room, totally within his power, gave him a rush of almost barbaric pleasure. He had sworn when Diane de Verette betrayed him that he would allow no other woman to come close to his heart. Catherine had almost persuaded him to break that vow, but he had learned his lesson just in time. When they were married, she would discover that her intended victim was not quite as gullible as she had imagined. And his revenge was going to taste very sweet.

He rode his gelding back to Wellespont at a gallop, his thoughts all centred upon the intoxicating pleasures of revenge. It was not until he had consigned the lathered and sweating horse into the care of a groom that it occurred to him to wonder why all his schemes for punishing Catherine somehow involved a speedy marriage and long nights in her bed before he uttered his final, cutting rejection. As he walked up to the house, he was considering the disquieting fact that far and away the most effective revenge would be simply to refuse to marry her.

For some reason, this particular method of punishment did not appeal to him in the slightest, and he managed to convince himself that the practical difficulties of breaking his engagement were too great to be contemplated.

By the time he had bathed and changed, his plan of action was clear to him. He would leave Richland Towers immediately after luncheon, with the excuse of seeking out the local bishop. Having obtained a special licence, he would claim unexpected pressure of business in connection with his marriage and would not return to Richland Towers until the day before the wedding ceremony.

His decision taken, he summoned his valet to pack his clothes, then flung himself into an armchair and spent a gratifying half-hour brooding over the many and various humiliations he would inflict upon Lady Catherine once she was his wife. Until this moment, he had never considered how many interesting variations on the sexual act he had learned during his years in South America.

A highly satisfactory vision of Catherine kneeling at his feet and pleading tearfully for his forgiveness somehow transformed itself into an erotic picture of Catherine naked in his arms, begging for the consummation of their love-making. He was quite relieved when a footman appeared at the door and announced that luncheon was ready.

All things considered, he could hardly wait to leave Richland Towers, and he hoped very much that he would find Lady Annabelle in London.

The Marques de Algarve Branca sipped a glass of excellent Madeira and re-read the formal announcement of Captain Moreton's betrothal. He knew nothing about Lady Catherine Richland and her family, but tomorrow he would make it his business to find out every detail of her past. He clipped the notice from the pages of the newspaper and added it to several other papers in a slim leather folder.

It was interesting to discover that his old enemy was about to marry. It added a new and stimulating element to the Marques's plans for revenge, since it seemed obvious that Captain Moreton's humiliation would be more complete if it somehow encompassed his wife.

When he was a youth, and his father had first been exiled, the Marques's plans for revenge had been primitive in the extreme. As he grew older, he had gradually grown aware that killing Captain Moreton would provide inadequate retribution for the scope of the man's crimes. Satisfactory vengeance required that, before he died, the Captain should suffer the same sort of public humiliation that the proud family of Algarve Branca had suffered. The Marques poured himself a second glass of wine, and leaned back in his chair. The existence of a wife added intriguing possibilities to the range of his planning.

It would be absolutely perfect if the Captain's marriage happened by some fortunate chance to be a love match. Such an eventuality would be out of the question in Portugal, of course, where the unions of great families were arrived at by more logical methods than the vagaries of human passion. The English, however, were as crazy in the ordering of their marriages as they were in almost every other aspect of their lives, and the Marques considered there was a good possibility that the Captain was actually in love with his bride-to-be. The thought was positively delicious in its ramifications.

But how was this wife to be worked into his schemes? Captain Moreton, the Marquis remembered, had been

seen frequently in the company of Lady Annabelle
Brigham. It was not much to go on, and it might prove to be
a fact of little interest. On the other hand, a former mistress
usually created great potential for mischief in a new marriage, particularly one contracted for foolish reasons of
sentiment rather than valid reasons of fortune and personal
advancement. Smiling slightly, the Marques tugged at the
bell-rope.

'Summon my carriage,' he said when a footman opened
the study door. 'I am going out.'

It was almost midnight, but all the Marques's servants
knew better than to question his orders. The footman
acknowledged the order without any indication of surprise,
bowing very low as he left the room.

The Marques smiled once again. He had no doubt that
this evening was going to prove extremely informative.

Edward Moreton arrived at Long Acres, his brother's
country estate, on a rainy Thursday evening. The Captain,
who had returned from London only a few hours earlier,
greeted him with cheerful smiles, hot mulled wine, a superb
dinner—and total silence on the subject of his forthcoming
marriage.

Lord Moreton did not attempt to press his brother for
confidences until the next morning, when they were travelling in the Captain's chaise to Richland Towers.

'I am sure Lady Catherine's family will be anxiously
awaiting your arrival,' he said with an attempt at casual-
ness. 'The wedding takes place tomorrow morning, and you
have scarcely seen your fiancée since your betrothal.'

'That is true,' the Captain agreed. 'I had urgent business
to attend to in London.'

'Ah, I see.'

Edward knew that his brother had been seen disporting
himself every night in the company of Lady Annabelle
Brigham, but he wisely refrained from asking if she had
constituted the sum total of the Captain's 'urgent business'.

'You must have missed the pleasure of Catherine's
company,' he suggested mildly. 'Your fiancée is a
charming young woman, and Diane is delighted that you

have chosen such an interesting sister-in-law for her.'

Captain Moreton's smile lacked any trace of warmth. 'I am naturally delighted to have been of service to Diane. But you are mistaken if you think I have missed Lady Catherine's company. You know that we met each other only a few weeks ago, Edward, so you surely cannot believe that she and I are making a love match. She marries me for my fortune, and I . . . I marry her because . . .'

'Yes?' Lord Moreton prompted. 'Why do you marry her, William?'

He shrugged. 'Because my mother wished for the match and because of certain circumstances at Wellespont that pushed the matter out of my control.'

'There is no possible circumstance which I can think of, William, that would compel you to marry a woman whom you do not wish to marry.'

'You are mistaken. There was a threat of scandal, and our mother felt responsible for Lady Catherine's reputation. She is, after all, her godmother. In a nutshell, Edward, the threat of a scandal was the reason for our betrothal.'

Lord Moreton grinned. 'William, fool yourself if you wish, but don't try to deceive me! I shall merely repeat that there is nothing on earth that could have forced you to offer marriage to a woman whom you did not wish to marry. Certainly not the vague threat of a possible scandal.'

The Captain shrugged. 'You may be right. Perhaps I have simply decided that it is time for me to marry. Having made my fortune, I have developed an aspiration to become a typical country squire. Do you not think that the role would suit me?'

Lord Moreton laughed. 'Not very well, and, to be honest, I think Lady Catherine would make an appalling country squire's wife. I give you a year to play at being the gentleman farmer; then the urge for adventure will strike, and you will once again be off and running. No doubt taking Lady Catherine with you.'

'Are you truly happy, Edward? Do you never regret your impetuous marriage?' The Captain asked his questions abruptly, not looking at his brother.

'I am truly happy,' Lord Moreton said softly. He hesitated before speaking again. 'You know, William, we have never really discussed my marriage, and I think, perhaps, that it is past time for us to rectify that omission.'

'What can there be for us to discuss? You married Diane out of expediency, and afterwards . . . well, afterwards I suppose that you fell in love with her.'

'No,' Lord Moreton said quietly. 'That is not quite right, William. The truth is that I was fascinated by Diane from the instant we first met, and I was sick to my soul because she was betrothed to you. The more we saw of each other, the deeper my attraction to her became and the more violently I resented her power over me. I spent many long nights imagining subtle tortures I could inflict upon her. The trouble was that all my visions of punishment somehow ending up with my ravishing Diane, and Diane by some miracle falling willingly into my arms.'

Captain Moreton gave a convulsive start, which he covered by saying, 'London is full of beautiful women. You should have found yourself a new mistress.'

Lord Moreton sought and held his brother's gaze. 'I had a mistress at the time, William. In fact, I had several. But no other woman succeeded in relieving the yearning that Diane aroused in me. Have you not discovered that uncomfortable truth for yourself?'

The dark rush of colour along his brother's cheekbones told its own story, and Lord Moreton said quietly, 'Until I fell in love with Diane, I had never found myself in a situation where my intuition was utterly at war with my reason. Believe me, William, I have learned that the heart is invariably much wiser than the head. As a combat-weary old soldier, I have a recommendation to make to you. Trust your instincts about Lady Catherine, and you will save yourself a great deal of unnecessary pain.'

The Captain smiled politely enough, but he chose to ignore his brother's remarks. He pointed out that they were approaching the far western boundary of the Richland estate, and in their discussion of the practical arrangements for the wedding ceremony, all chance of further confidences was lost.

*   *   *

It had started to rain heavily the day after Captain Moreton's departure, and Catherine found that the gloomy weather fitted perfectly with her mood. The constant downpour kept her confined to the house, and she tried to convince herself that it was only inactivity which made the days seem so long and dreary. The complete absence of any letter from the Captain had nothing to do with her depression, she assured herself.

She was not entirely convinced by the logic of her own arguments. Nevertheless, despite the doubts she cherished about her prospects for future happiness, she never regretted her betrothal. As far as she was concerned, her betrothal had achieved its more important objective—Jane was no longer required to marry Mr Craddock.

Jane's stunned gratitude when she heard the news amply compensated Catherine for the misery she had endured in trying to decide what to do about her stepmother's ultimatum. Unfortunately, Catherine's own situation gave no indication that it would end as happily as her sister's. The Captain Moreton who returned to Richland Towers on the eve of their wedding was the same icy stranger who had left it eight days previously. He arrived with his brother late on Friday afternoon, and swept into the drawing-room, where Catherine was sitting with the Dowager.

'You look wonderful, my dearest Mama,' he said, kissing his mother fondly. 'Considering that you have not consumed a drop of goat's milk in more than a week!'

The Dowager's eyes twinkled. 'It is undoubtedly pleasure at your forthcoming marriage, William, that has enabled me to survive the deprivation.'

'Ah yes, my marriage. What a pleasure it will be for us all!' The Captain shot a mocking glance towards Catherine. 'Lady Catherine,' he said, bowing low over her hand, but not carrying it to his lips. 'Long Acres awaits the pleasure of your arrival tomorrow. I trust everything is in order for our wedding?'

She lifted her head proudly, aware that several interested eyes were fixed upon them. 'Yes, it is,' she said with a bleak, formal courtesy that matched his own. 'The bishop is already a guest here at Richland Towers, and the ceremony is to take place at nine o'clock tomorrow morning. I believe that is what you requested in a letter from your lawyer to my father.'

She did not wait for him to comment, but turned to Lord Moreton, smiling as she extended her hand. If the Captain could smile at everybody except her, she could certainly return the compliment.

Captain Moreton stirred impatiently. 'The drive this afternoon took longer than we had planned,' he said. 'If it is not inconveniencing the household too much, Lady Catherine, I should like to bathe before dinner. Will you excuse me if I go to my room?'

'Certainly,' Catherine said. 'You are in the King Charles suite once again. I am sure you remember how to get there, although your previous stay with us was so unexpectedly brief.'

'My stay was brief, but my memory of everything which occurred here is indelibly engraved upon my mind, Lady Catherine. Some of your conversations were particularly memorable.'

She sensed the hidden thread of anger behind his words, but could not even begin to guess at the cause. His gaze was so cutting that she turned quickly away. 'Lord Moreton, you are in the South Bedroom. I shall be happy to show you to your room if you, too, would like to rest before dinner.'

The Dowager rose to her feet. 'There is no need to disturb yourself, my dear. I have a few things to discuss with Edward, so I shall escort him upstairs. William, do you come with us?'

'Yes, Mama, I am coming now.' He bowed briefly in Catherine's direction, his gaze utterly cold. 'Until this evening, my lady.'

CHAPTER
TWELVE

THE MORNING of Lady Catherine Persephone Richland's wedding to Captain the Honourable William Edward Moreton dawned brilliant with renewed sunshine. The countryside, freshened by the previous days of rain, gleamed green and gold in the dancing sunlight, and the wedding guests all congratulated each other on this auspicious start to a marriage which was clearly ordained in Heaven. The bride's gown of cream lace over beige satin was deemed to be in the height of good taste for a widow, and fashionable enough in style to satisfy even the most demanding of tastes. Her quantity of veiling was considered just right: enough to demonstrate her modesty, but not so much as to seem absurd considering the fact that she was a widow, and therefore by definition an experienced woman of the world. The bridal attendants were declared positively charming in their simple gowns of pale lemon yellow. Jane, the guests concluded, while too plump to be considered as beautiful as either of her sisters, was rosy-complexioned and far from ill-looking when got up properly. And the bridgegroom, supremely elegant in a morning suit of pale grey superfine, was announced to be such a fine figure of a man that the size of his fortune was sometimes not commented upon for at least two minutes together.

The bride and groom did not linger at the reception after the ceremony. Captain Moreton's estate was less than forty miles from Richland Towers, but it was considered only prudent to set out as early as possible so that there would be time to complete the five-hour journey long before nightfall. Farewells were quickly exchanged, and the Captain's travelling chaise rolled out of the drive to a chorus of heartfelt good wishes. Only the Dowager and Lord Moreton looked thoughtful as they watched the chaise pick up a somewhat reckless speed.

The Captain's concentration was clearly fixed on his

driving, and Catherine did not attempt to introduce any conversation. In truth, her feelings had reached such a state of bewildered numbness that she was barely capable of rational thought.

From time to time he enquired curtly into her comfort, and she replied with polite inanities. When she finally mentioned that she was thirsty, he stopped the chaise at the next village and bought her a beaker of chilled apple cider, which she drank gratefully while the horses were changed.

When she guessed that they were only three or four miles from his estate, she summoned up the courage to break the painful silence.

'Would you tell me a little about the people I shall be meeting at Long Acres? I don't even know the name of your housekeeper.'

'Mrs Noyes,' he said briefly. 'The butler is Cowper, and my estate manager is called Peter Brownfield. I have asked the cook to prepare a light supper for us. I imagine you will be tired and will want to go early to bed.'

She looked down at her pale grey kid gloves, which matched her grey pelisse, trimmed with emerald-green braid. She wondered why she had spent so much time choosing her outfit, when he had not even glanced in her direction.

'Yes,' she said huskily. 'I am a little tired. An early night would be welcome.'

His mouth compressed into a tight, forbidding line, and Catherine sighed as she turned once again to watch the passing scenery. Men's moods, she decided, were exceptionally difficult for a mere woman to fathom.

The Captain's estate lay almost on the Gloucestershire border, and she already knew from conversations with the Dowager that it had come into his possession on the death of his maternal grandfather ten years earlier.

'This is the eastern boundary of Long Acres,' the Captain said abruptly. 'The house is on the other side of the village, about a mile from here.'

She looked around with renewed interest, and saw at once that his long absence abroad had not led to any neglect of his property. The cottages were sturdily built, the cows in the meadows were fat, the hedgerows neatly trimmed, the drainage ditches efficiently placed and, in the soft light of summer dusk, the budding wheatfields rippled like a green sea. The Captain had clearly adopted the most modern agricultural techniques and had also employed a great deal of local labour to put the new scientific techniques into practice. She was immensely glad to realise that visiting starving cottagers was not going to form any part of her new wifely duties.

Long Acres was about eighty years old, an early Georgian building that stood about half a mile from the village, surrounded by a small pleasantly landscaped park. She had half-expected the entire Long Acres staff to be lined up waiting to greet her, but she had forgotten about the informality that always seemed to creep into even the best-run bachelor households. Only the butler, the house-keeper and the estate agent waited in the hall to welcome them, and Peter Brownfield made polite excuses about returning to his own small house almost as soon as the introductions were complete.

'Lady Catherine is fatigued from the long journey and the early start to our day,' the Captain said to the house-keeper as soon as the agent had departed. 'Will you show her to her bedroom?'

'Yes, sir. Her ladyship's maid arrived in the carriage this morning with all her ladyship's luggage. And Cook has prepared a light supper, if you would care to eat it later. Breast of chicken poached in white wine and a sorbet, your ladyship, if that meets with your approval.'

'It sounds most welcome,' Catherine said. She did not look at her husband when she spoke. 'Do you think we could be ready to eat by eight o'clock, Captain Moreton?'

'That should present no problems, I think. Summon Mrs Noyes when you are ready, and she will conduct you to the dining-room. Since there are only the two of us, we shall keep everything as informal as possible tonight. You appear very—fatigued.'

'And you are all kind consideration, sir.' She bit her lip, not having intended to speak so sarcastically in front of the servants, but it had been a trying day and she wished that she might have received some small measure of genuine support from the Captain. His frigid courtesy left her feeling weary to the depths of her soul. Tears of mingled exhaustion and misery were beginning to gather at the corner of her eyes, and she walked swiftly towards the stairs. She did not want to embarrass herself or the servants by crying in the main hall of her new home.

'If you would be good enough to lead the way, Mrs Noyes,' she said evenly. 'You will appreciate that I am anxious to rest a little before we eat.'

'Of course, my lady.' The housekeeper showed her new mistress to a pleasant, spacious bedroom decorated with cream-striped silk wallpaper and unusual rose-coloured Turkey carpets. A small fire burned in the grate, dispelling any risk of dampness, and her maid was seated in a comfortable wing chair close to the hearth. For some unfathomable reason, the cosy elegance of the room increased Catherine's feeling of depression. If Captain Moreton's attitude towards her had only been different, she could have been so happy here. As it was, he clearly felt nothing but regret for the marriage that had been thrust upon her.

Mary stood up and bobbed a tiny curtsy. 'It's good to see you have arrived safely, my lady. Mrs Noyes, would you be so kind as to prepare some hot tea for her ladyship?'

'Certainly. I will send Fanny up with it directly. If you need anything else, my lady, you have only to ask.'

Catherine murmured her thanks, then sank on to the bed and pulled off her bonnet, running weary fingers through her hair.

'You look exhausted, my lady. What has been happening since I've been gone?'

'I've been getting married.' She cut off a gasp of laughter that was uncomfortably tinged with hysteria. 'I don't know what's the matter with me, Mary. We have travelled only thirty-eight miles today, a journey that took less than five hours, and yet I feel as if I have been jounced around in that chaise for ever. Even my teeth feel tired!'

Mary examined her mistress shrewdly, and what she saw made her suspect that the journey was the least of Lady Catherine's present worries. 'You will feel better when you have had a bath,' she said, keeping her voice severely practical. 'The hot water is already here by the fire, my lady, waiting to be poured. And the tea will help to revive you.'

By the time Catherine summoned the housekeeper to escort her downstairs, she felt outwardly like a new woman. She wore a simple evening gown of brown shot silk that emphasised the brilliant green of her eyes and flattered the soft, silvery fairness of her hair. Mary had said that she looked beautiful, and the gasp of appreciation from the housekeeper confirmed the maid's praise. Mentally, however, she remained in a torment of doubt and confusion. What would she do if the Captain continued to ignore her? A few weeks ago, she would have claimed that life could offer her nothing more desirable than a quiet position as mistress of a prosperous country estate. Now she knew that her comfort and independence would be meaningless if they did not include some degree of friendship with the man who had become her husband.

Captain Moreton rose to his feet as she entered the dining-room, and they stared at each other in a silence laden with unspoken questions.

'You look . . . refreshed . . . my lady,' he said finally. He glanced towards the housekeeper. 'You may tell Cowper to serve the food now.'

'Shall we sit down at the table?' he asked Catherine when Mrs Noyes had left the room. 'Would you care for some wine?'

'Some claret, please, if you have it.'

He poured it from a crystal decanter that stood on the sideboard, but when she lifted the glass, he put out his hand and stilled her movement.

'First, a toast,' he said. 'My dear wife, do you not think we should offer a toast on this momentous occasion?'

'Certainly, Captain Moreton.' She struggled to remain calm although his fingers seemed to turn her skin to flame at the point where they touched her hand. 'Shall we toast our future happiness together?'

'Oh, I have a much more interesting toast to propose

than that, my lady. How about a salute to your incredible acting ability? Since it cannot be acknowledged upon the stage, let us at least acknowledge it in the privacy of our own home.'

'I think you praise me for talents I don't possess, Captain Moreton. I have no idea why you should think I have any ability as an actress. However, if that is the toast you wish to propose . . .' She allowed her voice to tail away into silence as she raised her glass to her lips and defiantly tossed back the entire contents in a single series of swallows. The wine left a small glow in the pit of her stomach, and she was suddenly aware of anger beginning to coil tightly inside her.

'Come, Captain,' she said softly. 'You do not drink.'

His gaze lingered for several seconds on her lips, then he swung away from her and put his glass down on the sideboard with a slight clatter. 'I seem to have lost my thirst,' he said curtly.

A servant flung open the double doors at that moment, and the butler entered carrying a large silver tray laden with dishes. A footman followed him into the dining-room, and as soon as they had served the golden chicken breasts, tiny green peas and buttered rice, Captain Moreton dismissed them.

'Thank you, we can serve the rest of the food ourselves. We shall ring if we require anything further, Cowper.'

'Yes, sir.' The two servants withdrew, leaving Catherine and the Captain to stare at each other across the width of the table.

The Captain's expression became more mocking than ever. 'I see that Cowper has left us a bottle of champagne,' he said. 'How enterprising of him! Would you care for some, my lady?'

'Yes, why not?' she said, her eyes sparkling with temper. She was heartily sick of his perpetual mockery, which seemed directed at her without any adequate cause. Perhaps he was justified in resenting the fact that they had been forced into marriage, but in truth the marriage was no more her fault than his. Circumstances and the Dowager had conspired to bring about their union. It was unfair of him to place all the blame on her, and she raised her chin with unconscious defiance.

'By all means, let us drink the champagne. A wedding is usually considered cause for celebration, is it not?'

'Indeed, I believe it is. And you have every reason to celebrate this wedding, do you not, my lady? It must seem that you have achieved your objective with almost laughable ease.'

Her defiance was immediately pricked by a debilitating rush of guilt, and her hand shook as she picked up her fork. She wondered precisely what he meant by his hurtful remarks, and yet was afraid to ask. She took refuge in deliberate incomprehension.

'I'm not sure that I understand you, Captain Moreton. Do you mean that we should celebrate because the scandal my godmother feared has not materialised?'

His smile was tinged with bitterness. 'No, my lady, I did not refer to the non-existent danger of scandal, or even to my mother's strange complicity in bringing about our betrothal. You are to be congratulated, by the way, on your skill in keeping my mother ignorant of your true purpose in coming to Wellespont. She is not an easy person to deceive, even if she does find it pleasant to have a companion who speaks fluent Greek.'

For a moment her gaze locked with his. 'You are mistaken about me, Captain Moreton.' She paused, then added, 'I do not speak Greek at all. I merely read and write it.'

He bent his attention to a bowl of peaches, selecting one with apparently infinite care. 'I fear we are in danger of forgetting that this meal is supposed to be a celebration. It is certainly not the moment for serious discussion. Do, pray, eat some of your dinner. My cook will be desolate if you don't do greater justice to his efforts. This menu is undoubtedly the culmination of days of planning.'

She obediently swallowed a mouthful of spring peas, washing them down with champagne when it seemed likely that they might stick in her throat and choke her. She followed the peas with a piece of chicken. She thought that, if she could have tasted it, it might have been delicious.

'Your cook has prepared an excellent meal,' she said with
a determined effort to introduce some normal conversation. 'You seem fortunate in the efficiency and friendliness
of all your servants, Captain Moreton.'

'My brother found the cook for me in London, just
before I returned to England. The housekeeper and
the butler have both been here for more than twenty
years, and they have taken pride in training the younger
servants.'

They managed to produce a few more polite exchanges
about the domestic arrangements of Long Acres and the
need for local employment of the village girls. It struck
Catherine as the height of absurdity that they should be
discussing the virtues of the Long Acres domestic staff on
their wedding night, but even this stilted discussion was
preferable to the biting undertone of his more personal
comments. She wanted to ask him what she had done to
make him so angry, but guilt—and fear of how he might
answer—kept her silent. How could she ask him to explain
his behaviour, when he would never respect her, or feel
affection for her, if she confessed the truth about her
stepmother's ultimatum.

She sipped at her champagne, assailed by a sudden
nostalgic memory of the day she had married Matthew.
They had been so young and carefree, she thought. Neither
of them had wanted to leave the post-wedding party at
Richland Towers until the very last minute, so they had
danced until late in the afternoon and drunk a little bit too
much wine.

It had been after nightfall when they finally arrived at
Matthew's small house near Bath. How happy they had
been as they sipped tea in the tiny drawing-room, relaxing
before they went upstairs to bed! They had laughed
together, breathless with the strange, shy intimacy of marriage after so many years of being best friends. Later,
Matthew had come to her room and held her close, telling
her how much he loved her and how much fun they would
have as man and wife. He had kissed her lightly on the
cheek, and she had felt warm and safe in his gentle
embrace. It had been a week before their marriage was

actually consummated, because she was frightened and he had not wanted to hurt her.

The painful sweetness of the memory was so sharp that for a moment she could not breathe, aching with tender regret for Matthew and all she had lost.

'What is it?' Captain Moreton's curt enquiry cut into her reverie. His voice was harsh, and it sliced through her nostalgia with surgical brutality. 'Regretting your situation already, Lady Catherine? Isn't it a bit too late for second thoughts?'

She put down her fork and clasped her shaking hands in her lap where they couldn't be seen. 'No, of course I don't regret our marriage, Captain Moreton. What is there to regret?'

'What indeed! In the circumstances, my lady, I would suggest that it is a little early for melancholy silence and tragic sighs.'

She was suddenly resentful of his power to intrude on the bittersweet pleasure of her memories, and she was seized by an intense desire to hurt him. Some primitive feminine instinct told her that he would not be pleased to know that she had been daydreaming about her dead husband. She looked up, her eyes glittering with unspoken challenge.

'I was thinking about Matthew,' she said. 'I was remembering my first wedding night and the joy we shared together. I found the comparison—striking.'

For an instant she saw his knuckles gleam white as his hand clenched the stem of his crystal wine goblet, and his anger made her obscurely happy. 'It is a little early to be making comparisons,' he drawled, his voice dangerously soft. 'I have not yet called upon you to fulfil any of the more interesting wifely duties.'

She felt heat flame in her cheeks. 'I am well aware of that, Captain Moreton. I am a widow. I know precisely what the married state entails.'

'I am sure that you do, my lady. However, if at any time you feel too sentimental about the loss of your late husband, I recommend that you remember the rewards that are available to my wife, if she plays her part well. You have hardly begun to enjoy the delights of your new position, my dear. If the prospect of sharing my bed becomes too repellent, think of the money which is now yours to command. Did your father tell you that you are to receive a quarterly allowance of five hundred pounds? Does that news not help to return a little sparkle to those bewitching green eyes of yours?'

'Five hundred pounds a quarter! Captain Moreton, I cannot possibly accept such an enormous sum. I would have no idea how to spend it!'

He laughed without mirth. 'No doubt practice will soon make perfect, my lady.' He got to his feet and strode to the sideboard, pouring himself a large glass of burgundy. 'Have you finished pushing that helpless piece of chicken round your plate, or do you intend to torture it any further?'

'I have finished eating, thank you.'

'The night is still young, Lady Catherine. If you do not wish to eat anything more, what plans do you have for our mutual entertainment?'

'You already know that I have no accomplishments that can be considered entertaining, so if you will excuse me, I shall go to bed. As I told you earlier, I am a little tired tonight.'

The Captain's voice was suddenly smooth as silk. 'But not, I trust, too tired to demonstrate what I suspect will prove to be your major accomplishment, Lady Catherine.'

'My major accomplishment? I don't understand . . .'

'Please, spare me the protestations of pseudo-innocence,' he said shortly. 'Go to bed, if that is what you wish. Perhaps I shall join you later. On the other hand, perhaps I may not.'

He topped up his glass of burgundy and carried it over to the window, his back towards Catherine. She stared at the rigid line of his spine and the darkness of his thick, curling hair. Then, with a small sigh, compounded half of regret and half of frustration, she left the room and abandoned her new husband to his drinking.

CHAPTER
THIRTEEN

As SOON AS she was undressed, Catherine dismissed her maid. The small fire had long since burned out, but she walked over to the fireplace and paced up and down beside the ash-filled grate, too tense to consider going to bed and too tired to consider reading.

Lady Catherine Moreton. She repeated the name to herself several times, but it still lacked all semblance of reality. She could not believe that she was now Captain Moreton's wife. Captain the Honourable William Edward Moreton. William. A man whom she scarcely knew, whom she hesitated to call by his first name, was now her husband. However she expressed the idea, it became no more believable. She wondered if he would come to her tonight as tradition demanded. She hoped that he might, so that the ordeal would be over for both of them as soon as possible.

When she left the dining-room, it had seemed that he would not disturb her. Perhaps he considered the prospect of consummating their marriage too uninteresting a task to undertake until he was between mistresses. And according to the Countess, he was not between mistresses now. A certain Lady Annabelle Brigham was satisfying his masculine needs every time he appeared in London, and he had been in London consulting with his lawyers until the day before the wedding.

Catherine stopped her pacing and stared into the embers of the dead fire. Not for the first time, she wished that she could visualise precisely what a mistress actually did. It was difficult to compete with the mysterious Lady Annabelle when she had no idea what basic skills the competition required.

It was well known that gentlemen were prepared to pay astronomical sums to beautiful women who were also talented courtesans. But Catherine could not for the life of her imagine any gentleman paying huge sums of money for the mere privilege of jumping into a woman's bed and making love. She had never seen any signs that Matthew derived much pleasure from the whole curious exercise, and only her deep affection for him, and the hope that they might one day have children, had enabled her to tolerate the humiliating invasion of her body.

She shrugged resignedly, deciding once again that the question why a man paid a woman to become his mistress was likely to remain unanswerable as far as she was concerned. Perhaps most courtesans had spectacular feminine accomplishments, she thought. Perhaps they were brilliant conversationalists, or played the piano, or sang sweet songs to the accompaniment of the harp before climbing into bed with their lovers. In that case, she acknowledged ruefully, Lady Annabelle had won the battle for Captain Moreton's attention before it had even begun. In the field of feminine accomplishments, Catherine knew that she could stake no claim.

Glancing up, she caught sight of herself in the full-length cheval glass in the corner of the bedroom, and stared warily at her reflection. Was she really trying to compete with Lady Annabelle for Captain Moreton's attention? she asked herself. If she was totally honest, would she have to admit that she was hoping to capture his heart?

Her eyes looked huge and her cheeks were flushed, probably from the vulgar nature of her own thoughts, she reflected wryly. She lifted the filmy gauze pleats of her négligé, then watched it drift back against the slender line of her hips. The pale pink silk covered her body from neck to toe, but the material was so sheer that the outline of her body was visible as a shadow beneath the soft folds.

She had no idea what had caused her to order such an unconventional set of garments. Her mouth curved into a tiny smile as she remembered how outraged the Richlands' dressmaker had been when Catherine described the sort of night-clothes that she required for her trousseau. Shocked to her respectable core, the woman had allowed only married seamstresses to work on pieces of clothing that she did not hesitate to describe as flagrantly immoral.

Would Captain Moreton find her négligé immoral,

Catherine wondered, or would he find it pretty? Even as the thought crossed her mind, the strange heat she had learned to recognise flared beneath her skin. She touched her fingers to her lips, remembering all too clearly how she had felt when the Captain kissed her. It had been like nothing else she had ever experienced. Certainly nothing like Matthew's chaste kisses. What would it be like to submit to the Captain's love-making, she wondered. Was it possible that women, as well as men, sometimes enjoyed the undignified act?

The sound of a door opening caused her to spin on her heels, her négligé flaring out round her. Captain Moreton stood on the threshold of the door that connected their two rooms, tall and unaccountably commanding in the flickering lamplight. He wore a dressing-gown of fashionable crimson Chinese satin, and in his hand he held a glass of wine.

His expression seemed dark, almost brooding, as he pushed the door closed behind him and advanced further into her room.

'You look surprised, Lady Catherine,' he said mockingly. 'This is our wedding night. Why would you be surprised to see me?'

Not really surprised, Catherine thought, as her heart began to beat with almost frantic speed, but certainly not ready. Five weeks ago, this man had been no more to her than a name spoken by her stepmother. Now he was her husband. Events had moved too fast for her emotions to catch up with physical reality.

'No answer, my lady?' He halted several feet away from her, putting his glass on a near-by table, and she swallowed over the sudden constriction in her throat. How impossible it was to accept that this tall stranger had every right to be in her bedroom. How incredible it was to think that under his dressing-gown he probably wore nothing except his nightshirt. The thought was absurd in its irrelevance, but it did not make her want to smile.

She stared, unable to speak, as his gaze roamed over her slim body. She was frightened when she discovered just how much she wanted him to find her beautiful, how much she wanted him to take her into his arms and kiss her.

'You look even more desirable than I had imagined you would,' he said. 'You are an exceptionally alluring woman, Lady Catherine. Sensuality cloaked by the appearance of shyness is the ultimate aphrodisiac for me, as it is for most men.'

His voice was oddly husky, and Catherine felt her body suffuse with heat. The sensation was acutely uncomfortable, and yet she hoped it would not go away. She knotted her hands into a tight ball, forcing herself to ignore the racing of her pulses and the frantic beat of her heart. Now, perhaps, was the appropriate moment to try to straighten out some of the misunderstandings between the two of them.

'I would like to take this opportunity to apologise for the way our betrothal came about, Captain Moreton,' she said. She knew that she sounded prim, and a little breathless, but she could not help it. 'I give you my word that I shall try . . . try in every way to be a dutiful wife.'

'Dutiful!' His mouth twisted into a sardonic smile. 'Oh no, my lady, you can do better than that. Tonight you shall not fob me off with duty. We may not have any love to share, but at least we shall have passion. Your eyes have been promising me that for weeks.'

In three strides he covered the few feet of space that kept them separate, and pulled her into his arms. She had time only to think of how cool his hands felt through the thin fabric of her négligé before his mouth descended and covered hers in an urgent, compelling kiss.

A burning wave of pleasure swept over Catherine's body, leaving her soft and pliant in his arms. The same liquid heat that she had felt when he kissed her in the rose garden coursed through her veins, melting her bones, so that she was forced to cling to him for support.

He lifted his head for an instant. 'Open your mouth,' he whispered, and she found it impossible to disobey his command. His tongue touched the tip of hers, and a delicious languor stole over her body. Her limbs burned with a cold fire, and yet she could not feel the flames, could not feel anything save the thrusting demand of his tongue inside her mouth.

She wanted the kiss to last for ever, and she gave a dazed little moan when he finally moved away from her. Her breasts ached in a way she had never felt before, and there was an uncomfortable throbbing sensation deep inside her. She knew suddenly that she wanted him to put his hands on her breasts, and the realisation sent a blush rushing from the base of her throat to the roots of her hair. Is that what a mistress did? she wondered. Did a mistress invite her lover to put his hands on her breasts? And did they both enjoy the sensation?

The Captain touched the smooth braids that hung over her shoulders. 'Loosen your hair for me,' he said thickly. 'I confess that I have dreamed of seeing it spread out on the pillow next to me.'

'My hair?' It was hard for her to think, even harder to speak coherently. 'But Mary has just plaited it ready for the night.'

'Do you wish me to play lady's-maid?' He laughed softly. 'If that is your fancy, I am reliably informed that I am quite skilled in the role. Come, sit at the dressing-table and I shall undo your hair.'

She had no will left to resist him when he led her to the velvet-covered stool in front of the dressing-table. He removed the embroidered ribbons which tied the ends of her plaits and quickly unfastened the loosely worked braids. Then he picked up a brush and began to stroke it through the silky, waist-length strands of her hair.

The rhythmic swish of the brush found an echo in the deepest, most hidden recesses of her body. For quite a while she stared fixedly at her hands, which lay clasped in her lap, but her eyes were dragged inexorably upwards until—at last—she looked into the mirror and her gaze locked with his. She saw the dark colour that slashed across his high cheekbones, and her throat became inexplicably dry. Her lips parted, and she felt compelled to moisten them with her tongue. She heard the rasp of the Captain's indrawn breath, and he halted his brushing in mid-stroke. His hands tightened on her shoulders.

'Are you ready, my lady?' he murmured.

'Ready?' She spoke the word as a question, but her voice shook so badly that she did not know if he had understood her meaning. She tried to stand up, intending to walk away from the hypnotic images in the mirror, but to her bewilderment she felt her shoulders sway backwards until they rested against his chest.

Slowly, he set the brush down on the dressing-table and clasped his hands round her waist. He raised her effortlessly from the stool, then pushed it to one side and drew her back until her body touched his along the entire length of her spine. She bit her lip to hide a gasp of pleasure as she watched his hands slide up her body and cup the underside of her breasts.

His thumbs reached upward to caress her nipples, and she discovered that she could not bear to watch the mirror-images any longer. She closed her eyes as a convulsive shudder of pleasure ripped through her. He bent his head, his mouth seeking out the hollow at the base of her neck, and she turned suddenly in his arms, reaching up to pull his mouth against her own.

'You have a truly curious sense of duty, my lady,' he said softly, and she thought she heard a hint of laughter in his throaty whisper.

'I like it when you kiss me,' she said, then wondered why the first complete sentence she had spoken all night should have to be such an inane one.

'Then let me kiss you again,' he said. 'But properly, this time.'

Before she had any idea what he planned to do, he swept her up into his arms, his lips taking passionate possession of her mouth as he carried her across to the bed. He tossed back the covers and lowered her gently on to the down-filled mattress. He sat beside her, cradling her in his arms, as his mouth moved with devastating persuasion over the slender column of her throat. When he reached the lace-trimmed neckline of her négligé, he untied the satin ribbons with fingers that trembled slightly.

Catherine had thought there was nothing left that could shock her, but when she saw that he planned to take off not only her robe but also her nightgown, she fought away the debilitating waves of pleasure and sat bolt upright. Since babyhood, she had never been wholly naked in front of a man, and she could not quite believe that the Captain's authoritative gestures meant what they seemed to mean. She clutched at the padded lapels of his dressing-gown as she struggled to give voice to her objections.

Unfortunately, coherence once again eluded her. 'Captain Moreton!' she stuttered. 'My nightgown!'

His smile was almost tender, and he touched her lightly on the cheek. 'I see that it is beautiful and I will not rip it, Catherine. Look, if you will lift your arms so . . .

'But you are wearing your night-clothes, so why must I remove mine?' Even to her own ears, the question did not seem to be phrased quite right. Her voice emerged as little more than a husky murmur, and she was not entirely surprised when he simply laughed.

'You think that we should dispense with our clothes simultaneously?' he said quizzically. 'The truth is that I was hoping that you would undress me. But I feel in a generous mood, and even though you have neglected your tasks so disastrously, I am willing to complete them for you.'

Without giving her any chance to protest, he stood up and untied the belt of his robe, slipping out of it in a single, economical movement.

Catherine was totally unable to conceal her gasp of amazement. She had suspected that Captain Moreton might be wearing only a nightshirt beneath his dressing-gown. In her wildest fantasies it had never occurred to her that he might be wearing nothing at all. She realised that she was staring at his naked body, and hastily averted her eyes.

He leaned towards her and she put out her hands to push him away, but he misinterpreted her gesture and simply took advantage of her outstretched arms to remove her nightgown. He threw it carelessly over a near-by chair, and then looked down at her, all laughter dying out of his face as he pulled her against his hair-roughened chest.

'Ah God, Catherine, my imagination did not do you

justice! Your body is beautiful beyond belief. I burn with need for you.'

He kissed her again, and his hands were hot as they covered her breasts, caressing her nipples until they throbbed in unison with the blood pounding in her ears. His hands moved to her waist and stroked softly down towards her hips. When she felt the moist touch of his mouth against her breast, her body became rigid on the bed until his hands expertly coaxed her thighs apart, teasing her closer and closer to a sensation for which she could find no name.

She clung to him without any idea of what was happening to her own body. The feelings he had aroused in her were so new and so intense that she could not judge if they were pleasure or pain. She only knew that she wanted something to happen, something that would ease the need that twisted her senses into a tighter and tighter knot. Of their own accord, her hands clutched at his shoulders and her hips began to writhe against him, desperately seeking relief from the ache that tormented her.

'Dear heaven, Catherine, you must be still or I shall not be able to wait any longer! Are you ready? Do you want me to take you now?'

His words were a hoarse whisper against her lips. She did not quite understand what he meant, but some instinct suggested that he would know how to provide her with the release she craved. And at that moment, nothing else in the world mattered save that she should find release.

'I want you now,' she murmured, hoping he would understand what she meant, hoping he would know what to do. Her hand reached out in a tentative caress, and he pressed a swift, hard kiss into her palm.

'God help me, you are everything that I despise, Catherine, but I desire you as I have never desired any other woman. Your body may lie when it hints at love, but it lies so beautifully that I no longer care.'

She scarcely heard what he said, and was completely indifferent to the fact that she did not understand him. Words were irrelevant to the way her body felt at this moment.

'William, hold me close,' she murmured urgently, unconsciously wriggling so that her breasts rubbed against the muscled expanse of his chest. 'Please make love to me.'

'Sweet Catherine, it will be my pleasure,' he said huskily and, for a brief instant, the whisper of laughter had returned to his voice. It vanished quickly. He moved between her thighs as he finished speaking, holding her hips arched tightly against him as he thrust into her yielding softness. Catherine felt her body begin to quiver, and before long her limbs shook uncontrollably as he continued to move rhythmically inside her. At last, the tight painful knot in the pit of her stomach exploded into a tumultuous burst of pleasure.

'William . . .' Her breath mingled with his as she murmured his name, and his arms tightened, holding her safe until the tremors of joy had passed. With a low groan, he thrust deeper inside her and she felt a fresh wave of sensation begin to build inside her body. She was burning again, and only he could extinguish the blaze.

'Dear heaven, but you are beautiful,' he said huskily.

'So are you.' She had just enough control over her thoughts to know that she had admitted something that would better have been kept silent. She bit deep into his shoulder to avoid crying out her pleasure as his body went rigid and then shuddered in convulsive release against her. She tasted his sweat on her tongue and the ecstasy spiralled higher, carrying her up until the world became a silent, spinning void and they were at the centre, with William the only source of light in a blissful, endless darkness.

The clock on the mantelpiece chimed the hour, and Catherine floated slowly back to the reality of her bedroom. William's head rested against her breasts, his eye-patch a black shadow against her pale skin. There was a ridge of thick scar tissue along his shoulder, and she ran her fingers over it in a tentative caress. She wanted to ask him how he had received such a terrible wound, but she felt his body grow tense beneath her fingertips, and so she remained silent, sensitive to his need for privacy.

Hesitantly, she reached out to touch the narrow velvet ribbon which held his eye-patch in place, but William jerked his head away and got up from the bed. He walked silently to the chair where he had thrown his dressing-gown, and she watched, fascinated by the play of muscles beneath his tanned skin as he donned the robe and then reached into the pocket and extracted a white doe-skin pouch. He loosened the tasselled silk cords at its neck, and tossed it carelessly on the bed.

'I have a wedding gift for you, my lady,' he said, his features appearing all hard angles and dark shadows in the flickering lamplight. The pouch landed on her stomach, and an emerald necklace tumbled out, the jewels glittering green and cold against the warmth of her flesh. She thought she heard a faint sound from William, but when she looked up, his expression was as controlled as it usually was.

'I trust you will consider my little gift sufficient re-imbursement for the outstanding performance you just gave in bed. I confess that I had not hoped for such —excellence.'

She told herself that she must be imagining the harsh sarcasm of his voice. It was impossible—it must be impossible—that he had not felt the numbing sweetness of what they had just shared. She cupped the emeralds in her hands and smiled hesitantly at him. The design of the necklace was opulent, almost garish, and would never have been her choice, but she guessed that he must have wanted his wedding gift to be lavish, and tried to sound appreciative.

'Thank you, William,' she said. 'Emeralds are my favourite stone, and this is . . . Well, it's—um—very nice.'

'You seem less than overwhelmed, my dear Catherine. Is the strand not long enough? Are the jewels smaller than you anticipated?'

'N-Not at all, William. I anticipated nothing. And this necklace is . . . it is certainly very long and large. No one could have anticipated anything more . . . anything bigger.'

'In any event, my dear Catherine, there is no reason for you to despair. Consider these emeralds merely a token payment. If you always make love so—enthusiastically—I have not the smallest doubt that I shall eventually become quite reconciled to the high cost of marrying you. If you continue your performance in bed as you have begun, the stream of trinkets I bestow upon you may soon become a veritable flood.'

It was no longer possible to ignore the fact that he intended to insult her. She tucked the sheet under her arms and sat up in the middle of the bed. 'Would you be good enough to explain precisely what you mean, Captain Moreton?'

'Please do call me William, my dear. There can surely be no further cause for formality between the two of us when we have come to know each other so—intimately—over the past hour or so.'

She was holding the necklace so tightly that the jewels cut into her hands, but she was unaware of the pain. 'You seem very angry with me, and I would like to know why. Would you please tell me what I have done?'

'Catherine, please spare both of us this charade of wounded innocence. You deliberately trapped me into marriage, and you did it for the sake of my money. You are mistaken, however, if you think that I am angry with you. Why should I feel anger when I went into the marriage fully aware of your true nature and your true motives for marrying me? But I want you to understand from the start that I am not interested in playing the role of besotted husband which you seem to have assigned to me in your little drama. Our marriage is a commercial transaction, so let us behave accordingly. I have always prided myself on treating my mistresses generously, and I see no reason why my wife should not enjoy a similar standard of compensation, provided she exerts herself to please me. I do hope that you haven't been disappointed by the profit your stratagems have achieved so far? Even if the necklace seems a mere trifle, a wedding ceremony is not to be sneezed at.'

'My stratagems? William, you must believe me! I have employed no stratagems where our relationship is concerned. If you refer to the unfortunate incident which precipitated our betrothal, I swear to you that I had no idea you were in the rose garden at Wellespont, truly I did not! And I would *never* agree to marry a man simply because he was wealthy. If you knew me at all, you would realise that money is not important to me. Many other things are infinitely more crucial to my happiness.'

'You sound so passionately sincere, my dear, that I feel more than ever that the stage has lost a great talent. But since it pleases you to protest that you didn't marry me for my money, I must confess that I am curious to know just what prompted you to accept my proposal. If it wasn't for my fortune, precisely why did you marry me, Catherine?'

The truth came to her even as he posed the question. 'Because—because I l-love you,' she blurted out, shock making her stumble over the simple words.

His laughter did not quite conceal his bitterness. 'I'm disappointed in you, Catherine. Surely you could have thought of some slightly more plausible reason? But don't struggle to invent a more convincing lie. I know why you came to Wellespont to visit my mother. Your stepmother contrived the invitation solely so that you could be introduced to me. Are you prepared to deny that you planned all along to compromise me? To trap me so that I was forced to offer you a proposal of marriage?'

Catherine closed her eyes to shut out the ice-cold anger reflected in his gaze, but a stubborn sense of pride kept her from lying—or from excusing her own actions. 'No,' she said quietly. 'I do not deny that I came to Wellespont at my stepmother's behest and with the express purpose of meeting you.'

'And compromising me.'

She swallowed hard, wondering how long he had known the truth, and how he had discovered it. 'That was my original intention,' she admitted.

His voice was heavy with irony. 'But then your plans changed, I suppose, almost as soon as you met me. You fell in love with me at first glance, I do not doubt it.'

'Yes,' she whispered painfully. 'I suspect that is exactly what happened to me, although I had never dreamed that it might be so.'

She heard the hiss of his expelled breath and forced her eyes open. The contempt in his expression was almost more than she could bear to see.

'Our life together would be a great deal more enjoyable,

Catherine, if you would abandon this somewhat tedious pretence of love at first sight. I am not interested in your love, or even your affection. I have never asked for it, nor could I ever return it. I am interested only in enjoying what I have paid for—which is the use of your delectable body and, eventually, your services as the mother of my children. I would like to point out that most people would consider that I am paying very well for these minor privileges. The services with which you provide me are not in short supply. There are innumerable young women in England who have impeccable lineage and tolerably attractive bodies.'

For a split second after he had finished speaking, Catherine's heart was seared by a pain so acute that she wondered how she was able to bear it. Then rage replaced the hurt. If he was determined to consider her scheming and mercenary, she would live up to every one of his expectations. With trembling hands, she picked up the necklace and coiled it round her neck. She looked across the room and saw herself reflected in the mirror, the jewels glowing darkly against the creamy pallor of her naked skin. She felt the hurt of William's rejection as if it were an arrow piercing her soul, but she had no intention of letting him see the wounds he had inflicted.

She flicked her hair away from her face, and looked arrogantly towards him. She raised her shoulders, then lowered them in a languid shrug.

'It is a matter of complete indifference to me if you would prefer not to give our relationship the gloss of pretended affection. I simply thought you would prefer our marriage to have the appearance of being normal.'

Tears were forming in the back of her throat, and she looked hurriedly away in case any trace of them appeared in her eyes. She saw her négligé on the floor and drew it on, disguising her haste to cover her body by sliding off the bed and walking towards the cheval glass in the corner. She patted the emeralds caressingly as she preened herself in front of the mirror.

'This necklace certainly makes an enjoyable beginning to our relationship,' she said. 'But I am sure you have already understood that it is only the beginning. My favours won't come cheaply. After all, I am your wife, not merely your mistress. As the future mother of your children, I look forward to being well rewarded.'

She saw the look of disgust, mingled with resignation, that passed fleetingly across his features, and almost regretted the pride that had made her deny the truth of her love. Perhaps, even if he rejected her, it would have been better to explain the whole truth about her sister and why she had gone to Wellespont.

From the corner of her eye, she watched as he picked up his glass of wine. He drank deeply, then walked slowly towards her, coming to a halt immediately behind her. One hand traced the outline of the necklace where it rested against her throat and dipped down to the hollow between her breasts. His other hand drifted slowly, insultingly, across her stomach. He lifted her hair and bent to nuzzle the delicate skin at the nape of her neck.

His touch was a torment to her. 'Please don't do this,' she whispered.

'Why not? I have discovered that I desire you again, and the necklace you are wearing is surely worth more than one quick tumble in your bed. I look forward to a long night of mutual pleasure.'

Only a few hours earlier she had not known what physical desire really meant. Now she was making the discovery that she could tremble with longing for a man whom her mind was commanding her to hate.

'Have you nothing to say—my sweet, lying, Lady Catherine?'

She shook her head, unable to speak, and her silence seemed to infuriate him. He spun her roughly round in his arms, and his mouth claimed hers in a hard, punishing kiss.

She wrenched her head sideways to avoid his lips, but his strength was immeasurably greater than hers, and he did not hesitate to use it to enforce his will. He pulled her so tightly against his body that the gold setting of the necklace cut into her flesh, and she concentrated on feeling angry at his brutal treatment. She twisted violently against him, then realised too late that her movements only enflamed them both.

'Don't do this,' she said despairingly. 'William, I don't want to make love to you again. Not like this.'

'We have never made love,' he said harshly. 'How could we, when there is nothing between us save greed and anger?'

'William . . . please . . . You must acknowledge that —just now—there was something more between us than that.'

For an instant his body stilled, then he seized her hands and held them pinned behind her back. Her négligé fell open, and his gaze rested hungrily, insolently, on the soft curves of her body. 'Yes, I will admit there was something more than greed between us,' he said with deliberate cruelty. 'I will admit that you offered me passion over and above the call of duty. If you will give such passion to me again, you can have a bracelet and earrings to match the necklace I have already given you. Does the thought not excite you?'

'No,' she murmured despairingly. 'It doesn't excite me at all.'

'Your body proclaims you a liar,' he said softly, running his hands tauntingly over her breasts, his thumbs lingering on her erect nipples. 'However much you may try to deny it, I can see that you are already very excited indeed.' He stroked his fingers along her arms, and the silk of her robe slipped against her skin, unbearably erotic beneath his questing touch.

She did not protest when he picked her up and once again carried her to the bed, although her vision was blurred by tears. If she had not loved him, she might possibly have been able to resist the expertise of his seduction. As it was, her heart conspired with her body to undermine every defence, and she lay silently in his arms, aching with unspoken passion.

But his victory over her was not complete. She could not prevent her physical response, but he had to drag every caress out of her and, in the end, even though it was torture to conceal the intensity of her pleasure, she did not cry out, nor did she reach for him. Her hands clutched the sheet beneath her and she bit her lip until it bled—but she did not beg for his kisses. The blissful, terrifying ecstasy waited for her just as it had done before, but this time she met it alone.

Afterwards they lay unspeaking on the bed, their bodies fused into an intimate tangle of limbs, their minds utterly separate. She tried to think what she would do if he gave her another piece of jewellery in payment for her supposed services, but her mind refused to contemplate how she would react to such an insult.

In the end, the problem did not arise. After lying beside her in silence for several long minutes, William rose and shrugged into his dressing-gown. He paused at the door that joined their two rooms, and she sensed that he hesitated momentarily before he spoke.

'Good night, Cath. . . my lady. Sleep well.'

She did not reply. She turned her head into the pillow, and when she finally heard the click of the latch, allowed the dry, wrenching sobs to pour out of her.

It was dawn before she realised that she wept not because of William's callous treatment, but for the futility of her unwanted love. When she accepted the truth, her tears stopped.

CHAPTER
FOURTEEN

THE EXPERIENCES of his wedding night convinced William that his wife was a dangerous woman. He knew it would be all too easy to become a slave to the joys of her love-making and, in a confused attempt at self-protection, he vowed that he would burn in hell before he returned to her bed.

He had not bargained for the effect Catherine's subtle sensuality would exert upon him, and her constant presence rapidly became a torment he found hard to ignore. He spent hours in the saddle, touring his estate, simply so that he could keep away from her. And he spent hours at night, pacing the floor, trying to convince himself that he had no desire to open her bedroom door and lose himself in the softness of her embrace.

In the end, it was the arrival of a pressing letter from the Foreign Secretary that precipitated the breaking of his vow a mere six days after he had made it. George Canning apologised sincerely for interrupting Captain Moreton's newly-wedded bliss, but the Government needed his presence in London as soon as possible.

The Foreign Secretary's letter reminded William of several facts he already knew. Dom Pedro, the twenty-four-year-old son of King John of Portugal, had defied his father by declaring the Brazilian Empire independent of its mother country on 22 September 1822. Most of the great Brazilian landowners had accepted Dom Pedro as their Emperor, and the young monarch was already working on a draft of the new nation's first constitution.

The Foreign Secretary's letter contained other information that was new to William. It seemed that King John of Portugal, furious with his son and even more furious at the loss of a huge empire, had appealed to the British Government for military help in quelling what he termed *a treasonous rebellion*.

As if this were not troublesome enough, the fledgling

nation of Argentina had simultaneously sent one of its
senior ministers to London to request assistance in the
border disputes that had developed among the former
Portuguese and Spanish colonies. Señor Bernardino Rivadavia had already met Captain Moreton in Buenos Aires,
and had specifically requested his presence in London. The
Foreign Secretary was only too pleased to comply with
Señor Rivadavia's request. His letter pointed out ruefully
that there was nobody in the entire British Government
who had any up-to-date experience of conditions in South
America. Although British troops had fought in Argentina
as recently as 1808, several of the Government's official
maps were so inaccurate that nobody was quite certain
where the boundaries of the old colonies actually lay. In
these circumstances, Mr Canning urgently requested the
honour of Captain Moreton's presence at the forthcoming
discussions. He added a brief postscript congratulating
Captain Moreton on his recent marriage and expressing
the hope that Lady Catherine would join her husband in
London. If so, Mr Canning would send invitations to
both of them for the reception and ball he was giving on
Friday next at eight o'clock in the evening.

William would have considered it his duty to go to
London even if his marriage had been perfect and his
honeymoon idyllic. Given the actual state of affairs, he
seized avidly upon the excuse offered by the Foreign
Secretary's invitation and immediately began preparing for
his departure.

At dinner, he announced to Catherine that he would be
leaving for London early on Tuesday morning, with a stop
overnight somewhere in the vicinity of Reading. He had
wrestled all afternoon with the problem of whether to ask
Catherine to join him, and the briefness of his announcement reflected the fact that he had not yet managed to reach
a decision.

His deliberate brusqueness brought a flush to her cheeks,
and he saw her eyes cloud over as she attempted to mask
her reaction. He was furious with himself for the stab of
sympathy that pricked at his heart, and even more furious
when he heard himself speak.

'I shall have business to attend to when I am in town; nevertheless you are welcome to come with me if it would please you to do so.'

Her smile was dazzling in its sudden radiance, and he quickly looked away. 'I have always dreamed of visiting London,' she said breathlessly. 'If it would not interfere with your plans too much, Captain, I should very much enjoy a stay in town with you.'

He concealed a ridiculous surge of pleasure by speaking even more curtly than before. 'Your presence will have little effect upon me one way or the other,' he said. 'You will no doubt wish to shop and see the sights. I shall be engaged in a series of meetings with the Foreign Secretary.'

'Your mother plans to be in town for a few days before she leaves for Brighton, and I am sure she will help me to find my way round. You need not worry that I shall intrude upon you when you are busy.'

He conquered the ludicrous impulse to say that he would be delighted to show her the sights of London by swallowing his glass of burgundy far too fast. 'The Foreign Secretary plans to give a ball next Friday evening and has invited us both to attend,' he said, setting his empty wine-glass back on the table. 'Would that amuse you? It would serve well as an occasion to introduce you formally to London society.'

She gave him another of the radiant smiles that always turned his heart over. 'Amuse is probably not the right word,' she said, her voice husky. 'I don't doubt that I shall be terrified, since I have never before had occasion to attend anything more formal than our local country assemblies. But I am honoured that the Foreign Secretary has invited me, and I should dearly like to go. I have a new dress that I have been longing to wear, and this will be the perfect occasion for it.'

She looked so happy and so excited that for a moment William was tempted to forget everything that he knew about her and simply accept her smiles at face value. Then he remembered how cynically she had set out to trap him into marriage and how perilously close he had come to losing his heart. He looked away, carefully hardening his defences. Her excitement, he reminded himself, was caused chiefly by the chance to flaunt herself in public in an expensive new gown. The remainder of her radiant smiles were probably inspired by gleeful anticipation of visiting the many stores and warehouses where she could spend his money.

'We may be in town for several weeks,' he said. 'For my own part, I imagine I shall be extremely busy. But with all of London's merchants anxious to display their wares to you, I am sure you will find numberless ways to entertain yourself. You will find that being the wife of the fabulously wealthy Captain Moreton is a much more rewarding role in London than it is here in the country.'

The excited sparkle died out of her eyes, just as he had intended it should, but he felt an unexpected pang of regret for its passing. She looked at him with a touch of hauteur.

'The role of your wife must always be a gratifying one, Captain. How could it be otherwise, when you are all kind attention?'

She rose from the table, and two footmen sprang to move back her chair. 'Will you excuse me, sir? The servants cannot work on Sunday, of course, so that leaves me only tonight and Monday to prepare for our departure. I must consult with my maid and the housekeeper before I go to bed this evening.'

He was obscurely annoyed by the loss of her company, but could think of no valid reason to demand that she should stay. They exchanged courteous good nights for the benefit of the servants, and he watched her leave the room with a bitter sense of frustration. He knew that he had somehow lost an opportunity to breach the barrier that separated them, and yet he had no idea where he had gone wrong. In fact, he had no clear idea why he should want to breach it. He was willing to acknowledge that he desired Catherine's body, but he knew from years of experience that desire did not require friendship or mental intimacy.

As soon as the sound of her footsteps died away, he slumped back in his chair. 'Get me the brandy, Cowper,' he said. 'And you servants can all clear off. I shan't need you any more tonight.'

'Yes, sir.' The butler placed a decanter of brandy next to his master's elbow, and with discreet gestures, ordered the other servants to clear the table. Within two minutes, William was alone with his thoughts and his brandy.

He spent almost an hour trying to get drunk, then realised that he was having no success in forgetting about Catherine, so there was little point in continuing to pour excellent French cognac down his increasingly reluctant throat. He got to his feet and discovered that the dining-room walls were rocking gently.

'Damned house,' he muttered. 'It's worse than a damned ship in the middle of the Atlantic.'

He strode upstairs, moving fast if not always entirely in a straight line, and found himself standing outside Catherine's door. He entered without bothering to knock.

His wife was sitting in front of her dressing-table, while her maid brushed out her hair. The silky strands cascaded down Catherine's back, and the heat of the brandy circulating in William's veins suddenly changed to an entirely different kind of fire.

'You may leave us, Mary,' he said, embarrassed to hear the hoarseness of his own command.

The maid bobbed a curtsy, and left without saying a word. He watched, his body burning, as his wife rose from her seat in front of the mirror and turned to face him.

She clutched the folds of her dressing-gown tightly to her. She was wearing another of those incredibly sensuous négligés, he noticed, transparent and floating like the one she had worn on their wedding night. This one was a pale silvery green, and he could see the rapid rise and fall of her breasts quite clearly beneath its sheer folds. The urge to feel the softness of her body beneath his hands was irresistible, and he walked quickly towards her, letting the door slam shut behind him.

'D-Did you want something, Captain Moreton?'

He felt an unexpected surge of tenderness when he heard the fright in her voice. He wanted to sweep her into his arms and tell her that with him she need never be frightened of anything, because he would always keep her safe. He deliberately pushed the tenderness aside.

'Yes, I want something,' he said. 'I want to make love to you, Catherine.'

She stepped back, her green eyes huge in her thin face. 'I don't want you to make love to me,' she whispered. 'Not now. Not when you are still so angry with me.'

All lingering trace of sympathy was swept away by a surge of sheer, naked desire. 'You mistake your position, my lady,' he said coldly. 'I did not ask either for your opinion or for your permission. I simply told you what I planned to do.'

'But not like this. Please, William, not when when there is so much—hurt—still between us.'

He laughed, but there was no trace of amusement in the sound. 'Don't worry, my lady. I have taken the precaution of providing myself with something that will take care of any pain you may feel at being forced to submit to me.' He withdrew a package from the tail pocket of his evening coat and tossed it on to the dressing-table.

'Earrings and a bracelet, my dear, to match your necklace. Are you not anxious to examine them?'

Her face was suddenly stark white in the flickering candle-light. 'No. I am not at all anxious to see how you plan to pay me off tonight.'

A dozen conflicting emotions raged inside him, but in the end, desire won over everything else. Silently he dragged her against his body, experiencing a strange mixture of self-loathing, anger and longing as he felt her tremble in his embrace.

'I am not going to do anything you will not like,' he murmured as he bent his head to kiss her. 'Catherine, have you forgotten already what it was like between us?'

'No.' Her voice was little more than a sigh against his mouth. 'How could I forget something so wonderful?'

At that moment, he knew that he would willingly sacrifice pride and honour for the sake of another night spent making love to her, but anger at his own lack of self-control made him momentarily savage, and he forced her lips ruthlessly apart, probing hungrily with his tongue until he felt the first enticing quiver of her response. As soon as her mouth softened, his heart began to race, and he was aware that he needed something more from her than forced submission. He wanted the sort of passionate response she had given him the first time they made love.

His hands became gentle as they caressed her body, and his kiss was deliberately restrained, although he desired her with an intensity that only increased when he felt her hands creep inside his evening jacket and run hesitantly over his spine. He wondered if she could even begin to guess at what the touch of her fingers through the fine linen was doing to him.

He slipped off his jacket and tore impatiently at the elegant folds of his cravat. He noted ruefully that his hands were shaking as he fumbled with the diamond studs that fastened the front of his shirt. Dear heaven, he could not remember ever feeling such need for a woman! He was startled when he felt Catherine's slender fingers close over his hands.

'Would you like me to help you?' she asked huskily.

She did not wait for a reply, and his breath expelled in a sharp hiss as she quickly removed the jewelled fasteners and dropped them on her dressing-table. She pushed aside his shirt and ran her fingers lightly over his tanned chest, only stopping her tantalising stroking when her fingers came in contact with the high waistband of his trousers. Even in the dim light, he could see the enchanting flush that crept into her cheeks.

'Don't abandon your quest now,' he murmured, his voice softly teasing. 'It is just becoming interesting for both of us.' When she made no answer, he kissed her again, a long, intoxicating kiss that left him desperate for more intimate contact.

She did not resist when he swept her into his arms and carried her over to the bed, and he sighed with satisfaction when her robe fell open and he saw the shadow of her breasts beneath the transparent silk of her nightgown.

'Catherine, do you want to make love with me tonight?' he asked urgently. For some reason, he badly wanted to hear her say out loud that she desired him.

'Yes, I want us to make love. *Please!*'

He had extracted the response he wished for, and yet,

oddly, he felt no gratifying rush of masculine power, only an increased awareness of how much he desired her. He pushed her robe off her shoulders and passed commanding hands over her body, shaping the swell of her breasts, the flatness of her stomach and the warmth of her thighs.

'William . . . I—I can't stop shaking,' she said, her words partially muffled by the pillow.

'Neither can I,' he admitted. His mouth quirked into a tiny smile. 'Perhaps, if we hold each other, we can find a cure for our mutual problem.'

'Perhaps.' She buried her face deeper into the pillow. 'But not if you wear so many clothes.'

He laughed softly, caressing her lightly on the cheek before standing up to undress. She did not protest when he leaned over and untied the ribbons of her nightgown, although her fingers clenched convulsively against his chest. He stroked the delicate fabric away from her body, his touch expert and unhurried as he removed the concealing silk. When he finally lay down beside her, she curled her hands round his neck, twining her fingers in the thickness of his dark hair.

'I think I like . . . I like the way your body feels against mine,' she whispered, and he did not need to look at her to know that she was blushing again.

'And I *know* I like the way you feel against me,' he said, gathering her tightly into his arms.

The gentleness of his kiss changed swiftly to passion, and her trembling transformed itself into a burning, pulsating heat that leaped over the barriers between them, welding them so closely that he no longer knew precisely where his body stopped and hers began.

He only knew that when she quivered beneath him in the final, abandoned movements of ecstasy, he lost his heart irretrievably and for ever.

CHAPTER
FIFTEEN

CATHERINE AND William arrived at the Moreton town house in Grosvenor Square at four o'clock on Wednesday afternoon. Lord Moreton, the Dowager, and about two dozen servants were all waiting to greet them.

They had entered London from the west, passing through the villages of Maidenhead and Slough, and Catherine had spent the last two hours of the journey in awestruck silence. She was overwhelmed by the size, splendour, efficiency, noise, filth and squalor of London. None of the stories she had heard, none of the accounts she had read, prepared her for the reality of driving through a city which contained more than a million people. She ate dinner in a daze, and when she retired to bed that night, it sounded to her country ears as if at least three-quarters of London's citizens were disporting themselves on the street beneath her window.

When she finally woke on Thursday morning, the Dowager told her that both Edward and William had already left for consultations with Mr Canning at the Foreign Office. While Catherine ate breakfast, the Dowager enthusiastically outlined the route for a brief tour of what she considered London's major attractions.

'We cannot do anything too exhausting, because you must be in tip-top form for the reception tomorrow night. You may never want to come back to London after this visit, Catherine, but it's always as well to create the best possible impression when you make your début. I am so glad to have this chance to give you a taste of the delights the city holds before I leave for Brighton.'

'Jane is very much looking forward to spending the summer with you, Godmama. It is kind of you to have invited her.'

'Nonsense, I am never kind! I simply want to make sure I have a captive listener for my speculations about the

Ancient World. Those weeks you and I spent together at Wellespont have utterly spoiled me. I cannot wait for Jane to arrive so that I shall have the company of somebody who can respond intelligently to my questions.'

Without giving Catherine a chance to reply, the Dowager swept to the front door, where the butler informed them that the barouche was waiting.

They drove first to Westminster Abbey. The Dowager seemed to thrive on the noise and bustle of the city, but Catherine—fascinated as she was—thought she would never become accustomed to the frenetic pace of activity in the streets. She was deeply impressed by the soaring gothic façade of the Abbey; she was awed by the magnificence of St Paul's and the blood-stained antiquity of the Tower. She was suitably dazzled by the variety of shops in Regent Street and the incredible choice offered by Farmer and Roger's Great Cloak and Shawl Emporium, but her overwhelming impression was of neither historic monuments nor prosperous merchants. It was of the incredible volume of traffic and the vast number of beggars.

She knew that the crippled veterans of the Napoleonic wars and the emaciated, filthy children would haunt her dreams for long nights to come.

'I had not realised that we should see so many hungry children,' she said to the Dowager, as the carriage rolled past three thin little boys fighting over a muffin that had fallen from a pedlar's tray. 'I had always heard that London was the richest city in the world, and I wasn't prepared to see so much misery.'

'London *is* the richest city in the world,' the Dowager said gently. 'Catherine, in Greece and Turkey—in fact in most of southern Europe—the vast mass of people live on the constant edge of famine, in the country as well as in the towns. In an English village, unless the landlord is very inefficient, cottagers go from birth to death without ever feeling the pangs of real hunger. And in London, commerce is so successful that there are many, many people who are neither rich nor of noble birth and yet they earn sufficient money to live comfortably in well-built houses, with warm clothes and good food. In the whole of Greece there are probably fewer prosperous shopkeepers than there are in a single street in London.'

'But in just one day we have also seen scores of people—perhaps even hundreds of them—who don't earn sufficient to support themselves and their families!'

'Regrettably, that is true, and when William was in the army, he fought long and hard for the establishment of pension funds for disabled soldiers. It's disgraceful to think that we have men wandering the streets who are unemployable and hungry because they were wounded fighting to save England from Napoleon's mad dreams of glory.'

'The soldiers are a sad enough sight, but what about the children? Nobody is ever going to provide a pension fund for them, and yet it isn't their fault that they are hungry.'

'Catherine, I don't know the answer. The Church does have some foundling hospitals, but nowhere near enough. Edward and William have both decided that part of the problem is too many untrained young men and women drifting to the big towns in search of better lives—and ending up unable to cope with the demands of city living. They have both instituted schemes on their estates to educate all the children, and to provide work other than labour in the fields for the young people who seem brightest and most eager to learn. Diane has established a school at Wellespont where even the girls are taught to read and write, and she has had considerable success with it. Girls from her school are greatly in demand as nursemaids and abigails, not to mention as wives! Some of the local farmers can scarcely read and write themselves, so they consider it a real step up if they can marry one of Diane's girls.'

'What about the young men? Once they've been to school and learned to read and write, can they find useful employment on the estates?'

'Quite often, but not always, of course. However, both Edward and William invariably find the young men secure jobs somewhere not too far from their homes. In fact, there have been no young people running off to London from either estate since my sons took over the management, and they have convinced me that if every landlord took his responsibilities seriously, there would be far fewer children starving on the streets of London.'

The Dowager and Catherine ate dinner alone that night, since Edward and William were both detained at the Foreign Office. Catherine was almost relieved when bed-time came and the men still had not returned. She was too tired to erect a blockade round her emotions, and she suspected that if William had come to her room, she would have ended up sobbing out her love against his bored and unyielding shoulder.

By Friday evening, however, her mood had changed to one of greater optimism, and as Mary helped her to dress for the ball, she admitted to herself just how badly she wanted this night to be a success. She wanted William to think she was the most beautiful woman at the reception. She wanted him to admire her and desire her, because that might lead to the hope that he might one day learn also to love her.

She had not spent so long getting ready for a party since she was seventeen, but she thoroughly enjoyed her prep-arations. It was fun to smooth essence of strawberry lotion on to her bare shoulders, and to allow Mary to brush a trace of cream rouge on to her lips. How shocked her sisters would be if they knew she was using something as wicked as French cosmetics! She decided that she rather liked the daring sensation of being a painted woman. She glanced into the mirror, examining her pink and glossy lips, and wondered why it had taken her twenty years to pluck up the courage to wear something so flattering and enjoyable.

By the time Mary had finished her ministrations, Catherine scarcely recognised the sophisticated, elegant stranger who stared silently back from her dressing-room mirror. Even her figure seemed different. She had gained weight over the past few weeks, and although she would never be either buxom or fashionably plump, her collar-bones no longer stuck out at sharp angles, and her arms were slender rather than thin.

She stepped away from the mirror, watching the subtle, iridescent ripple of her skirts as they were reflected in the candlelight. Her dress was made from Chinese shot silk, woven in muted shades of copper and bronze. It was cut low over her bosom, and hugged her ribs tightly as far as her waist, before flaring out over several petticoats in the new, fuller style.

Mary went into the bedroom to fetch her mistress's jewel-case and returned carrying the heavy leather box. 'I thought you would want to wear some of the emeralds which Captain Moreton has given you,' she said. 'Emeralds are the perfect complement to that outfit, my lady.'

Catherine's first reaction was to reject her maid's advice. Her memory of their wedding night was painfully vivid, and she did not want to wear anything that would remind her of William's scornful expression as he had tossed the jewelled collar on her bed. However, she knew that Mary was right in one respect: emeralds were the ideal jewels to enhance the subtle colour effects of her dress and, in the end, she reached reluctantly for the earrings.

She slipped them into her ears, shaking her head gently to observe the effect. The stones were larger than anything she had ever worn, but there was no denying that they formed an eye-catching contrast to the dull sheen of her gown. After a long moment of hesitation, she picked up the heavy emerald necklace and held it against her throat. It was far too garish a design for her taste, and she was on the point of returning it to the dressing-table when Mary reached out and stilled her hand.

'Let me fasten the clasp, my lady. It looks magnificent with that gown.'

'But it is so . . . so opulent.'

'Your dress has no decoration at all, my lady. No frills, no embroidery, nothing. These emeralds give the touch of lavishness which your outfit needs. I am certain that you will be the envy of all the other women at the reception.'

A short tap sounded at the door, and Mary hurriedly fastened the clasp.

'There is no time to select anything else, my lady. Here, let me help you put on your cloak.' With swift, efficient movements, she draped the stiff taffeta cape over Catherine's shoulders. 'There. You would not wish to keep the Captain waiting.'

But when the servant opened the door, Catherine saw

that it was her godmother, not William, who stood in the hall.

'Please come in, Godmama,' she said, smiling shyly. 'You look so elegant that I am sure you will outshine us all!'

'There is no fear of that!' the Dowager said. 'My dear child, you look positively magnificent.'

'Thank you. That is a compliment of the highest order, I think!'

The Dowager smiled. 'Indeed it is. It is gratifying to see that marriage to my son has restored all your former beauty to you. I hope it will not be too long before your happiness is restored in just as full a measure.'

Catherine forced herself to respond lightly. 'How could I not be happy, Godmama, when we are in London and preparing to attend such an exciting party?'

The Dowager did not respond immediately. She wandered over to the empty fireplace, staring pensively into its depths. 'My dear,' she said at last. 'There is something I want to tell you, or perhaps to ask of you. Could you please request your maid to leave us for a minute or two?'

Somewhat surprised, Catherine nodded to Mary, who left the room. 'What is it, Godmama? There is nothing wrong, I hope?'

'Not in the way you mean, perhaps. However, I am being assailed by an attack of guilty conscience, which is a most unusual experience for me. I want to confess something about the circumstances leading up to your marriage.'

'My marriage? To William?'

'Yes. When you first came to Wellespont, I was distraught to see what the loss of your mother and your first husband had done to you. For the first two weeks of your visit, I worried about you constantly. Then William arrived home after almost seven years away from us, and I stopped worrying about you for a day or two, because I was too busy worrying about my son.'

She smiled ruefully. 'I normally believe strongly in allowing people to ruin their own lives without any assistance from me. But with you and William I was quite unable to follow my own excellent rules. You were both so miserable, and both so dear to me, that I found myself in the novel situation of not knowing whom to worry about first.'

'William is an amazingly successful man in every way, Godmama—I cannot think that there was any reason for you to worry about him. He has everything a man could possibly want!'

'That is just not so, Catherine. To the world, William may have seemed successful, confident and content, but I could see that he was suffering. I always knew that he had been hit hard by Diane's marriage to Edward, but I had not realised until he came home just how deeply he had been wounded. The scars round his heart were obviously very thick, and I wondered whether he might no longer be capable of feeling the more gentle emotions. For two or three days I told myself there was nothing I could do —nothing that I ought to do. Then, when I finally took a good look at you both again, I discovered that the strangest things had been happening while I had been locked away in my room, worrying. You suddenly looked alive, Catherine. Not as vibrantly alive as the beautiful seventeen-year-old I remembered, but at least not the pale ghost you had been when you arrived at Wellespont. And as for my son . . . Well, he seemed to be spending a great deal of time pretending to ignore you, although I knew you rode together every morning. In fact, he spent so much time pointedly ignoring you that he quite forgot to brood over his sister-in-law. When you were in a room together, it was obvious to me that neither of you had eyes for anyone else. Edward and Diane both noticed the same thing.'

Catherine smiled wryly. 'I think your observations were only half correct, Godmama. It is true that I found William a fascinating man, but he gave me his attention only because he is innately courteous.'

The Dowager snorted. 'Courtesy, my dear, had absolutely nothing to do with what William was feeling for you. A man does not agree to marry a woman out of courtesy.'

'But that is exactly what happened in William's case, Godmama. You were there! You know that he married me because of what occurred in the rose garden at Wellespont, and for no other reason.'

'Ah yes! The incident in the rose garden. That was what I

wanted to speak with you about. Catherine, you have far less experience of the world than my son, and I knew you would believe me if I warned of an impending scandal. But William must have known there was absolutely no risk to either of your reputations. The servants at Wellespont are so loyal that they would never have gossiped even if they had known what had occurred. But, in fact, they knew nothing. Servants at Wellespont are not expected to work in the middle of the night, dear child. Only your maid happened to be up late and happened to see where you had gone. Even she didn't know that William was also in the rose garden. Only I knew he was in the habit of going there late at night to smoke a cigarillo.'

Catherine looked at the Dowager, her expression bewildered. 'Then why did you insist that we had to marry? I don't understand . . .'

Incredibly, the Dowager's wrinkled cheeks darkened with a blush. 'I thought you and William were ideally suited,' she said simply. 'I thought I knew what was best for both of you, and so I broke my own cardinal rule and manipulated other people's lives to fit what I believed would be good for them. My conscience has been bothering me ever since. At the time, I was convinced that you were on the verge of falling in love with each other, and I continue to sense some very powerful emotions flowing between the pair of you. But your eyes remain sad, my dear, and that troubles me deeply.'

'Godmama, you trouble yourself unnecessarily. If my eyes are sad, well, I still miss Mama and Matthew—I'm sure I shall always miss the laughter and the warmth of their company—but I don't grieve for them any longer, and it was Wil . . . It was my stay at Wellespont that helped me to understand that the time for mourning was past. So, you see, you have nothing with which to reproach yourself. On the contrary, I have everything to thank you for.'

The Dowager's gaze was suddenly full of understanding. 'I will not ask if you love my son, Catherine, since I believe I already know the answer to that question. I can't tell you that William loves you in return, because, over the past seven years, he has learned to conceal his feelings so effectively that even I cannot penetrate his disguise. But I told you this story so that you would understand that William did not marry you because he was forced to do so. He married you because he chose to.'

If only the Dowager knew the whole truth about their convoluted relationship, she would not be so certain that she understood William's motives, Catherine thought with sudden weariness. She forced the pessimistic thought away and gave her a friendly smile.

'There is no reason for you to be concerned,' she said. 'William and I are both very well pleased with our marriage. It is an arrangement that suits us both admirably.'

The Dowager looked at her godchild for a long time in silence. 'Be gentle with him, Catherine,' she said at last. 'He gives the appearance of being solid steel through to the core of his being, but in his case, appearances are deceptive.'

'You mean he is steel only half-way through, and after that he is merely iron?'

The Dowager laughed, accepting the change of mood, but the laughter did not quite reach her eyes.

'Come, child. I have delayed us long enough. The gentlemen are already waiting downstairs and we do not want to give them just cause for complaint. Men are always so odious when they complain about the feminine lack of punctuality.'

William and Edward were taking wine in the drawing-room when the ladies arrived downstairs. The brothers were dressed similarly in white silk stockings, formal knee-breeches and close-fitting tail coats, and the resemblance between them was startling. Both were tall men, powerfully built, and unusually dark for Englishmen. At a distance there seemed little to distinguish them except for William's eye-patch and the tan which bronzed his complexion.

She looked from one man to the other as the Dowager and Edward made small talk. She wondered, since they looked so similar, why a brief, cynical glance from William could make her heart lurch with love, whereas Edward's welcoming smile aroused no feelings in her other than polite acknowledgment and a touch of warm affection.

Neither she nor William joined in the conversation while they all waited for the carriage to drive round to the front of the house, but her gaze was drawn irresistibly towards her husband. When their eyes finally met, her cheeks suffused with heat as she saw a gleam of desire break through the rigid control of his expression. It was strange to think that only a few weeks ago she would not have recognised the leap of passion that tightened his features, even stranger to realise that, until her wedding night, she would not have understood the cause of the answering heat that ran like liquid fire through her veins.

There was a slight drizzle falling, and they hurried to enter the carriage without getting wet. The reception was being held at Lansdowne House, with the Marquess of Lansdowne acting as host along with the Foreign Secretary. The drive, which normally should have taken no more than ten minutes, required almost half an hour to complete because of the crush of carriages waiting to set down visitors under the portico.

George Canning, who was known for the elegance of his address, was at his most debonair when he greeted Catherine, apologising charmingly for interrupting her stay at Long Acres and assuring her that the discussions with the Argentinian and Brazilian envoys could never have progressed so smoothly if Captain Moreton had not been present to offer his invaluable advice. Mr Canning then personally escorted her across the room to introduce her to Bernardino Rivadavia of Argentina, leaving William deep in conversation with the Spanish Ambassador.

Catherine was a little nervous at being flung so precipitously into the thick of London's social activity, but she found Señor Rivadavia a fascinating man, and quite easy to talk to. He was much younger than she had expected, and passionately devoted to the cause of providing responsible government for the citizens of Argentina.

He, in turn, was intrigued by the ethereal beauty of Captain Moreton's wife, and fascinated by the quickness of her intellect. He was an accomplished philanderer, and would have liked very much to flirt with her, but she seemed unaware of his skilful overtures and, catching the Captain's gaze fixed hungrily upon his wife, he came to the sad conclusion that theirs was undoubtedly a love match. He spared a moment of regret for the strange English habit of encouraging love matches within the governing classes, then resigned himself to doing no more than requesting the pleasure of partnering Lady Catherine for a pair of country dances.

'Your necklace is remarkable for the perfection of its emeralds,' he said when they had been dancing for a few minutes. 'And the setting is most unusual. It reminds me of the designs we make in my own country.'

Catherine smiled. 'My husband owns an emerald mine in your part of the world, Señor Rivadavia, and I believe this necklace was made by a South American jeweller. You are quite right. The design is not at all typical of our English taste.'

'Indeed? But it must please you to know that you are unlikely ever to see such a necklace anywhere else in this country, since only your husband has access to the necessary jewels. The stones and the setting are each unique.'

She smiled a polite acknowledgment, but she hated to remember the circumstances in which William had given the necklace to her and quickly turned the conversation to a more agreeable topic.

'It is such a relief to dance with somebody who is as kind and patient as you,' she confided. 'Especially since you are such an expert dancer. This is my first London ball, you know, and I was afraid that I might make a complete spectacle of myself.'

Señor Rivadavia, who was accustomed to thinking of himself as fatally attractive to the ladies, had never before heard a beautiful young woman tell him that he was kind and patient. There was a glint of wry humour in his eyes when he responded, 'I am delighted, my lady, to know that you consider me a satisfactory partner.'

When the country dances ended, he looked around for her husband, locating him at the foot of the Grand Staircase, still immersed in conversation with the Foreign Secretary. He escorted Catherine to the Captain's side, but before William could speak, Mr Canning requested the pleasure of dancing the minuet with her.

Catherine accepted with a shy smile, relieved that she knew the measures of the old-fashioned dance well enough to concentrate on the Foreign Secretary's conversation. She need not have worried. Mr Canning set his mind to being agreeable, and she found his company thoroughly enjoyable. It was hard to believe that this sedate, middle-aged gentleman was the same man who had once fought a duel with Lord Castlereagh and the same man whose policies in South America were provoking such cries of outrage from Spain and Portugal. Her only moment of tension occurred when he commented upon the unique splendour of her emerald necklace, but she passed off his compliments with a light remark and they parted from each other in excellent humour at the end of the set.

Mr Canning thoroughly enjoyed his dance with Lady Catherine, and he informed several of his friends that Captain Moreton had married a diamond of the first water. Even before the minuet was over, Catherine had been declared a delightful young woman and amazingly beauti-ful, although a trifle too pale to be perfect, but the Foreign Secretary's approval was all that was needed to set the seal on her success. Upon second glance, her pallor was dis-covered to be intriguing rather than excessive, and her green eyes were agreed to be exceptional.

Several matrons made a point of congratulating the Dowager on her son's forethought in marrying a woman whose colouring so perfectly matched the jewels that were his chief source of income. Catherine was forgiven for the extraordinary size of the emeralds in her necklace, and the guests commented instead upon the exquisite crafts-manship of the setting. Before long, the Dowager had the satisfaction of seeing her daughter-in-law beseiged by gentlemen of all shapes, ages and sizes wanting to dance with her. Secure in Catherine's success, the Dowager heaved a sigh of relief and retired to the card-room with an old crony.

The Dowager's retreat to the card-room came five minutes too soon. Catherine was dancing with a stout young prince attached to the Spanish Ambassador's suite when a slight stir at the doorway marked the arrival of some latecomers. She was looking at her partner rather than towards the entrance, so she had no idea who had come in, but she heard the ripple of excited comment spread through the ballroom and, for a moment, had the strangest sensation that the whispered comments somehow encompassed her. The sensation became stronger when—inexplicably—she felt her partner's hand tighten momentarily against her waist, but he said nothing to justify her suspicion, and she forced herself to ignore the irrational prickle which stole down her spine.

As soon as the dance ended, the Spanish prince moved with unflattering promptness to escort her from the floor. Their exit was barred, however, by the crush of people ahead of them, and Catherine overheard a man behind them remark, 'Good lord! That Portuguese fellow is here, and he's brought Lady Annabelle with him. Even if he's a foreigner, he ought to know better than that! Dashed bad form when everybody knows that Lansdowne doesn't approve of loose women.'

An amused feminine voice responded, 'Yes, but did you see what Lady Annabelle was wearing? As far as I'm concerned, my dear Bertie, that makes this entire evening worth while.'

Catherine had no opportunity to discover which precise item of Lady Annabelle's dress had aroused so much interest. Her escort, with scant regard for the courtesies, forged a path through the crowds in front of them and almost pushed Catherine to the side of the ballroom.

'The Dowager, your chaperon, she is not here!'

It seemed to Catherine that there was an inexplicable note of panic in the young prince's voice.

'I dare say she has gone in search of refreshment,' she said soothingly. 'She mentioned to me a short while ago that she felt very thirsty.'

'I will find her! I will find your husband. He will know what to do!' Without waiting for any response, the prince melted into the crowds in the doorway, leaving Catherine entirely alone.

She felt both mystified and slightly annoyed at his strange and unmannerly behaviour. She was also perturbed to realise that her earlier sensation of being the cynosure of all eyes was growing steadily stronger. Despite the crush of people in the ballroom, the area around her had developed into a little oasis of space and silence.

Her isolation was so conspicuous that Catherine began to hope that the prince would soon succeed in finding the Dowager. She scanned the room, hoping to see either her husband or her brother-in-law, but neither of them was in sight. Mr Canning was similarly absent, and she concluded that they must all be closeted in some private room, discussing matters of state.

Her gaze roamed absently over the dancers grouping themselves for the quadrille, then halted in blank, horrified astonishment on the plump figure of an auburn-headed young woman bouncing merrily around at the end of the set. She wore a cream satin dress with a bodice that was nowhere near large enough to cover her generous endowment of bosom. Her gown, however, was not what fascinated Catherine. Every time the woman moved, an emerald necklace—big enough to overshadow almost any other piece of jewellery in the room—dipped and sparkled against the flamboyant swell of her breasts.

Lady Annabelle! Catherine thought. Dear heaven, this is the woman who is William's mistress!

In common with half the other eyes in the room, her gaze fixed itself hypnotically upon the emerald necklace, which looked almost obscenely opulent against the white mound of Lady Annabelle's flesh. Not only was it obviously worth a king's ransom, it was also identical to the necklace she herself was wearing! Moreover, there could scarcely be a person in the room who was not aware of that face—and precisely what it signified.

Catherine's stomach twisted tight with humiliation. With the exertion of superhuman control, she managed to avoid tearing her necklace from her throat and crushing it underfoot. She realised that the area around her was becoming increasingly empty, and her humiliation changed suddenly into a flame of agonising, white-hot rage. How dare

William give her—*his wife*—a piece of jewellery identical to something he had given his mistress! Had he never stopped to consider the scandal which would inevitably ensue if his wife and mistress were both present at the Foreign Secretary's ball, wearing identical jewels?

Rage made her temporarily unaware of her surroundings, and intent only upon finding the Dowager, she walked swiftly towards the main doors, indifferent to the murmur of fascinated speculation which followed in her wake. She halted her flight only when her path was blocked by a short, dapper gentleman of somewhat foreign appearance.

'I beg your pardon,' she said stiffly, attempting to circumvent the man without actively acknowledging his presence.

The gentleman laughed softly. 'It shall be granted only on one condition,' he said, his English heavily accented although grammatically perfect. 'You must be my partner for the next dance. Fate has thrown the most beautiful woman in the room into my path, and I refuse to ignore the gift.'

His manner seemed lightly flirtatious and, unlike the poor Spanish prince, not at all embarrassed. She thought he must be one of the few people in the room not to have noticed the startling resemblance of her necklace to Lady Annabelle's, but she was not tempted to accept his offer to dance. She needed to be alone so that she could think. Should she go home? Stay here, but take off her necklace? Alternatively, perhaps, she might plan how best to murder William and Lady Annabelle. She swallowed an inappropriate sob of laughter, recognising that she hovered dangerously close to hysteria. She pressed her hands to her cheeks and drew in a deep, calming breath.

'I am sorry, sir. I believe we have not been introduced. I think I should probably rejoin my husband and the other members of my party.'

He swept her an exaggerated bow. 'I can find any number of elderly dowagers who would be willing to introduce us formally if you insist.' His eyes twinkled. 'For myself, I am happy to believe that you are a proper person for me to know, and I will not insist that you produce your credentials.'

'Sir, my godmother will be wondering where I am . . .'

He interrupted her smoothly. 'I am the Marques de Algarve Branca, at your service. My estates lie a few miles distant from Lisbon, and I am in England to assist our Ambassador in gaining British support to quell the rebellious factions in Brazil. Does that sound respectable enough to qualify me as your partner for the next dance?'

She forced a smile, although her attention was not really upon what he had said. His name ought to hold some significance for her, she felt, but she could not for the life of her imagine what it might be.

'I am Lady Catherine Moreton,' she said distractedly. 'The wife of Captain the Honourable William Moreton. Our home is in Wiltshire.'

'The wife of Captain Moreton? What a happy coincidence, my lady! My father once knew your husband well.'

'Did he? Did they meet in London, Senhor Marques?'

'No, in Lisbon. Unlike me, my father never travelled to London.'

'And how long have you been here, sir? Your command of our language is excellent.'

'Thank you. On this occasion, I have been here only two weeks, but I have studied the language since childhood with a succession of English governesses.'

The fiddlers struck up the opening chords of a waltz, and his dark eyes gleamed. 'Ah, the gods are definitely on my side tonight! I can claim not just a country dance, but a waltz!' He swept into another bow. 'I beg, Lady Catherine, that you will allow me to demonstrate that Portuguese skill in this dance can sometimes rival that found in Vienna.'

The words of refusal already hovered on her lips when she saw William re-enter the ballroom. She watched him as he strode purposefully towards the dance floor, walking directly to Lady Annabelle's side. Catherine held her breath as she saw him bow politely and offer the woman his arm. Even at this distance, she could see Annabelle's flirtatious smile as she tapped William's arm with her fan. He made some quick comment, and Annabelle curtsied to her previous partner before walking off with William in the direction of a small ante-room.

Catherine expelled her breath in a harsh, involuntary gasp. It was bad enough that her husband should have created this impossible situation. It was utterly intolerable that he should publicly seek out his mistress!

'It is good of you to ask me to dance,' she said through clenched teeth. 'I should be delighted to test your skill at the waltz, Senhor Marques.'

The Marques did not appear to notice the somewhat fierce manner of her acceptance. He escorted her on to the floor, and although he was scarcely as tall as Catherine herself, swept her into his arms with a dignified flourish. Well aware that at least half the people in the room watched her progress across the dance floor, some streak of obstinacy forced her to appear indifferent to their curiosity. She could not stop people from talking about Lady Annabelle and the identical necklaces, but she could deny them the satisfaction of appearing to be humiliated.

It seemed a very long time until the waltz ended, and she had almost no idea what she replied to the Marques's attempts at conversation. It was imperative that she should find the Dowager.

Years of training enabled her to smile courteously at her partner. 'Thank you, Senhor Marques, for a most enjoyable dance. I can hardly believe that you learned to waltz in Lisbon. I didn't know it was a city much given to dancing.'

'It has its occasional moments of celebration. Lady Catherine, I see that Dom Sebastian has just returned to the ballroom. Dom Sebastian is a distant cousin of our King John, and he is also our Ambassador to the Court of St James. Would you do me the honour, my lady, of allowing me to introduce you to His Excellency?'

Despite her urgent desire to find the Dowager, she could not possibly refuse such a request. Accordingly, Catherine placed her gloved hand on the Marques's sleeve and allowed him to escort her towards the balcony at the far end of the ballroom. They had not proceeded very far, however, when William stepped into their path, his face set into its harshest and most forbidding lines.

Catherine hesitated for a moment before inclining her head in bare acknowledgment.

'Captain Moreton,' she said. 'I would like to present my partner to you. Senhor Marques, this is my husband, Captain the Honourable William Moreton. Captain, this is His Excellency the Marques de Algarve Branca.'

'Senhor Marques.' William gave the briefest possible nod, and he did not hold out his hand.

'Captain Moreton.' The Marques smiled as he raised himself from a deep bow. 'I have heard much of you from my father and from other friends.'

'Indeed? The late Marques and I met on only one occasion.'

'But that was such a memorable occasion, Captain Moreton! Believe me, your activities and your reputation were indelibly imprinted upon his memory.'

William's expression became momentarily bleak. 'I did my duty as I saw it, Senhor Marques. I imagine your father did the same.'

'Perhaps. However, why waste time referring to events which were finished seven long years ago? Napoleon Bonaparte is dead, and the world is a rapidly changing place for us all. You see me now, a member of Portugal's embassy to the Court of St James, a situation that would have seemed impossible only two or three years ago.'

'I congratulate you upon your appointment, Senhor Marques, and wish your Ambassador every success with his mission. If you will excuse me, I wish to have the pleasure of dancing the next set of country dances with my wife.'

'But certainly.' The Marques was all smiles. 'To dance with the Lady Catherine is a joy of the first order. I felicitate you upon your recent nuptials, by the way.'

William bent his head in a gesture that was barely courteous. 'Thank you. Goodbye, Senhor Marques.'

'Let us not say "*Goodbye*", Captain Moreton. Let us say rather "*Até logo*". It is an expression my countrymen use to indicate that they look forward to seeing each other again soon.'

The Marques ignored William's thunderous expression and bowed low over Catherine's hand.

'I thank you for the pleasure of your company, my lady.

Later, you must allow me the privilege of introducing you to my Ambassador.'

'I should be honoured, Senhor Marques.'

Even had she wished to say anything further, she would have had no opportunity. William gripped her by the elbow and practically marched her on to the ballroom floor.

'I don't wish to dance with you,' Catherine said.

'You have no choice in the matter if you wish to save any shred of your reputation. No society hostess will ever invite you to one of her functions unless we are seen to be in perfect charity with each other. If you wish to enter the world of the *ton*, my lady, you will dance with me, and smile as if your life depended upon it.'

Catherine stood like a piece of wood within his arms. 'How dare you speak to me so! Why is *my* reputation at risk when it is you and your mistress who have caused this humiliating situation?'

'My mistress,' he said through clenched teeth, 'is none of your business. There are, however, several other subjects on which I have a great deal more to say to you. For one thing, I do not want you to have anything further to do with the Marques de Algarve Branca. He is not to be trusted.'

'What has he done that is so terrible? Paraded his mistress on his arm at the same reception as his wife?'

His mouth tightened into grimness. 'Believe me, my lady, the Marques is not a safe man for you to know, and that is why I have asked you not to see him again. His family has every reason to dislike the Moretons, and although he is mistaken, he thinks he has special cause to dislike *me*.'

There was unaccustomed mockery in the brittle smile she flashed at him. 'Poor man, I am almost tempted to offer him my sympathy. There are so many of us in the same situation.'

'Catherine, for your own safety I have no choice but to forbid you to see the Marques de Algarve Branca. I would remind you that you are my wife, and it is your duty to obey me in this simple command.'

'Naturally, obedience to your commands must always be one of my primary objects,' Catherine said tightly. She recognised the angry glitter in her husband's eyes, but she did not realise that the anger was directed exclusively towards himself and she was infuriated by the seeming injustice of his behaviour.

'You may feel that Lady Annabelle is none of my business, Captain Moreton. For myself, I should like to spend a little longer discussing her. Tell me, is it the fashion in the high circles you frequent to deck out wives and mistresses in identical pieces of jewellery? Does it make for ease of identification if you suffer from a moment of absent-mindedness? You must forgive the naïveté of my questions. Remember I am only a country bumpkin, unused to the elegant manners of the *ton*.'

'You betray your gaucheness, my lady,' he said tautly. 'I repeat that Lady Annabelle is none of your business.'

She was white to the lips. 'And her necklace? Am I to understand that it, too, is *none of my business*?'

'Her necklace need not concern you. If you will give me *your* necklace when we return home tonight, I shall arrange to have it reset.'

'You may burn it for all I care. I shall never wear it again!'

He shrugged. 'As you wish.'

She drew in an incredulous breath. 'And, as far as you are concerned, that is all there is to be said on this subject?'

He hesitated for a moment. 'Catherine, the middle of a ballroom floor is scarcely the place to conduct this conversation.'

She did not hear the faint note of appeal in his voice, and she felt her anger bubble over. 'I did not ask to dance with you, Captain Moreton. In fact, it is difficult for me to think of anything in the world that I would find less agreeable.'

'Is that so? Then in this, at least, we are of one mind.'

His unwarranted harshness was finally too much to bear. Indifferent to the shocked babble of comment from the onlookers, Catherine tore herself from his grasp and ran from the room. She was vaguely aware of bumping into the Spanish Ambassador, but the tears she had repressed ever since first seeing Lady Annabelle welled up and flowed down her cheeks, blinding her to his astonished gaze and blinding her equally to William, left white-faced and alone in the middle of the floor.

The Marques de Algarve Branca walked inconspicuously from the ballroom, a tiny smile of triumph curving his full lips. The first stage of his plan was complete, and, all things considered, it had been a very satisfactory evening.

CHAPTER
SIXTEEN

THE DOWAGER waited until the servants had all gone to bed before tapping softly on William's bedroom door. Despite her need to speak with her son, she had half hoped that he might be with Catherine. Her hopes were dashed when her knock was answered immediately.

'I am sorry to disturb you at such a late hour,' she said 'But I think we must talk for a little while.'

He stepped aside. 'You haven't disturbed me, Mama Please come in; I was merely reading.'

In recent weeks, the Dowager had found it difficult to read her son's mood, but tonight she could easily detect the storm of painful emotions concealed behind his cool words. She walked over to the window, wondering how best to say what needed to be said, but he spoke before she could collect her thoughts.

'I'm glad you came, Mama. I owe you an apology, if you are prepared to accept it. What happened tonight was . . contemptible.'

'I certainly found the situation embarrassing, although not for myself. It seems to me that it is Catherine who deserves your apologies.'

There was a small silence. 'She will not talk to me,' he admitted finally. The colour in his cheeks darkened. 'Her bedroom door is locked.'

'Could you honestly expect otherwise?' the Dowager asked quietly. 'William, your relationship with Lady Annabelle is none of my business, but your treatment of Catherine is very much my affair. How in the world did you come to commit such a gross error of judgment as to bestow identical pieces of jewellery upon your wife and your mistress?'

'What can I say, Mama? There is no rational justification no explanation that I could expect you to understand.'

'You might be astonished at what I understand, William

I, too, was once young and very much in love with a husband who did not seem aware of my existence. We are both proud, you and I, and a little too arrogant for our own good. There was no folly that would have been too absurd for me to commit during the months that I strove to attract your father's attention. You are older than I was at that time, but I imagine your wisdom in matters of the heart is not much greater.'

'When I met Catherine, I thought I was still in love with Diane,' William said slowly. He poured himself a glass of Chablis, staring abstractedly into its depths. 'I did not plan to fall in love with her, you know. She is not at all in love with me.' The Dowager made no comment, and his voice dipped lower. 'I gave her the necklace at a moment when I was furious with myself, and so I hit out at her to protect my own feelings. I was angry enough not to think of the possible consequences.'

'Even so, William, I cannot imagine how you neglected to warn her before she dressed tonight.'

He took a deep swallow of his wine. 'Spain and Portugal are determined to declare war upon their former colonies in South America. Edward and I have been so preoccupied with our meetings at the Foreign Office that I quite literally forgot about the wretched necklace. Besides, Annabelle is not usually invited to receptions given by the Marquis of Lansdowne and the Foreign Secretary.'

'Unfortunately, William, it is Catherine who will pay the price for your forgetfulness. London society is not forgiving.'

'God knows, Mama, that I have no right to ask for your assistance, but for Catherine's sake do you think there is anything you can do to help put matters right?'

'It is difficult to think of a convincing explanation of why your wife was wearing the same necklace as your mistress. However, I shall pay a few strategic morning calls and do my very best to smooth matters over. What are your own plans for tomorrow?'

'I have meetings with George Canning and the Spanish Ambassador that are likely to last most of the day. Edward does not join us until the afternoon.'

'Perhaps, in the circumstances, it is just as well if you are out of the house before Catherine wakes up. I'll talk to her when I have paid my morning calls and put in a good word for you, although you scarcely deserve it. I shall attempt to explain that love has a disastrous effect upon the mental processes of the masculine mind.'

For the first time that night, a faint smile touched William's mouth. 'In my case, you would be speaking only the truth.' A frown quickly replaced his smile. 'Mama, something about this incident has been worrying me all evening. Were you in the ballroom when Lady Annabelle arrived?'

'No, I was talking to a friend in the card-room.'

'Unfortunately, neither was I in the ballroom. Edward and I were both upstairs with the Foreign Secretary, but Edward happened to return for a few minutes just as Annabelle arrived. She came with the Marques de Algarve Branca, you know, and Edward is almost certain that the Marques waited to make sure that we were out of the ball-room before announcing his arrival.'

The Dowager looked up sharply. 'Do you suspect that he planned somehow to cause trouble?'

William shrugged. 'He has every reason to dislike our family. After all, we were responsible for discovering his father's treason.'

'I do not like to believe in coincidence,' the Dowager said slowly. 'On the other hand, I cannot see how he could have planned this scandal, or even what he hoped to gain by it.'

'I agree. I sought Annabelle out as soon as Edward warned me of what had occurred. She is a good-natured woman, and she left the reception willingly when I asked her to do so. Unfortunately, she isn't very intelligent, and the Marques could easily have deceived her as to his true intentions. She told me that he had been paying her assiduous court for the past couple of weeks.'

The Dowager looked thoughtful. 'I assume that the Marques could not possibly have known that Catherine possessed a necklace just like Lady Annabelle's?'

'No possibility at all. And yet I cannot shake off the feeling that he plans some sort of revenge, and that

Annabelle's presence at the reception yesterday was merely the first step in a carefully-wrought plan.'

The Dowager rose to her feet, smoothing out a wrinkle in her satin skirt. 'Well, we can resolve nothing tonight, I fear. However, when you speak to Catherine tomorrow, I recommend that you explain the truth about your relationship with the Algarve Branca family. Explain how you and Edward unmasked a plot to rescue Napoleon. Explain that the former Marques was a ringleader in the plot and that the Portuguese Government exiled the entire Algarve Branca family. If the Marques does plan some sort of revenge, it is better if Catherine knows everything.'

'It may be difficult to persuade her to listen to me.'

'Difficult, perhaps, but not impossible. You see, I happen to know that Catherine loves you, and when a woman is in love, she is prepared to forgive a great deal.'

'I hope you are right, Mama, since she has a great deal to forgive.'

The Dowager paused in his doorway. 'Twenty-five years of happy married life taught me several useful things, William. Above all, it taught me that the marriage bed is a wonderful place in which to apologise.' She smiled slightly. 'You may care to remember that the housekeeper has duplicate keys to all the doors in this house. Good night, William. Sleep well.'

Only Edward was in the breakfast-room when Catherine arrived downstairs the next morning. He was dressed for a journey, drinking coffee as he paced up and down the room.

'Catherine!' he exclaimed as soon as she walked in. 'William and my mother are both out, and I have just received bad news from Wellespont. Diane has taken a severe fall. The doctor is with her, but she is in bed and asking for me.'

'Oh, I'm so sorry!' Catherine said. 'Of course you must go to her at once. How did the accident happen?'

'I'm not sure of the details. The message comes from her maid and is not very clear, but it seems Diane tripped while she was at the schoolhouse.'

'If she is asking for you, matters cannot be too bad.' Catherine tried to sound reassuring. She had never imagined that her brother-in-law could look so white and shaky. 'Take heart, Edward. To ask for you, she must at least be conscious.'

'I suppose so.' He strode impatiently into the hall. 'Where is the carriage? It is fifteen minutes at least since I summoned it.'

'It will be here shortly, I'm sure.' Catherine hesitated. 'What of the baby, Edward? Does the doctor give any news?'

'So far, it seems that the child is safe. The maid does not mention it, at least. But it is Diane I care about, not some unborn infant which has yet to draw breath.'

The rattle of wheels announced the arrival of the carriage from the mews.

'Your hat and gloves, my lord,' said the butler.

Edward took them with a brief word of thanks, and Catherine followed him out on to the marble steps of the entrance.

'Please explain the situation to my mother and to William,' he said. 'And, Catherine, I am sorry about last night and the ruin of your début. I have not seen my brother this morning, so I don't know what explanation he has to offer. But when you see him next, will you please remember that he loves you very much?'

She could not meet his eyes. 'Yes, of course I shall remember.'

Edward was not deceived, and he took her hand into his. 'Once, many years ago, my brother imagined himself to be in love with Diane. Believe me, Catherine, that love was an illusion. His innermost feelings remained untouched until he met you.'

She was quite sure that Edward was wrong, but she deeply appreciated the fact that, in this moment of crisis, he still spared time to comfort her.

'Thank you for all your kindness,' she said softly. 'Now, please hurry home to Diane, and tell her that we look forward to hearing good news from Wellespont shortly.'

Edward stepped quickly into the carriage. The groom

lifted the steps and sprang up beside the driver, who whipped the horses into instant motion. Catherine watched until it was out of sight, before returning slowly to the breakfast-room.

She served herself with bread and a slice of ham before sitting down at the table. She had planned to ignore William completely if he attempted to speak to her, but it was disconcerting to discover that he was not even in the house to be ignored. How could any man publicly humiliate his wife, then depart without leaving any message to explain his absence? Catherine began to feel excessively ill used.

She abandoned the attempt to eat and got up from the table, glancing at her watch. It was well past noon. 'Is the Dowager still sleeping?' she asked the butler.

'Her ladyship summoned the barouche about half an hour ago, my lady. I understand she has some calls to pay.'

'Thank you,' Catherine said. It was bad enough to be deprived of the satisfaction of ignoring her husband. It was even worse to be deprived of the Dowager's bracing company.

She walked into the drawing-room and stared gloomily out of the window. The sun shone on the pavement with annoying cheerfulness. The afternoon stretched ahead of her with daunting emptiness, and she wondered what on earth she could do to fill it. Sighing, she picked up a book and settled herself listlessly on one of the window-seats. She was startled when the butler's booming voice announced the arrival of His Excellency the Marques de Algarve Branca.

'Lady Catherine! What an unexpected delight to find you at home. And alone, too!' The Marques swept into the room, all smiles and dapper deference.

'Senhor Marques.' Catherine extended her hand, her thoughts in a turmoil. Her last conversation with William was painfully clear in her mind, and she remembered that William had ordered her to have nothing further to do with the Marques de Algarve Branca.

'I have called in hope that you will take pity upon me, Lady Catherine. I have just now taken possession of a new curricle, and I long to drive it somewhere. Would you do me the honour of accompanying me on a short outing?'

Catherine had no particular desire to drive anywhere with the Marques. However, she had a burning desire to annoy William, and the Marques's invitation presented the perfect opportunity.

'That sounds delightful,' she said. 'I was just thinking that the afternoon was too warm and sunny to waste indoors.'

'The wind is a little chilly, at least to my Portuguese blood. You will need to dress warmly, Lady Catherine, despite the sunshine.'

'If you will wait while I collect my hat and pelisse, Senhor Marques, we can be on our way very shortly.'

He smiled his agreement and she hurried upstairs to change into a dashing new carriage outfit of emerald-green broadcloth, the sleeves braided with jet ribbon and the high-standing collar trimmed with a froth of white Brussels lace. When she came downstairs, the Marques took one glance and professed himself overcome with admiration for her elegance.

His curricle was splendid, with pale yellow upholstery ad wheel rims picked out in silver. He was a competent driver, and she complimented him sincerely on his skill at the reins.

'We have all the afternoon ahead of us, Lady Catherine. Would you care to come with me as far as Kew Gardens? I am fortunate to have been given permission to visit them, and we should be back long before nightfall.'

An irrational shiver trembled down her spine, and she shook it away impatiently. Just because William had warned her to avoid the Marques, that was no reason for her to follow his advice.

'I have never been to Kew of course,' she said, 'although I have heard from those privileged to see them that the gardens are splendid. Thank you, Senhor Marques, for your invitation.'

The gardens were as magnificent as Catherine had heard but although the Marques exerted himself to be entertaining, she did not find his company appealing. Irrationally, the more lavish his flattery became, the more she wished that she had never accepted his invitation. However, it was not until the afternoon was well advanced that she was able to establish the precise cause of her uneasiness. At the Marques's suggestion, they had seated themselves on a rustic bench to admire a vista of budding white roses, and she suddenly realised how strange it was for him to have invited her out on this excursion. *She* had accepted the invitation because she was angry with her husband and determined to defy his arbitrary orders, but why had the Marques extended the invitation in the first place?

She wondered briefly if he hoped to start an affair, but dismissed the thought almost as soon as it occurred. Despite his unending flow of compliments, she did not think that he found her desirable. The subtle undercurrent of sexual tension simply was not present when he looked at her.

Even though she was making little response, the Marques continued to chatter eloquently about the beauty of the roses, but when she twisted round on the bench, she found that he was not looking in the direction of the flower-beds. He was surreptitiously examining his watch, his fingers strumming tensely against the gold case. As soon as he saw that she was watching him, he slid the timepiece back into his waistcoat pocket and gestured towards the sloping expanse of lawn.

'In Lisbon we do not have such wonderful green grass and trees as you have here, but in early summer the countryside is full of wild flowers in the most vivid shades imaginable. I think you would like the colourfulness of Lisbon, Lady Catherine. The garden of my home is full of magnolias which my great-uncle brought back from Brazil, and in spring they bloom in a profusion of pink and purple.'

Catherine discovered that she was heartily sick of discussing the horticultural wonders of the world. 'Why did you invite me to come here with you today, Senhor Marques?' she asked abruptly.

His voice was smooth as silk when he replied, making her aware of the clumsiness of her question. 'Dear Lady Catherine, did I not explain already? I have a new curricle which I was anxious to try out, and I wished to see the famous gardens while enjoying the pleasure of your company.'

'There are any number of people who would have been only too delighted to accompany you, Senhor Marques.'

'Ah, yes. But I chose *you*, Lady Catherine,' he replied softly. 'Your presence here today was quite essential to my happiness.'

Another shiver snaked down her spine, and she jumped quickly to her feet. 'I think, Senhor Marques, that it is time for us to return to town. I would not want to be late, since my husband is expecting me.'

'Goodness, we certainly would not want to keep Captain Moreton waiting!' The Marques's dark countenance was smiling. 'Allow me to offer you the support of my arm along these paths, Lady Catherine. There are some unexpected bumps that we are likely to encounter.'

She did not recall precisely where they had left the curricle, but at one point in their long walk it seemed to her that the route they took back was exceptionally circuitous. She reminded herself that her sense of direction was not strong and the paths were notoriously winding, and soon managed to convince herself that her impression was mistaken. It was absurd to imagine that the Marques had some reason to delay their return to town.

The curricle was exactly where they had left it, in the charge of a stocky Portuguese groom who spoke no English and appeared not to have moved a muscle from the moment they had left him. The Marques helped Catherine into the carriage, the steps were lifted up and the journey home proceeded uneventfully until they reached the centre of town.

Catherine had decided that her uneasiness was nothing more than the product of a guilty conscience, when the Marques took the curricle sharply round a corner and tooled swiftly down Regent Street. She sat up with sudden attention.

'Senhor Marques, I have not been long in town, but this does not seem to be the correct route for us to take.'

'How so, Lady Catherine?'

'Moreton House is in Grosvenor Square. Should we not have turned left at the last crossing?'

'Your sense of direction is excellent, my lady. But we are not going to Grosvenor Square.'

'Not going to . . . But where are we going? It is far too late to drive anywhere else this evening. In a few minutes it will be dark!'

'You need not worry about the harmful effects of the night air, Lady Catherine. We shall soon be safely indoors.'

The panic she felt transformed itself into a strange, icy calm. 'Where are you taking me, Senhor Marques?'

'To my house, Lady Catherine. I think you will find it very comfortably appointed for a bachelor establishment.'

A sickening lump of dread settled in the pit of her stomach, but she made no conventional protests. She was quite sure that the Marques did not have seduction on his mind.

'Why are you doing this?' she asked quietly. 'What do you hope to achieve by forcing me to accompany you to your home?'

'Several things, Lady Catherine. But chiefly the ruination of your family and the restoration of my own family's fortune.'

She drew in a deep, shaky breath. 'Those are grand ambitions to build upon such a simple foundation.'

'Oh, but my plans have not been simple at all, Lady Catherine. Indeed, I pride myself on the fact that— complex as they have been—I have worked them all out to the smallest detail.'

'You surely cannot expect me to walk meekly into your house, knowing that you plan something dreadful?'

'Your co-operation is not important, Lady Catherine. I can enforce your compliance if you do not give it willingly.'

She mentally assessed the speed at which they were travelling and the distance between her seat in the curricle and the road. Two seconds of thought were sufficient to convince her that any attempt to jump from the carriage would achieve nothing, unless she were intent upon committing suicide. Silently she turned her face forward again. She would have to find some other method of escape.

'That was a wise decision,' the Marques said mockingly, 'although João would have grabbed you even before you jumped. The instructions I have given him were very clear and quite specific. I have found with peasants that it is always desirable to keep things simple.'

As he spoke, he drew the carriage to a halt in front of a narrow town house close to St James's. A liveried servant stood by the iron-fenced entrance. The Marques clicked his fingers and the servant ran forward to hold the horses' heads. At the same time, João jumped down from the curricle and the Marques gripped Catherine's arm. With a quiver of disbelief, she felt the steel blade of a dagger press against her side, the point sharp enough to penetrate the thick wool of her pelisse.

'Please do take care descending from the carriage,' the Marques said. 'I should be desolated if any—accident —befell you.'

'Why?' she asked bitterly. 'Would my death interfere with the successful conclusion of your plans?'

'Not really,' he said. 'And you would be well advised to remember that fact.' The dagger pressed insistently against her ribs. 'Please hurry, Lady Catherine. I am anxious to show you to your room.'

From the corner of her eye, she noticed two gentlemen passing by on the opposite side of the road, and opened her mouth to scream. Instantly the Marques's hand clamped over her mouth and he pressed her close to his body in a grotesque parody of an embrace. The dagger ripped through the fabric of her bodice, its point leaving a thin, shallow scratch along her ribs.

'Tut, tut, Lady Catherine, I had not thought you were so foolish.' The Marques pushed her ahead of him into the house, where a blank-faced maidservant waited in the hall. She curtsied deeply as the Marques entered. After one swift, appraising glance, Catherine realised that she would derive no more help from the maid than she had from the grooms.

The Marques's arm tightened round her waist, and he flicked the dagger against her skin to indicate that she should precede him up the stairs. The maid, who was the only servant in sight, followed them. So far, she had not spoken a single word, and Catherine became aware that the whole house was eerily silent. The Marques's servants, she reflected, certainly did not sing with happiness as they went about their tasks.

The Marques conducted her into a small bedroom, pleasantly furnished with a modern bed and elegant, upholstered armchairs.

'Please sit down, Lady Catherine. In a moment, Maria will bring water to tend to your wound.'

'Your kindness overwhelms me.'

His smile made her heart contract with fear. 'I should warn you, Lady Catherine, that in the past I have not been known for my kindness.'

She refused to give him the satisfaction of displaying her fright, but she sank into a chair, glad to be left to her own devices for a few minutes. The Marques and the maid began a rapid, incomprehensible conversation in Portuguese, and she let the guttural sounds flow over her head. Rescue could not be far away, she reminded herself. The servants at Moreton House all knew that the Marques had taken her driving. The Dowager was probably home already, and William would return from the Foreign Office at any minute. He would soon come pounding on the Marques's door, demanding her release. Catherine pressed her fingers against the painful ache in her side and willed herself to remain calm.

The Marques's soft voice broke into her thoughts. 'You will be interested to hear what Maria has been telling me.'

She managed to inject a note of boredom into her voice. 'I doubt it, Senor Marques.'

'Ah, but you are so wrong, Lady Catherine. You see, Maria's news concerns your husband. The so brave and daring Captain Moreton.'

Involuntarily, her head jerked up. 'My husband?'

'Yes. Maria paid a visit to Moreton House this afternoon. She had a most important note to deliver to the Captain. Fortunately, she found him at home.'

Icy chills spread out from her stomach and enveloped her entire body. 'What did the note say?'

'It asked Captain Moreton to come alone and on foot to a certain isolated corner of Hyde Park. The Captain thought the note was from you—a plea for help. Your husband is a gallant man, Lady Catherine, although a trifle impetuous. He dashed off at once to the rescue.'

Her lips moved stiffly. 'What happened in Hyde Park?'

'Naturally, your husband did not find you, Lady Catherine, since you were not there. You were at that moment admiring the roses at Kew.'

She was appalled to think how carelessly she had accepted the Marques's invitation. Her mouth was so dry that it was hard to speak.

'Where is my husband now?'

'He is—somewhere safe.'

'Is he . . . Is he hurt?'

'I have not seen him, Lady Catherine. Two of my helpers were waiting for him when he arrived in Hyde Park, and they detained him on my behalf. You will be happy to hear that they had strict instructions not to kill him. Maria tells me that he put up a most impressive struggle. Your husband may lack cunning, Lady Catherine, but he is blessed with a powerful supply of muscle.'

'In straightforward language, Senhor Marques, where is my husband detained, and when do you plan to release him?'

'Those questions are to the point, my lady, and to some extent the answers to them depend upon you. To be utterly frank, my dear, your husband's life depends upon your co-operation.'

Catherine fought back the impression of moving through a nightmare. 'How can I co-operate with you when I am held prisoner?'

'Oh, come now—*prisoner* is such a harsh and uncomfortable word! Please do try to think of yourself as my guest. Believe me, I intend to offer you every comfort. The Algarve Branca family was previously noted for its hospitality.'

She bit her lip, fighting back the urge to cry out. 'Tell me plainly, Senhor Marques. Where is my husband, and why is his life in peril? What has he ever done to deserve your enmity?'

'You really do not know, do you? It seemed incredible, but I realised when we met at Mr Canning's ball that you had no idea that your husband caused the ruination of my father and the almost total loss of the Algarve Branca fortune.'

'How could that be? My husband was in Lisbon only once, and that visit lasted no more than a few days.'

'His short stay was enough to wreak havoc in the lives of every member of my family. He saw to it that my father was condemned as a political outcast, and in consequence, our family life was ruined.'

Understanding dawned upon Catherine. 'Your father was involved in the plot to rescue Napoleon Bonaparte from the British garrison on St Helena!'

The Marques shrugged. 'It is true that my father was a leader of the Court faction which supported the French Imperial cause, but I had no such leanings, and when your husband engineered my father's downfall, it was I who suffered the consequences. My family lost lands and income with a value in excess of ten thousand English pounds.'

'I am sorry for you, Senhor Marques, but your father chose to pursue a dream of political power, and he paid the inevitable price of failure. I cannot see how my husband is to blame for that. Moreover, you don't appear to have suffered too badly. You are, after all, accredited as an envoy to the British Government. To hold such a position, your King must have decided that you are not responsible for your father's actions.'

'Oh yes, King John is delighted to have me pressing his cause here in London. But His Majesty has not seen fit to restore to me a single acre of the land that his predecessor confiscated.'

'Then it seems to me that your grievance, if you have one, is with King John, not with my husband.'

A very European shrug of the shoulders was his only direct response. 'Almost at the same time as I set sail for England, I heard that Captain Moreton was leaving South

America carrying a fortune in emeralds with him. The coincidence seemed an act of Providence, to say the least, and I decided there and then that the English Captain should repay the debt that my monarch refused to honour. You and your husband will go free, Lady Catherine, when I have been paid the ten thousand pounds that you owe me.'

'Even if my husband authorises the release of such an enormous sum, how can it benefit you? You cannot possibly expect your crime to go undetected. You will be arrested and accused of abduction within hours of setting us free!'

'If you think about what you have just said, Lady Catherine, you will understand that it is not a comforting proposition from your point of view. The punishment for abduction in this country is death by hanging. Obviously, if I thought such a punishment were likely, I would never set you free.'

He pulled out his watch and looked at it quickly. 'I regret that we cannot continue this interesting little chat any longer, but it is time for me to pay a visit to your husband. For your own sake, I suggest that you spend the next few hours praying hard for the success of my plans. As your own comments indicated, my failure is the equivalent of a signature on your death-warrant.'

He took her hand, ignoring her efforts to pull away, and bowed over it with an elegant flourish.

'I am your servant, Lady Catherine. I look forward to reporting back to you when I have spoken with your husband.'

CHAPTER
SEVENTEEN

THE MARQUES descended the stairs, reflecting with pleasure on the report Maria had given him. Captain Moreton had left Grosvenor Square at five o'clock and gone straight to the Park. In accordance with the Marques's instructions, two men had been waiting at the designated rendezvous. The Captain had been seized, force-fed laudanum and taken to the house in St Giles. Lord Moreton was now off on a wild-goose chase to Wellespont, and the Dowager had been diverted by a similar urgent plea for help. Everything had gone exactly according to plan.

The Marques reclaimed his hat and gloves from a silent servant and strolled out into the street to summon a passing hackney. It had been amazingly easy to involve Lady Catherine in his plans. It was extraordinary, he thought, that Captain Moreton had told his wife so little of his past. This reticence of the English was a characteristic which he found altogether delightful. Keeping themselves to themselves was a national preoccupation that extended from the highest reaches of the aristocracy down to the humblest crossing-sweeper or link-boy. The Marques considered it a characteristic to be treasured.

After only two months in London, he had decided that the English were incredibly unsophisticated. They had not had a real revolution for almost two hundred years, and their casual attitude towards personal safety reflected the peacefulness and security of their lives. It had made his task of capturing the Captain almost childishly easy. An English aristocrat—even one who had foiled the plot to rescue Napoleon Bonaparte—was certainly no match for a nobleman brought up in the scheming, treacherous environment of the Portuguese Court.

By this point in his ruminations, the Marques had reached the middle of Regent Street. He stopped a passing hackney and gave the driver a direction off Rosemary

Lane, close to St Giles-in-the-Fields.

The pleasant rural-sounding names belied the true nature of the district he wanted to visit, and the hackney-driver protested vigorously. 'That ain't no place for a gent! There's only magsmen and bludgers in there.'

'Nevertheless, it is where I wish to go. There will be a golden guinea for you, if you get me there promptly.'

The coachman said nothing more. He merely grunted, whisked his whip over the rump of his nag, and set off in the required direction.

The Marques leaned back against the tattered leather squabs and allowed a shiver of pleasurable anticipation to quiver down his spine. He would soon be confronting Captain the Honourable William Edward Moreton, and the confrontation was going to be unbelievably sweet.

When he first regained consciousness, William was aware only that he felt intolerably thirsty. If he had been able to speak, he would have called out for water, but the gag in his mouth made speech impossible. After a while he became aware of sounds, then, as the effects of the drug slowly cleared, he opened his eyes and stared into the darkness surrounding him. He was lying on the dusty wooden floor of an empty room. Not quite empty, he realised, as he glanced towards one corner and met the steady red-eyed gaze of a large rat.

His hands and feet were both bound, although the rope round his legs seemed to be tied quite loosely and there was little question that with sufficient effort he would eventually be able to free himself. But first he needed to find out what had happened to Catherine.

He rolled over on to his back, closing his eyes and forcing his tense muscles to relax. He had no doubt that he would shortly be receiving a visit from the Marques de Algarve Branca, and he wanted to be in the most steadfast frame of mind to face that visit.

He was furious with himself for having walked so blindly into the Marques's trap. If he had not been wild with anxiety on Catherine's part, he would never have left the house without letting somebody know where he was going.

The note, however, had been quite explicit: if he wanted to see Catherine alive again, no one was to know why he was leaving the house, or where he was going, and the note itself was to be returned to the maid as evidence that Captain Moreton agreed to co-operate.

Stopping only to check that Catherine had indeed left the house with the Marques earlier that morning, he had rushed out to the appointed rendezvous. Love, he thought —especially unrequited love—could make men behave very foolishly.

The sound of a key turning in the rusty door-lock made him instantly alert, but he turned his face towards the mildewed wall and closed his eyes, feigning unconsciousness. His unusually swift recovery from the effects of the drug was almost the only advantage he could count upon. That, and that fact that seven years of exile from England had left him stronger and more resilient than the Marques could possibly imagine.

He heard a few quick, light footsteps, then felt cold water splash over his face. Desperately he wished that he had not been gagged, so that he could have swallowed some of the drops and appeased his raging thirst. As it was, the water did little more than remove the last comfortable traces of drug-induced languor. He found that he was sore from toe to skull, and he had no difficulty whatsoever in producing a pitiful moan as he slowly rolled on to his side. A sharp kick in the ribs convinced him that it would be wise to speed up his pretence of regaining consciousness, and he quickly opened his eyes.

The Marques de Algarve Branca stood in the middle of the squalid room, a smoking oil-lamp hanging from a hook in the ceiling above his head. He was alone, but not un-protected. He held a pistol that was pointed squarely at William's heart.

'Good evening,' he said. 'What a pleasure it is to see you again, Captain Moreton. You look . . . less well . . . than you did on the last occasion we met.'

William closed his eyes, but another brutal kick to his ribs suggested that it might be wise to open them again swiftly.

'Yes,' the Marques said softly. 'I prefer that you should

look at me, Captain Moreton. We have a lot to discuss.' He raised his voice, turning his head in the direction of the door. 'Butcher! Come here!'

The nickname was not reassuring, but the appearance of the man who entered was worse. Butcher looked gruesome enough to strike fear into the sturdiest heart. He was exceptionally tall, heavily built, his face and hands encrusted with filth. He wore a blue flannel sailor's jacket that was shiny with the accumulation of years of grease, and tattered breeches tied at the waist with a coiled leather thong. The man's expression, however, was vacant rather than fierce, possibly because his mouth hung permanently open, revealing a row of blackened tooth-stubs and a gap where he should have had a tongue.

'Remove the gag, Butcher,' ordered the Marques.

The giant grunted, then lumbered over to William's side, fumbling at the knotted rag with fingers that were black and leathery with dirt. The stench from his body was so overpowering that William retched as the man bent over him.

Feeling distinctly queasy, William hauled himself into a sitting position, his back resting against the damp wall. He was vastly relieved when Butcher moved to a point some three feet away. As long as he remembered not to breathe too deeply, the smell was almost bearable.

'Where is my wife?' he asked, as soon as he could force his dry mouth to shape the words.

'I expect Lady Catherine is safely in bed,' the Marques said. His full lips curved into a slow, suggestive smile. 'She is a very beautiful woman.'

To the Marques's disappointment, Captain Moreton's expression did not alter by so much as a flicker. 'If you have harmed my wife,' he said, his voice low and totally controlled, 'you know that I shall kill you.'

'Your wife is unharmed—so far. I have no particular liking for injuring innocent people. You, on the other hand, destroyed my father without so much as a passing thought for what must happen to his family.'

'On the contrary, it was concern for his family that caused my brother and I to spare his life. Your father was a traitor to his country and an enemy to my country's interests. He had devised a plan to rescue Napoleon from St Helena that would have unleashed a new generation of war upon the weary peoples of Europe. In the circumstances, I think he was treated with considerable leniency.'

'Your definition of leniency is a strange one, Captain Moreton. My father was utterly disgraced. He lost all his hereditary positions at Court and all his lands save for the tiny estate of Algarve Branca. Three years ago, when my father died, I inherited the responsibilities and obligations of a marquisate with no income and no capital to support it. I estimate the losses you caused our family to be somewhere in excess of ten thousand pounds. You, Captain Moreton, are going to return to me the money that you stole from my father. I understand that you fortunately have assets which make the payment of such an enormous sum relatively easy.'

'I would as soon have dealings with the devil!'

'Insults have little effect upon me, Captain. Over the last seven years I have endured many that are far worse than any your simple English mind could dream of. Let us not waste time trading childish remarks, but rather let us proceed as quickly as possible to the practicalities of this situation.'

'By all means let us do that. You surely cannot hope that my absence will go unnoticed . . .'

'On the contrary, Captain Moreton. I have naturally taken steps to ensure that your absence will excite no comment whatsoever. If you are wise, you will not look for rescue. False hopes of that kind will merely delay the inevitable conclusion of our business. Captain Moreton, I hope you will not force me into a situation where I am compelled to allow Butcher to demonstrate the unique range of his talents.'

William watched Butcher scratch his belly. 'What is your price for setting my wife free?' he asked tersely.

'As I have told you, Captain Moreton, my price is merely repayment of the ten thousand pounds that you owe me. I have in my breast pocket a letter which instructs your man of affairs to release to me gold and jewels of the appropriate value. You have only to sign it and address it, and the first stage of our business will be concluded.'

'Even if I agreed to sign it, my bankers would never agree to release such a huge sum of money without a personal visit from me. Furthermore, I do not have gold and jewels of sufficient value to meet your ransom demand.'

The Marques stroked his left hand slowly along the ivory mount of his pistol. 'I do hope you are wrong, Captain Moreton, because unless my very reasonable request for repayment is met, I am afraid something unpleasant is quite likely to happen to Lady Catherine. And I feel sure that we would both of us prefer her to come through this little—er —*contretemps* completely unharmed.'

William spoke through clenched teeth. 'My wife has nothing to do with this. Your quarrel, if you have one, is only with me.'

'That is true. But it seems that she, like my mother and my sister, may well become the innocent victim of a situation entirely beyond her control. The women in my family had nothing to do with my father's political views, but my mother is now the widow of a disgraced man and my sister languishes as a spinster, for want of a dowry. I do hope, Captain Moreton, that for Lady Catherine's sake you are going to find some way to phrase the final paragraph of this letter so that the necessary funds are forthcoming.'

'I will sign nothing until I have seen Catherine.'

'I give you my word that Lady Catherine is as yet totally unharmed.'

William looked up mockingly. 'And your word, Senhor Marques, is supposed to set all my fears at rest?'

With a sudden deadly flare of rage, the Marques turned to Butcher. 'Beat him!' he ordered. 'But mind his hands!'

William had no more than a couple of seconds in which to still his breathing and blank out his mind, a trick for enduring pain that he had learned from his Indian guides in South America. Seven years ago, his sense of honour would have forced him to endure as many strokes of the lash as Butcher could inflict. Survival skills learned in the rain-forest had taught him greater wisdom. If he were going to escape, he would need to be in the best possible physical condition. He needed to stop the beating as quickly as he convincingly could. By the fourth whistling stroke of the whip, he had managed to produce the appearance of unconsciousness.

Butcher, gurgling with contentment, would have continued with the lashing, but the Marques stopped him, ordering him to procure some water.

'Imbecile! These English aristocrats are all weaklings and I have no use for a dead body, at least not yet. I need him to sign these papers. Throw some water on his face and see if it revives him.'

Butcher's grunt gave no clue to whether he had understood the reason for the Marques's annoyance, but he obediently shuffled out of the room in search of the requisite water; this time, when it was thrown in his face, William managed to swallow a couple of mouthfuls. It tasted cool and surprisingly fresh, and he tried hard not to think where it had come from. He could survive days without food, if need be, but he would need some water if his brain were to continue functioning efficiently.

He opened his eyes to find the Marques still watching him closely. 'Having considered the matter, Captain Moreton, do you think that you now might like to sign the letter to your bankers?'

William moved his shoulders and allowed himself to wince very visibly at the pain. It was imperative that the Marques should not think he was surrendering too easily. 'I cannot write with my hands tied behind my back,' he said, keeping his voice surly.

'True. Butcher, untie his hands. But remember, my dear Captain, that my pistol has a hair-trigger and it is pointed right at your heart. Please move very slowly, so that I am not made nervous. We shall both of us regret it if my finger trembles.'

'Give me the letter,' William said, when his hands were free. 'I must read it before I sign it.'

'Certainly. But remember, if you should do anything so foolish as to tear it up, it will avail you nothing, and it will be Lady Catherine who suffers while a new one is prepared.'

William read through the letter. 'How did you know who my bankers are?'

'For a man as wealthy as yourself, Captain, such information is not hard to come by. You will see that I have taken great pains to express my request in such a way that the bankers are not likely to refuse it.'

'How do I know that you will release my wife when I have signed this letter?'

'I shall not release her when it is signed, Captain Moreton—you cannot be so naïve as to imagine that I would! I shall bring her here to join you some time late tomorrow night. You will both be released when the money is safely in my hands. I have a ship waiting for me at Tilbury, and shall be leaving England as soon as you have paid your debt to me. I have arranged to send word that you may be set free once I am on board. You have my word upon it.'

'My life, and that of my wife, staked against your word,' William said bitterly. 'You will forgive me if I say that it does not seem a very equal bargain.'

'I will ignore that slur upon my honour, Captain Moreton. Pen, ink and a small table have been provided for your convenience.' The Marques gestured to a shadowy corner of the room. Other than the broken remnants of a cast-iron stove, the table constituted the only piece of furniture in the room.

Even though the Marques clearly had a low opinion of his intelligence, William realised that it was necessary to voice some objection if his compliance were not to seem suspiciously easy. 'Why should I trust your word that you will release me? You must know that I will notify the authorities as soon as I am free.'

'You will not be released in time to prevent my departure from England, and once I am in Portugal, your Government has no authority to apprehend me.' The Marquis glanced again at his pistol, and then across the room at the grinning Butcher. 'Besides, Captain Moreton, I would suggest that you have little option other than to hope my word can be trusted. Ten thousand pounds is an insignificant sum to stake against the chance of freedom.'

William, who did not consider acting one of his strong

suits, did his best to portray a man struggling to reach a life-and-death decision.

'My emeralds are not stored in the bank,' he said finally. 'They are housed in a special location known only to me and to my man of affairs. I shall have to change the wording of this letter slightly, otherwise the bankers will not be given access to those emeralds. And without the emeralds, I have not nearly enough money to pay you the ransom you demand.'

'You may write whatever instructions you consider necessary, Captain Moreton. Only remember that if the money is not forthcoming, you will not be released and Lady Catherine . . . well, I will leave it to your imagination to visualise what will happen to Lady Catherine.'

William added a final paragraph to the letter, and signed his name with evident hesitation. He sprinkled fine sand over the wet ink and injected just the faintest quiver of fear into his voice. 'Bankers do not move quickly, Senhor Marques. It will be two days before you have your money. What is to happen to me while I am waiting for my bankers to act?'

'You will remain here as my honoured guest,' the Marques said. 'Butcher and one of his very good friends will be posted outside the door, night and day, to see that nobody comes into the room to disturb you. I'm afraid that there are no cooking facilities in this lodging-house, so you may become a little hungry.'

'But I must have food! It is hours since I last ate!'

'Captain Moreton, please disabuse yourself of the notion that I am a fool. I *hope* for both our sakes that the instructions contained in this letter will produce the funds I require, but I am not certain of it. I do not intend to feed you until the money you owe me has been paid in full. If, at the end of two days, your bankers have not produced the appropriate sums of money, I shall return so that you may pen a new, more forceful, request for action. After two days without food, I imagine your mood will be suitably co-operative.'

'But I'm already hungry and thirsty . . .'

'Console yourself with the thought that once the money is

in my hands, you may return to Moreton House and enjoy a meal fit for a king. I have it on the best authority that your cook works miracles in the kitchen. If you ask me nicely, I may relent so far as to provide you with some water. But you will have to ask me *very* politely.'

William gritted his teeth, pretending a humiliation he did not feel. 'Please may I have some water,' he said flatly.

'You do not sound very humble, Captain Moreton. If you had heard my father begging for mercy from the British officers, you would understand what it means to beg. Try a little harder to be abject if you truly wish for water.'

As a younger man, William would not have been able to humble himself sufficiently to beg for anything. Fortunately, three years of back-breaking expeditions through the mountains and jungles of South America had radically altered his perspective. Survival was a great deal more important than anything else at this moment. Even so, it cost him a considerable effort to subdue his pride sufficiently to plead with the Marques. He could not look at his adversary when he spoke.

'I beg of you, please give me water.'

The Marques's voice was laced with contempt. 'You are much less brave in your dealings than you were seven years ago in Lisbon, Captain Moreton. It seems that without the might of the British navy behind you, your backbone lacks steel.'

William did not reply, and the Marques walked towards the door. 'Bring him a cup of water,' he said to Butcher. 'And when he has finished it, tie his hands behind his back again. I regret, Captain Moreton, that I shall not be able to see you tomorrow. I am holding a reception at my house, and Lady Catherine is to be my—er—partner. What with the visit I must make to your man of affairs and all the arrangements for my little party, you can see that my social calendar will be full.'

William turned his gaze to the small barred window.

'Go to hell,' he said.

CHAPTER
EIGHTEEN

CATHERINE DID not see the Marques again until the morning, and her night of captivity seemed painfully long.

It had taken her less than five minutes to determine that escape from her room was impossible. The door was locked and bolted from the outside and the window shutters were riveted in place by steel bars. She had even examined the elaborate carvings surmounting the fireplace. Unlike the heroines in Mrs Radcliffe's novels, Catherine quickly discovered that the sprays of wooden roses were exactly what they seemed to be. Unfortunately, they were decoration, and not cunningly concealed spring locks leading to a hidden escape tunnel.

She had just eaten a sparse breakfast of bread and coffee when the Marques came into the room. He waved the maid away without even glancing in her direction.

'Good morning, Lady Catherine. I am happy to see that you are looking so well rested. I think you will enjoy the activities I have planned for you today.'

She got up and walked as far away from him as she could. 'How is my husband?' she asked coldly.

'He is alive, Lady Catherine, although I would not say that he is in the very best of health. It is already several hours since he has eaten, you see, and the laudanum we administered does not seem to agree with his delicate English constitution.'

She would have liked to appear unmoved, but she made a tiny involuntary gesture with her hands, and he glanced with satisfaction at her whitened cheeks.

'Take courage, Lady Catherine,' he said mockingly. 'Captain Moreton was wise enough to agree to my demands. A letter ordering the transfer of ten thousand pounds to my estate is already in the hands of his bankers. If you are as co-operative as your husband, I may even permit you to see him tonight.'

She turned away, so that he could not see her face. 'Tell me what you want me to do, Senhor Marques, and I will do it.'

'My request is remarkably simple. I am giving a small reception this evening and I wish you to attend.'

'You wish me to attend a *party*?' she asked with genuine astonishment. 'How can you suggest such a thing when my husband and I are both your prisoners? Quite apart from any other consideration, you must know that I shall tell everyone what you have done.'

'I cannot imagine that you would do anything so stupid, my dear. The Captain is under guard. If I do not report that all is well at certain specified intervals, the guard has instructions to kill his prisoner. So you see, Lady Catherine, if you inform anybody of what I have done, you will cause me to be arrested, but you will also condemn your husband to certain death.'

She bit her lip, forcing back the rising threat of hysteria. 'Senhor Marques, if I attend your party tonight without my husband as escort, we shall give rise to endless gossip. And even if I remain totally silent about the true situation, there is surely a grave risk to the success of your plans. Why would you run such a risk over such a trivial issue?'

'Because you will be socially ruined, Lady Catherine, and I am prepared to risk quite a lot to see the Moreton family suitably humbled. You will find yourself exiled from London society, just as your husband caused my family to be exiled from the Portuguese Court. You will suffer as I and my sister suffered.'

Catherine could feel her self-control diminishing by the minute. 'I have nothing suitable to wear,' she said, seizing on the first, feeble excuse that sprang to her mind. 'Whatever sort of scandal you hope to create, you cannot expect me to attend your reception clad in a crumpled travelling-suit.'

He laughed softly. 'Ah, my dear Lady Catherine, I do not intend you to wear anything so dreary. You will write a note to your maid informing her that you and the Captain are both well and enjoying yourselves as my honoured guests. You will order her to pack a gown for you, and one of my servants will bring it here. Most important of all, you will instruct your maid to include your delightful emerald necklace in the portmanteau. It seemed to create so much interested attention when you wore it at Mr Canning's reception. I wonder what conclusions my guests will draw when they see you here in my house, unescorted, and wearing that notorious piece of jewellery?'

'They will not conclude that I am your mistress, if that is what you hope, Senhor Marques. Your guests, even the least perceptive of them, will realise that I am more fastidious.'

A dull flush suffused his olive complexion. 'It is somewhat unwise to insult me,' he said with an ugly little laugh. 'If you value Captain Moreton's health, you should be more careful how you behave towards me. Please remember, Lady Catherine, that I would not like anyone at my reception this evening to think that we are not friends.'

By some miraculous exertion of will, she brought herself under control and the gaze she turned upon him was coolly dispassionate. 'Bring me paper and pens,' she said. 'I shall write to my maid.'

'It is so encouraging to see you co-operating, Lady Catherine. Please be seated while I send Maria for the necessary implements. You know, I cannot help thinking that tonight we are going to enjoy a truly spectacular party.'

A stubborn streak of defiance—a refusal to show humility in the face of the Marques's threats—caused Catherine to order her maid to pack the most splendid of all her new gowns: a striking, low-cut, emerald-green crepe, draped over a slip of pearl-encrusted satin and decorated at the neck with white Mechlin lace. Helped by the impassive Maria, she dressed for the Marques's reception in total silence, refusing to acknowledge the shaking of her limbs and the permanent sensation of nausea lodged deep in her stomach. She noted with almost abstract interest how the emerald necklace gleamed against her skin with a vulgar, barbaric splendour, and she knew that by the time this evening was over, she would have no shred of reputation left.

She heard the squeak of the key as the Marques unlocked her door, and she walked to the centre of the room, raising her head in proud defiance as he entered. She had the satisfaction of seeing a moment of utter astonishment in his eyes, before his expression returned to its usual appearance of false deference.

He recovered quickly and raised her hand to his lips. 'What a pity that the good Captain is not here to see your beauty, Lady Catherine! I am sure he would be impressed.'

She pulled her hand away and wiped it ostentatiously against her gown, then walked purposefully towards the door.

'Shall we go, Senhor Marques? I believe it is time.'

From the moment she arrived downstairs, Catherine felt as if she moved through the scenes of a powerful nightmare. She had hoped against hope that her presence at the reception might pass without too much unfavourable comment. Within seconds of entering the drawing-room, however, she knew that all such hopes were utterly vain. Wherever she stood, the space around her immediately emptied of women and the men openly ogled her.

Bernardino Rivadavia from Argentina was the first person to speak to her. His smile was wary and a little shocked as he approached her.

'It is a pleasure to see you again, Lady Catherine, but where is the good Captain, your husband?'

The Marques appeared at her elbow. 'Yes, do tell us, my dearest Lady Catherine. Where is the so brave and valorous Captain?'

A trace of angry colour slashed across her cheekbones. 'He has been unavoidably called away,' she said. 'But I hope he will be back with me shortly.'

She tried to move on, but the Marques detained her. 'In the meantime, until Captain Moreton once again condescends to grace London with his presence, we bachelors must consider ourselves blessed by his absence. I'm sure you agree with me, Señor Rivadavia?'

The Argentinian inclined his head. 'How could I not?'

The Marques allowed his hand to rest suggestively on

Catherine's arm. 'I hope I may have the pleasure of partnering you in the first waltz?'

'Thank you, Senhor Marques, but I have no wish to dance . . .'

'Oh no, my dear Lady Catherine, I can't allow you to be so cruel as to deny my request.' He laughed lightly. 'Think of the terrible consequences! I positively *insist* that you dance with me. And how lucky we are! I hear the fiddlers striking up the opening chords at this very moment.'

Accompanied by a buzz of incredulous comment, the Marques de Algarve Branca led his partner out on to the floor. In a gesture that did not escape the notice of the eagle-eyed dowagers, he lifted one of her pale golden curls, untangling it from the place where it seemed to have caught on her emerald necklace. His fingers trailed slowly over her shoulders as he re-positioned it, and a collective quiver of delighted outrage trembled through the assembled guests.

Long before supper was served at midnight, Lady Catherine Moreton had scandalised society by dancing three more times with the Marques, all the while smiling brightly. Only the most acute of observers—a rather small group of people at this reception—might have observed the tight lines of strain about her mouth and the haunted look of misery in her supposedly brazen green eyes.

For his part, the Marques scarcely left her side except to fulfil his minimum obligations as host, and even the most liberal-minded people noticed that his hands had a distinctly Continental tendency to stray in the direction of Lady Catherine's narrow waist and other, even more indelicate portions of her anatomy.

Most of the guests were content to purse their lips and lay all the blame for such scandalous behaviour squarely on Catherine's shoulders. The Princess de Lieven, the only patroness of Almack's who happened to be present, made a mental note to rescind her offer of vouchers for the next assembly, and the Duchess of Barton pointed out to every-body how wise she had been not to invite Catherine to her forthcoming ridotto. Her friends nodded sagely and congratulated her upon her forethought.

Shortly before midnight, a servant was observed passing a note to the Marques, who was speaking to the Duchess of Barton at the time. The Marques hurriedly excused himself and crossed the room to Catherine's side.

To everybody's deep regret, his remarks were inaudible, but whatever he said produced an immediate and dramatic effect. Lady Catherine turned devastatingly white before getting up from her chair and following the Marques from the room.

The delicious possibility that Captain Moreton had arrived unexpectedly and challenged the Marques to a duel crossed one or two minds, but after several minutes of eager anticipation during which no untoward sound penetrated from the vestibule, all hope of such excitement was abandoned and the Marques's guests resigned themselves to the more mundane tasks of eating lobster patties and enjoying slices of cake cut from a spun-sugar confection cunningly designed to look like the Palace of Algarve Branca.

As soon as they were outside the dining-room, Catherine's precipitous flight halted. 'What has happened? What do you mean by saying that my husband's life is dangerously close to being forfeit? I have behaved exactly as you ordered me to—I have had no chance to do otherwise.'

The Marques did not answer, but grasped her by the wrist and dragged her into a small room at the end of the hall. He slammed the door shut, but he pushed it so hard that it sprang open again behind them. He paid the open door no attention as he spun around to face Catherine, his eyes black with fury.

'This is what I mean,' he hissed, thrusting a piece of paper almost under her nose. 'Your fool of a husband has attempted to trick me! His man of affairs released emeralds to me this afternoon that supposedly had a value of almost ten thousand pounds. Being a cautious man, I sent for an expert to value them, and *this* is his report!'

With some difficulty, Catherine managed to read the note the Marquis was waving in front of her. 'The two hundred and fifty-five emeralds your jeweller examined are all paste,' she said slowly.

'Yes! Worthless paste! Your husband may think that he has been very clever, Lady Catherine, but in fact he has only succeeded in making me angry. A foolish move on his part. I think that when this party is over, I shall take you on a visit to your husband. Perhaps your presence will convince him that it is not wise to play games with the Marques de Algarve Branca!'

'I have no knowledge of my husband's business affairs, Senhor Marques. My presence can have no impact upon his decisions.'

'It is not your knowledge that I require, my dear, it is your person. Let us see how defiant Captain Moreton feels when I allow Butcher to take you in his arms.'

'Butcher?'

'One of my hirelings. He is not a pretty fellow, and his manners are regrettably brutish.'

At some instinctive, subconscious level, Catherine realised that it would be disastrous if she allowed the Marques to take her to William's prison tonight. Although she had known her husband only for a short time, in some ways she already knew him well. She suspected that his tolerance for pain was quite high. She also suspected that his tolerance for watching others suffer pain was quite low. He would agree to almost anything the Marques demanded rather than watch her suffer at Butcher's hands. With some hazy idea of throwing herself on the mercy of one of the guests, she wrenched herself out of the Marques's grasp and ran for the door.

He caught her easily, pulling her into his arms and putting a hand across her mouth to silence her screams. For a man of only average height and build, his grip was powerful, and after a brief struggle, Catherine accepted that she had no hope of freeing herself.

The Marques did not notice that she had gone limp in his arms. His face was contorted by rage as he reached up to pull the bejewelled combs from her hair. Released from confinement, her curls tumbled haphazardly around her shoulders and the angry tension in the Marques's body underwent a subtle change. With a shudder of profound revulsion, Catherine recognised that the desire which had always been absent from his gaze was suddenly present i▪ overwhelming measure.

'Until tonight, I had not thought you worth ravishing,' h▪ said with ugly softness. 'Now I have changed my mind. Yo▪ are too fair for my taste, but your thin body is strangel▪ appealing, and it is a shame to think that Butcher is about t▪ spoil all this beauty before I have had a chance to enjoy it.'

His hand crept up from her waist and closed with gros▪ insult upon the curve of her breast. 'Oh yes,' he murmured 'I am sure I can afford to take ten minutes longer away fror▪ my guests.'

She managed to brush his hand away, but nausea close▪ her throat so tightly that she could not speak. She stared a▪ his thin, dry lips as they approached her face ever mor▪ closely, then, just before his mouth fastened over hers, a▪ returned to her lungs and she screamed with all the forc▪ she could muster.

He slapped his hand across her mouth, cutting off h▪ cry. 'Imbecile!' he hissed, his body trembling with the forc▪ of his rage. 'If you scream like that even once more, ▪ promise that you will never again see your husban▪ alive.'

There was a slight noise from the doorway, and th▪ Marques whirled round, still holding Catherine clasped ▪ his arms. He gave a hoarse, disbelieving cry.

'You!'

Captain Moreton inclined his head in ironic acknowled▪ ment. 'Indeed it is I, Senhor Marques. I would have bee▪ here sooner, had I known that you were entertaining s▪ many of my oldest and dearest friends.'

'You cannot have escaped,' the Marques croaked. '▪ isn't possible!'

'Not only possible, but quite easy. And if you immed▪ ately remove your hands from my wife's person, it is *ju*▪ conceivable that I may decide not to kill you.'

The Marques looked at the pistol pointed at his bell▪ then glanced at the implacable set of the Captain's feature▪ Slowly, reluctantly, he released his grip on Catherine▪ arms and she ran, stumbling a little, to stand beside h▪ husband.

William's gaze remained fixed on his quarry. 'Are you all right?' he asked, without looking at her.

'Yes! Yes, now that I know you are safe!' She took another step closer to her husband and gasped with horror when she saw the criss-cross of blood seeping through the tattered shreds of William's coat, and the soot that enveloped him.

'Your back!' she said. 'My God, what happened to you?'

'I shall explain later,' he said curtly. 'Get behind me, and move carefully. This pistol has a hair-trigger.'

She obeyed him without question and he spoke again to the Marques. 'You told me last night that a ship was waiting for you at Tilbury,' he said, his voice soft with menace. 'I give you until tomorrow evening to be on board. If you are still in England after that time, be warned that I shall lay this entire story before the authorities. I have seen a Portuguese gaol, and I am happy to report that ours are more comfortable. But not by very much, Senhor Marques.'

The Marques did not look at either of them. 'I shall be on the ship,' he hissed. 'And may the devil take both of you!'

'He is more likely, I think, to come looking for you. Goodbye, Senhor Marques.'

The happenings of the next few minutes provided conversation at the dinner tables and ballrooms of London's highest circles for weeks to come. The guests, alerted by the sounds of a scuffle in the hall and a series of muffled screams from the end of the corridor, surged out of the reception rooms to see what was going on, and those fortunate enough to be squeezed into the middle of the Marques de Algarve Branca's hall were able to dine out on their experiences for the rest of the Season.

Before their astonished eyes, the door to a small room at the far end of the hall was thrown open and the Marques de Algarve Branca appeared in the entrance. Lady Catherine Moreton swept past him, her infamous emerald necklace held in her hand.

'Here,' she said carelessly, allowing the jewels to drop i
a pile at the Marques's feet. 'Buy your sister a husband wit
my blessing.'

A tall, black-visaged man appeared at her side an
stepped indifferently over the glittering little heap of emei
alds. His appearance, Sir Archibald Nolan later asserted
could best be described as a cross between a chimney-swee
and an emissary of Satan. After pausing for a moment t
examine the assembled throng, the spectre swept uncor
cernedly into the hall. Lady Catherine Moreton, her ha
hanging almost to her waist, attached herself to one of h
arms. In his other hand, he carried a pistol.

The spectre bowed politely to the Duchess of Bartor
'Good evening, ma'am, I am delighted to see you lookin
so well. If you would be kind enough to move to one side s
that I do not touch your gown . . . Lady Catherine and
have been involved in a slight accident.'

The Duchess, who had never in her entire life been at
loss for words, stepped back in total silence, too ove
whelmed to speak.

'Good God! I do believe it is Captain Moreton!' e:
claimed the Spanish Ambassador, who happened to notic
that, beneath the layers of soot, the spectre was wearing
black velvet eye-patch.

While the rest of the guests assimilated this astonishir
piece of information, the Princess de Lieven moved pu
posefully forward. Before she could speak, the spect:
swept her another of his supremely elegant bows. Just as
his coat hadn't been hanging in shreds from his shoulder
as Lady Auden later remarked to her husband.

'I trust you will forgive us if we do not stop and convers
Princess. Lady Catherine and I are somewhat late for
pressing engagement.'

The Princess was not without a sense of humour. 'With
quantity of hot soapy water, I do hope? Pray do not let n
detain you, Captain Moreton. I can see that your *toile*
needs some attention if it is to meet the high standards
elegance that you have previously set for us all.'

'I am indebted to you for the compliment,' the Capta
said suavely, and the crowd fell back in wordless wond

as he and his bride continued their parade down the Marques's long hall.

From time to time, the Captain nodded politely to old acquaintances. Lady Catherine did not go so far as that, but she gave no sign of embarrassment despite the scandalous state of her hair and the fact that the lace of her gown was ripped in three different places. She simply stared straight ahead, her chin held high in the air.

'Pray take care, my dear,' the Captain was heard to say to his wife. 'There are a couple of footmen whom I was forced to dispose of on my way in. I dare say they are still lying on the floor.'

Lady Catherine showed her first sign of discomposure. 'Are they dead?' she was heard to murmur.

The Captain rubbed his knuckles reminiscently. 'No, just temporarily unconscious.'

Lady Catherine nodded, lifting her skirts slightly as she stepped over the recumbent bodies of the Marques's two most senior footmen.

The Captain and his bride finally reached the front door. They halted in the vestibule, and the Marques's butler, peering nervously from behind a marble pillar, was summoned by a click of the Captain's fingers.

'My carriage, if you please. We shall wait for it outside.'

The butler, who had feared that he might meet the same fate as his prostrate footmen, was intensely relieved to be assigned so mundane a task and one, moreover, that was so easy to accomplish. Sweating profusely, he bent his head almost to his knees in his eagerness to assure the Captain that the carriage would be at the entrance within minutes, in fact within seconds. He then flung open the front door and waited in an agony of hopeful suspense for the insane guests to leave before they did any further damage.

Captain Moreton turned in the doorway and faced the open-mouthed crowd. He raised his dust-streaked hand in a polite, almost regal, gesture of farewell, and a faint smile curved his lips upward, cracking the sooty layer of grease covering his face.

'I do hope you will enjoy the remainder of the party,' he said. 'It is your host's final night in London, as I am sure he will soon be coming to tell you. Good night to you all.'

He turned to Lady Catherine. 'Are you ready to leave, my dear?'

'Quite ready, thank you, Captain Moreton.'

They disappeared out of the lighted vestibule and into the darkness of the night, a sudden wave of excited comment bursting against their ears just before the butler closed the front door.

When the carriage arrived, the coachman jumped down to help his master and mistress inside. William then slumped against the seat, pain clearly visible beneath his coal-smeared features.

He carefully unloaded the pistol before tossing it on the seat beside him. 'I apologise, Catherine, for what you have endured at the Marques's hands,' he said flatly. 'I should have taken better care of you.'

'What *I* have suffered! William, for God's sake, I have suffered nothing. But you! Tell me what happened. Your back . . . Dear heaven, I have never seen anything like it! Do you have other injuries?'

He closed his eyes. 'Nothing of any significance,' he said wearily. 'My valet will take care of cleaning me up once we are home. If there are scars, they will scarcely be noticeable among the many that already grace my body.'

She did not quite understand the note of suppressed bitterness she sensed in his words, but she was all too well aware that he was exhausted to the point where speech was difficult, and she contented herself with murmuring something vaguely reassuring, and holding his hand clasped between her own. In view of the coldness of their last meeting, she considered the fact that he did not reject this small gesture of affection as grounds for celebration. She wondered what he would say when he found out that his abduction had been made possible by her illicit outing with the Marques de Algarve Branca. Despite her overwhelming joy at having him safe again, guilt over her own part in the episode prevented her joy from being complete.

The journey home lasted no more than a few minutes, and they were greeted upon their arrival at Moreton House by a full phalanx of agitated retainers, who crowded into every available space in the entrance hall, uttering cries of alarm as they took in the ghastly appearance of their master and the whiteness of their mistress's cheeks.

Catherine took one look at the milling servants and realised that their affection for the Captain had, in this instance, totally destroyed their usual impeccable discipline. She also realised that he was likely to collapse unless he were soon permitted to rest. She clapped her hands sharply, and the servants fell abruptly silent.

'Benson, Captain Moreton requires your services at once. I trust that there is adequate hot water available, since both the Captain and I require baths as soon as possible. Mary, I should like your assistance in my room. The Captain will have some bread and butter and a bowl of chicken broth as soon as it can be prepared. Thank you all for your concern, but it is late, and unless you have specific duties to perform, you should return to your beds.'

The firm, crisp commands had the desired effect. The crowd of servants dispersed purposefully in several directions, and Benson, after an approving nod in Catherine's direction, conducted his swaying master up the stairs.

Mary did not seem able to stop chattering as Catherine subsided on the bed and watched the scullery-maids pour hot water into her bathtub.

'Thank God you are home safe, my lady! Fair died of shock, we did, when the Captain came home, pounding on the door and demanding to know if that Portuguese Marques had taken you. Grabbed his pistol and was off like a madman when he heard we hadn't seen you since yesterday morning . . . Didn't stop for so much as a sip of wine or a change of jacket. And look what happened to your lovely new gown! It's a wonder that you escaped from that wicked man alive. It's a fine carry-on, I must say.'

Lack of breath finally caused her flow of recrimination to halt, and Catherine promptly burst into tears. Mary dismissed the goggle-eyed scullery-maid with an imperious nod of the head and gathered her mistress into her arms, stroking her back with swift, soothing strokes, and gently undressing her.

'There, there. I only spoke so sharp because we've all

been worried sick. It has been a terrible time for you, my lady, and for us servants, too. But that is all over now and the dear Captain is back safe and sound. You have nothing to look forward to now but happiness.'

'I thought he would die,' Catherine whispered. 'And I don't think I could have borne to lose him, Mary.'

'What nonsense is this? There is no reason for all these tears. You aren't going to lose the Captain—he's the sort what lives to be a hundred, you take my word for it, my lady. Tough as old boots, he is.'

Aware that this might not be considered a compliment by a lady of refinement, she added hastily. 'Of course, he's a real gentleman, and wonderfully good looking, too. Now, get into the bath and I will send for some nice hot tea.'

When her mistress was bathed and dressed in a warm nightgown and light woollen robe, Mary carefully brushed the tangles out of her hair, braiding it into two long plaits. Catherine obediently climbed into bed, but as soon as Mary had left the room, she rose and walked to the door that connected her room with William's.

She hesitated only for a moment before tapping gently on the light oak panels. It was not the done thing for a wife to request admission to her husband's bedroom, but in the circumstances she felt sure that her gesture would not be misinterpreted. The door was opened almost at once by Benson.

'How is he?' she asked, her gaze flying to the bed. William lay face down on the pillows, naked from the waist up, with crepe bandages already covering most of his upper body.

'He is in considerable pain, my lady,' the valet said softly.

As if to refute his servant's words, William swung his legs from the bed, standing up and putting his dressing-gown on. If either Benson or Catherine observed that he turned whiter than a sheet when he moved, neither of them was tactless enough to comment upon it.

'Thank you for all your help, Benson,' he said, as he tied the sash of his robe. 'Between the hot soup and your expert ministrations, I feel like a new man.'

'I'm pleased to hear it, sir.'

'Benson, has any word come from Wellespont about Lady Moreton?' Catherine asked. 'Do you know if she lost the baby she was expecting?'

'One of the grooms arrived from Wellespont only a couple of hours ago, my lady. It seems that the message Lord Moreton received was a false alarm. He and the Dowager both hurried down to Wellespont, thinking to find Lady Moreton on the verge of death. Instead, she was in the pink of condition, and her young sons are both equally well.'

'The Marques certainly spread his scheming net wide,' William said. 'It must have taken him weeks to construct such an elaborate plot. Thank you, Benson. You may leave us now.'

The valet looked at him searchingly. 'Yes, sir,' he said finally.

He extinguished the lamps, leaving only the glow of candles placed on the mantelpiece. He then gathered up a bowl of bloodied water and several macabre-looking linen towels before going quietly from the room.

His departure was followed by a long silence.

'Have you eaten?' Catherine asked, and when William nodded she said shyly, 'You look a great deal better now that you are clean.'

'So do you.'

She gave a tiny smile. 'You smell somewhat better, too.'

There was a touch of answering humour in his gaze. 'You do not think that I shall set a new fashion? I had wondered if the odour of London roof-tops might not become all the rage.'

'Roof-tops?'

'I escaped over the roof-tops,' he replied matter-of-factly. 'And I discovered during the process that chimneys give off an incredible quantity of foul-smelling soot along with those clouds of grey smoke.'

'How in the world did you manage to escape? The Marques told me that you were constantly under guard.'

William smiled grimly. 'It is true that there was always somebody posted outside my door, but the Marques made several fatal errors. He imprisoned me in a thieves' kitchen in the heart of the St Giles Rookery. He thought, quite rightly, that in such a place there was almost no chance of any search-party discovering me. You could comb through those courts and alleyways for a lifetime and never discover anything except filth and squalor, sickness and misery. But what the Marques did not consider is that slum buildings are never maintained in any sort of decent repair. There were thick iron bars on the window, but the bricks holding them in place were crumbled half away, and the window was covered not with glass but with oiled paper. As soon as I saw the type of building in which I had been imprisoned, I knew that escape would be relatively easy.'

'Easy! It does not sound so to me! Were you—Were you tied up?'

'Yes, but the rope round my legs was never properly secured, and the Marques was very careless about details. He had not bothered to clear out the room. There was an old cast-iron stove in one corner, and it required nothing more than perseverance to find a rough edge on which to saw through the rope binding my wrists. Once my hands were free, the only remaining problem was to dismantle the bars on the windows so silently as not to rouse the guard. I waited until I heard him snoring, then set to work fast. My prison was in the attic of an old building and it was obvious that I could not climb down, since the place was filled to the rafters with villains of every description. So, like a bird, I simply took off upwards. The houses in that section of town are built so close together that even a child could step from one roof to the next.' His voice became dry. 'Indeed, I shared my roof-top path with several agile young urchins who were kind enough to inform me that the bleedin' crushers were out in force that evening.'

'Crushers?'

'It is, I believe, thieves' cant for a guardian of the law.' He walked over to a low table, where a decanter reposed in the centre of a silver tray. 'Do you care for some brandy?' he asked, and poured a small measure into a glass, and held it out towards her.

She frowned. 'Ladies are not normally permitted to drink spirits,' she said.

'In the circumstances, I am sure you could consider it as strictly for medicinal purposes.'

'Then I think perhaps I should enjoy a little.'

He handed her the glass, and her fingers trembled as she took it.

'Are you cold?' he asked. 'The fire is laid. We could light it if you wish.'

'No,' she said, trying to smile and not succeeding very well. She took a sip of the brandy, and despite the vile taste, discovered that it imparted a pleasantly warm glow to her middle.

'I think I am probably shivering from nervous apprehension rather than from cold. William, I know it is selfish of me to insist upon making my confession when you are obviously in pain and close to exhaustion, but for my own peace of mind I must tell you that it is my fault the Marques was able to kidnap you so easily.'

'You cannot be serious!' he exclaimed after a moment of silence. 'I have caused you to be subjected to hours of abuse at the hands of that vile monster, and you try to tell me that *you* are to blame!'

'But I *was* to blame, William! At Mr Canning's ball, I was angry with you about Lady Annabelle's necklace, and then I was even more angry when you told me not to speak to the Marques again. So when he invited me to drive with him to Kew, I deliberately disobeyed you and accepted his invitation.'

'Leaving aside the question of Lady Annabelle's necklace, which, with your permission, we will discuss later, it is still I who should seek your forgiveness. I had no right to demand obedience from you without explaining why the Marques was to be feared, and by failing to warn you of what happened in Lisbon seven years ago, I exposed you to needless danger. Tell me the truth, Catherine. Did he harm you in any way?'

'Not at all,' she said, glossing over the scratches along her ribcage and the few terrifying minutes when she had known that the Marques intended to rape her. 'I think I am far too thin and pale to suit his tastes.'

'Then he is even more of a fool than I imagined,' William

said shortly. 'Are you sure that he did not hurt you? He was holding you very tightly when I arrived.'

'Only to prevent me from screaming. Truly he did not threaten me personally, except by saying that I should never see you alive again unless I did exactly as he commanded.'

There was a considerable pause before William spoke. 'And would it have worried you so very much if I had not returned, Catherine? You would, after all, have been an extremely wealthy widow.'

For the space of a few seconds there was absolute silence in the room but for the rhythmic ticking of the clock, then all the tensions of the past two days exploded inside Catherine at once. Without stopping to think, she raised her arm and hurled her brandy glass at William, her entire body shaking with the force of her fury.

'If you were not a wounded man,' she spat out, 'I would not be responsible for my answer to that question.'

He caught the glass with one hand and set it down on the table next to his own. 'I had never thought to be so heartily grateful that I am wounded,' he said drily.

She did not reply, and he picked up a napkin and dabbed reflectively at the cognac soaking into his dressing-gown.

'Was it such an unreasonable question?' he asked. 'After all, Catherine, you have told me on several occasions that you married me only for my fortune.'

'How could you be such a fool as to believe me? I don't care a tinker's curse for your loathsome fortune! I wish the Marques had taken it all! I married you because I love you, you obstinate, thick-headed, looby! Although I cannot for the life of me understand why I should love somebody so wilfully blind, so totally unsympathetic and so generally witless. I *love* you, do you hear! I love you!'

His hand stilled over the napkin. 'I hear you. Indeed, I suspect that half the household has also heard you.'

The sarcasm sprang automatically to his lips, but it did not serve the purpose. In the seven years since his betrothal to Diane de Verette he had never, even in the throes of passion, told a woman that he loved her, but he discovered that he needed to say the words to Catherine. After seven years of disuse, however, the simple sentence was not easy to pronounce. He drew in a deep breath. Once the words were spoken, there would be no going back.

'Catherine, I love you more than I have ever loved another woman,' he said. 'More than I ever imagined I could love anybody.'

He winced inwardly as he heard the flatness of his tone. So much for the polished address of a man noted on two continents for the skill and charm of his love-making! Even as he finished speaking, he admitted to himself that he was frightened—far more frightened than he had been as Butcher's prisoner. Once Catherine realised how blindly he loved her, he was vulnerable to hurt as he had never before allowed himself to be.

He could not bring himself to look at her, so he stared fixedly at the bottle of cognac.

'William?'

He felt her hand brush against his sleeve, and forced himself to meet her eyes. They were soft and a little shy, but glowing with the promise of tenderness and passion.

'William,' she said again, her cheeks suffusing with colour. 'I am so happy to know how you feel. When the Marques told me that you were his prisoner, and I thought that I might never see you again, I knew how silly I had been to allow pride to stand in the way of telling you my feelings.'

She reached out and touched his cheek in a fluttering, uncertain caress, then stared hard at her slippers. 'If—If you are not too tired, and if your injuries are not too painful, would you . . . could you make love to me?'

Ladies of quality were not brought up to request love-making from their husbands, and he could make a fair guess as to how much courage it had cost her to put such a request into words. He gathered her into his arms, raising her hands to his lips, and pressing his mouth against each palm in turn. At that moment he loved her so much that it was a physical ache inside him, but he also felt a warm, unaccountable urge to tease her.

'I am feeling very weak, dearest,' he said with a sigh. 'But if you were to persuade me, I might be able to oblige you.'

'P-Persuade you? I d-don't know how . . .' She gulped and tried again. 'I am not quite sure what I could do to persuade you, William.'

He caressed her flushed cheek tenderly, his throat closing tight with longing. There was more than a touch of wryness in his smile.

'Believe me, sweetheart, it will not be very difficult. Where you are concerned, I am easily persuadable.'

'Wh—What must I do?'

He tried not to look too eager. 'The first thing you must do is take off your dressing-gown.'

'That certainly sounds quite easy,' she said huskily. She wriggled out of his arms and unfastened the ties of her robe, allowing it to fall in a crumpled heap at her feet. She was wearing a long-sleeved nightgown of fine linen, buttoned high at the throat, and trimmed with a frill of broderie anglaise at the hem. It required all of his willpower not to reach out and snatch it off her.

He picked up his glass of cognac and swallowed quickly. 'Now you must take off your nightgown,' he said.

His attempt to appear unmoved obviously did not succeed. She gave him a look that was suddenly brimful of mischief.

'You know, I think I am beginning to understand *exactly* what I have to do. You must be an excellent teacher, William.'

She turned and walked slowly to the bed, pausing at the foot. With great deliberation, keeping her back towards him, she began to undo a few of the buttons at the top of her nightgown. When she still had about a dozen left to go, she moved to the side of the bed and swung around to face him.

Her blush darkened, but she looked at him steadily as she undid the final buttons. Still meeting his gaze head-on, she slowly pushed her nightgown off her shoulders.

'Have I persuaded you yet, William?' she asked, desire imparting a tiny quiver to her voice.

'You have persuaded me that you are a witch,' he said hoarsely, striding across the room and crushing her against his eager body.

They tumbled together into the middle of the bed and she

clasped her hands round his neck, urging his head down to receive her kiss.

'Am I hurting you?' she whispered. 'Your back?'

'No. Oh God, Catherine, it feels so good to have you beneath me once again. I want you so much that I die for you when you are not here!'

'It is the same for me.'

'Is it?' He gave an odd little laugh. 'Catherine, if you lied when you said that you love me, do not ever tell me the truth.'

'I didn't lie,' she said. 'When I am with you, I feel whole. Without you, I am only half alive.'

He had almost reached the point where he did not care if she spoke the truth. If she lied, she lied so sweetly that he never wanted her to stop. He held her locked tightly against his heart, kissing her deeply to assuage the sudden urgency of his need. But there was nothing violent about his kiss; it was as tender as Catherine had always dreamed it might be, and her slender body pressed ardently against his.

She helped him to ease off his dressing-gown, relieved to see that there was no fresh blood on his bandages.

'Perhaps we ought not to do this,' she said, with a regretful sigh. 'It is probably not very good for your wounds.'

'But it is wonderful for everything else,' he said, as he bent to kiss her breasts.

She fell back against the pillows, holding him close, all thought of protest forgotten. The knotted scar of his old shoulder wound rippled beneath her hands every time he moved, and she began to trace its length with gentle, purposeful fingers. When William realised what she was doing, tension tautened his entire body.

'The scar is very thick,' she murmured. 'Does it hurt you still?'

'No.'

One of the candles flickered with momentary brilliance and then went out. In the dim light of the remaining candle, it was difficult to read his expression, although the rigid stillness of his body conveyed the fact that her exploration of his scars was making him uneasy.

She kissed him softly, wanting him to understand that she needed to know his body as intimately as he had already learned hers. She gradually stroked her fingertips up his neck and along the tense line of his jaw. When she brushed the edge of his eye-patch, he made to push her hand away, but she resisted and, after a moment's obvious hesitation, he ceased his opposition. Neither of them spoke or moved as she reached into the thickness of his hair and untied the narrow silk strings that held the velvet patch in place. She lifted it carefully away from his face, then tossed it to the floor.

He twisted his head away with a convulsive movement, shielding his eyes with his hand.

'Does the light hurt you?' she asked. 'Oh, William! I'm sorry, you should have warned me.'

'No, the light doesn't bother me,' he said, still keeping the left side of his face averted from her. 'At least not immediately.'

'Then William, please . . . Will you look at me?'

His hand dropped back to his side, but still he did not turn. She saw his mouth tighten into a grim line of self-mockery, and then, after endless moments of waiting, he finally twisted his head towards her.

The first thing she saw was the livid scar that slashed across the top of his left eyebrow. She shivered, appreciating that if the cut had been even a quarter of an inch lower, there was no doubt that he would have lost his eye. As it was, the eye itself appeared relatively normal, only the unmoving droop of his lid indicating that it was permanently paralysed.

William saw her shiver, and with an ironic grimace, he turned away. 'Perhaps you wish now that you had not been so eager to reveal things better left decently hidden,' he said tightly. 'I learned long ago that women prefer the romantic mystery of an eye-patch to the unpleasant reality of a scarred and sightless eye.'

Her heart ached with tenderness for the hurt she sensed lying behind his harsh statement. Hot, painful tears pricked at the back of her throat and she was not sure if she would be able to find the right words to tell him that the scars on his body simply made her love him more rather than less. She leaned forward so that she could cup his face between her hands, then slowly drew his head towards her. She gazed at him for a long time before she stroked his eyes closed with her thumbs, dropping a kiss on each closed lid.

He gave a long shudder and she rejoiced inwardly as she felt some of the bitter tension seep out of his body. He reached for her hungrily, pressing her to him with almost agonised need. Her own body leaped in response when he covered her lips with a fierce kiss, locking their mouths and hearts together in mutual yearning. The flame of their love burned swiftly, consuming them both in its ultimate, explosive conflagration.

Afterwards, he did not turn away from her as he had always done in the past. He cradled her head against his shoulder, caressing her occasionally with the languid, intimate gestures of possession.

For a long time she allowed herself to bask in the contented exhaustion of total fulfilment, but eventually she stirred in his arms. She was heartily sick of the lies still festering between them, and was wise enough to know that some sort of barrier would always remain until she confessed the truth about Jane, and her stepmother's ultimatum.

She sat up in bed with an air of implacable determination. 'William,' she said, removing his hand from her stomach. 'There is something important I should explain to you. It concerns my visit to Wellespont and the way we first met.'

He put his hand back on her stomach and traced several lazy circles, the indolent movements belying the turmoil of his emotions. He acknowledged his cowardice, but he really did not want to hear what she had to say.

'Catherine,' he murmured finally. 'Sometimes it isn't a good idea to spend too much time talking about events that happened long in the past. I think we are both different people tonight from the man and woman who met at Wellespont. Do we need to talk about those two different people and what they did?'

For a moment she was tempted to allow the matter to slide. She had no particular wish to reveal either Jane's vulnerability or her stepmother's greed. But, in the end, a streak of practical wisdom prevailed. She understood almost by instinct that William might desire her, even love her in a limited way, but he would never really like her until he knew the truth about her past.

'Yes, I think we do need to talk,' she said. 'William, for both our sakes, I want to explain to you some things about my first marriage. I want you to understand why I behaved as I did when I came to Wellespont. We have never discussed my marriage to Matthew, and it is time that we did.'

His voice was hard. 'If you are about to tell me that you loved him deeply, there is no need. I am well aware of your passion for your first husband.'

'I did love Matthew deeply,' she admitted quietly. 'But as for the rest, you are quite wrong. I have realised for some time that I did not love him with any sort of passion. I enjoyed his company, I admired his goodness and his generosity to the poor, and I loved him as a friend. But when we made love . . . it was not like—it was not at all like what happens between you and me, William.'

He did not look at her. 'I have made love to more women than I care to remember, Catherine, but what happens between us—it has never been like that for me, either.'

'I'm very glad,' she said simply. 'But William, you must understand that when I married Matthew three years ago, I didn't know what it was like to love with passion as well as with affection. On the day I married Matthew, I thought that the world could not possibly hold any greater happiness for me. Then, four months after our marriage, Matthew developed an infection of the lungs. Two months after that, he was already coughing up blood.'

William's arms tightened round her. 'Did he have consumption?'

'No. The doctors said it was some other fatal disease of the lungs, more painful in its progress than consumption. It was as if the Fates had been angered by my happiness and were determined to punish me. A few days before my eighteenth birthday, my mother died of a sudden, totally unexpected fever. Matthew was too weak to accompany me to her funeral services, and in fact, he never again got out of bed. He died eighteen months ago, after weeks of excruciating pain.'

William cradled her head tight against his chest as he stroked her hair. 'Catherine, my very dearest, how can I tell you that I'm sorry? How can I find adequate words to express my sympathy for what you have lost?'

'Usually, I am able to remember the good times now without remembering the pain. You know, I have only recently been conscious of just how terrible it was for me when Matthew died. For a long time, I think I was slightly crazy with grief. I would sit in a room with other people, even members of my own family, and their faces would seem blurred, and it would be an effort to remember precisely who they were. If they spoke to me, their voices seemed to echo from the end of a long tunnel, so that I often didn't hear what they had said. When my stepmother first met me, she believed for several weeks that I was mentally defective.'

'Good God, Catherine, was there nobody for you to turn to? Nobody who was prepared to help?'

'Everyone tried to help,' she said. 'I received nothing but kindness from my family and friends. The vicar was a tower of strength. Even my father, in his own way, did his best to be sympathetic. But last autumn he remarried, and from that time . . . my stepmother . . .'

Her voice faded into silence and he prompted her gently. 'Remember that I have met your stepmother,' he said. 'Nothing that you say is at all likely to shock me.'

'Well, she decided that it was high time for Jane to marry, and, in many ways, she was probably right. However, Jane was appalled by the man my stepmother selected as her suitor. He was a new neighbour, a man called Mr Craddock.'

'Craddock?' he interjected. 'Of the shipping company?'

'Yes. Have you heard of him?'

'Indeed I have,' he said grimly.

'Then you probably know that he is an extremely wealthy widower who is rumoured to have laid the foundation of his fortune by shipping slaves illegally from western Africa to the southern parts of the United States. Quite apart from the dubious nature of his fortune, he is more than fifty years old. That is older than my father—indeed he is almost old enough to be Jane's grandfather. Naturally Jane was sick with horror at the prospect of such a match.'

'And rightly so. I cannot believe that your father willingly promoted it.'

'You must understand that my father has been obsessed for years with the need to produce a son. His title is an old one, and there is no heir in the direct male line. When my stepmother became pregnant within weeks of their marriage, she rose so high in his favour that her wishes began to prevail in everything. My father had no desire to thwart her plans and perhaps run the risk of some mishap to his prospective heir.'

'I gather that your stepmother promoted the match with Mr Craddock?'

'Very much so. I pleaded with the Countess to find some other suitor—somebody younger, whose fortune had been acquired less despicably—but she would not hear of it. That is, she would not hear of it until she learned that you had arrived in England with a fortune that rivalled Mr Craddock's.'

He crooked his finger under her chin, and gently urged her face upwards. He kissed her softly. 'It is here, I suspect that your story becomes especially interesting to me.'

'Yes.' Catherine drew in a deep breath. 'My stepmother struck a bargain with me. She said that she would cancel the announcement of Jane's betrothal on condition that I went to Wellespont and . . . and . . .'

'And *fixed my interest*?' he suggested, with a quizzical smile.

For the first time since beginning her confession, Catherine laughed. 'Oh no! The Countess was far too realistic to expect me to achieve anything so spectacular as that! Her plan was a great deal more practical and much more likely to be successful. She ordered me to compromise you so completely that you would be forced to offer me marriage. In exchange, she agreed that Jane's betrothal to Mr Craddock would be permanently cancelled.'

'Did she keep her promise?' William asked, knowing full well from the conversation he had overheard that the Countess had reneged on her bargain.

Catherine stirred uncomfortably, not wanting to portray her stepmother in too black a light. The Countess of Richland was greedy and fundamentally vulgar, but she was not really evil.

'Well, it has all been settled satisfactorily now,' she said finally. 'My father was very pleased about my marriage to you, and he agreed that the match with Mr Craddock was not suitable for Jane. He promised me that Mr Craddock would not be invited to Richland Towers again. And, as you know, Jane is to spend the summer in Brighton with your mother. I confess that I have high hopes she may meet somebody suitable while she is there.'

William understood that his wife would not be persuaded to recount the full villainy of the Countess and he felt a devastating rush of tenderness.

'Be warned,' he said, smiling a little. 'In her own eccentric way my mother is an inveterate match-maker, and she has the most unconventional ideas about who will make suitable partners. Jane will probably return from Brighton with a Greek revolutionary or a Turkish pasha in tow.'

'Even a Turkish pasha would be a vast improvement on Mr Craddock!'

'Possibly. Providing, of course, that he agreed to leave his other hundred wives safely in Turkey.'

Catherine laughed. 'Dear Godmama! She struggles so valiantly to conceal the fact that her heart is softer than melted butter! I have frequently wondered, you know, why she decided that we would suit each other so well.'

'Are you sure that she did?'

'Oh yes. She admitted to me only the other day that she deliberately engineered that entire proposal scene when she chanced to find us alone in the rose garden at Wellespont.'

'Thus playing right into your scheming hands?' William said, the warmth in his voice belying the condemnation of his words.

'William! You cannot think that I deliberately followed

you into the rose garden! I *swear* to you that I did not.'

'Goose! Of course I don't think that you followed me.' He hesitated for a moment, then raised her hands and kissed them lightly. 'Besides, Catherine, even if you did occasionally consider obeying your stepmother's orders, it would make no difference to how I feel about you. Sometimes we are presented with choices which are so difficult that there is no completely right answer and we must make the best decision that we can. Your stepmother contrived to put you in an impossible situation, and you dealt with it as well and as honourably as you could.'

'It is strange to think that we have reason to be grateful to the Countess. It is because of her scheming that we met and fell in love.'

'It is only my awareness of that fact which prevents me posting off to Richland Towers and telling her exactly what I think of her.'

She wriggled provocatively in his embrace. 'To take such a long journey alone seems a shocking waste of time. Can you not think of anything better to do than to post off to Wiltshire?'

He yawned. 'It is true that I have not slept in almost twenty-four hours . . .'

'I was not thinking of sleep,' she said crossly.

'Then I cannot imagine what you have in mind.'

She smiled. 'Are you sure?' She leaned forward, brushing the lightest possible kiss against his mouth before pulling quickly away. His eyes darkened as he leaned over her, pushing her down into the pillows of the bed.

'Lady Catherine,' he murmured. 'I have moments when I very much fear that you are embarked upon some evil scheme to turn me into a helpless slave to your love-making.'

'You have found me out,' she whispered. 'Do you think I have any chance of succeeding?'

'Lady Catherine, I think you already have.'

CHAPTER
NINETEEN

ᴇɴsoɴ, ᴇɴᴛᴇʀɪɴɢ the Captain's bedroom in the middle of the following morning, set a laden breakfast tray on the table in front of the hearth and drew back the curtains before walking over to the bed to awaken his master.

His hand was already on the Captain's shoulder when he recoiled from the bed with all the force of a man who had been shot. He glanced once again towards the bed, but the same incredible sight still met his eyes. Lady Catherine, her ivery-gold hair tumbling all over the pillow, was clasped in the Captain's arms, each of them so close to the other that there was scarcely room for more than a breath of air between them.

Benson backed towards the window, his feet becoming entangled in Lady Catherine's dressing-gown as he did so. He picked it up, blushing profusely, and placed it carefully on a chair. He did not dare to look for its matching nightgown, although he had the most lowering suspicion that Lady Catherine was not wearing so much as a single stitch of clothing. He did hope that his suspicion was wrong. After fifteen years of faithful service, he had finally learned to accept that the Captain never wore a nightcap and frequently slept without a nightshirt. However, the fact that a lady might do the same was simply outside the realm of his comprehension. And she the daughter of an Earl!

It was not, Benson thought, that he could be considered a prude, but he did expect his employers to conduct themselves with a certain amount of decorum. He accepted with equanimity the fact that Captain Moreton had kept a string of mistresses before settling down to matrimony. But there was a right and proper way of going about all things, and Benson was very keen on right and proper ways. An English gentleman was supposed to take his pleasures outside the home, and fulfilled his marital obligations inside

his wife's bedroom. The Captain, like any other marrie
man, should have gone to his wife's room and returned t
his bed—alone—long before his valet was likely to come i
and wake him.

As for Lady Catherine . . . Didn't she know that respec
able married women simply never ended up in their hus
band's beds? At least not in a well-regulated household
and Benson considered any household in which he serve
to be by definition well regulated.

He glanced a final time at the bed and pursed his lips. A
least Lady Catherine was decently covered by the sheet
whereas the Captain was mother-naked as far as the wais
To a man who did not discard his red flannel undershir
until the end of May and resumed wearing it on the first da
of September, such profligate nudity seemed to be askin
for rheumatism, if not for something much worse. Th
Captain, however, had always remained disconcertingl
free of all such afflictions.

Neither the Captain nor Lady Catherine had stirred fron
their embrace, which made Benson wonder what they ha
been doing all night to end up so exhausted at this advance
hour of the day. In all his years of service to the nobility, h
had never before encountered a husband and wife wh
remained locked in each other's arms at eleven o'clock i
the morning. Benson sighed. He had always considered th
Captain something of an idol, and he was sadly shaken b
this precipitous fall from grace.

Uncertain how to cope with the situation, he re-close
the curtains and quietly left the room.

As soon as Benson had shut the door, William extricate
himself from the tangle of Catherine's hair and sat up i
bed, a grin stretching his sleepy features. He leaned acros
and gently shook his wife awake.

'Sweetheart, I think you had better get back to your roor
before poor old Benson expires of an apoplexy. He came i
just now, and I'm afraid we shocked him terribly. He's lef
me some breakfast, so I can offer you a cup of coffee befor
you go.'

Benson would have been gratified to observe that Lad
Catherine—unlike her smiling husband—was not lost to a

sense of shame. She shot up in bed, her green eyes dark with dismay.

'Oh heavens, William! Benson in *here*! What on earth must he have thought! My clothes are all over the floor!'

'I imagine he thought that we had spent the night making mad, passionate love,' William said. 'If he did, then his thoughts were amazingly accurate. But I suggest you put on your dressing-gown, my love, for he is likely to return at any minute.'

Catherine was only too willing to comply. She found her nightdress under the bed and her dressing-gown draped tidily over a chair. She hurriedly put on both garments, and was tying the ribbons on her robe when there was an imperious knock on the door.

'Come in,' William called before Catherine had the chance to escape.

She threw him a glance that was intended to be crushing and was actually, William decided, totally enchanting. She clutched her arms around her waist and waited nervously for Benson to speak.

The valet walked across the bedroom with an air of lofty dignity that would have been well suited to the Archbishop of Canterbury at a royal coronation. He halted his progress some two feet from the bed.

'Good morning, sir. I have come to see if you are ready to be shaved.'

William grinned. 'Certainly. Whenever you feel like it, Benson.'

Benson inclined his head, then turned towards Lady Catherine. He had remembered during his agitated pacing of the hall corridor that Lady Catherine had acted with extreme courage while the Captain was in the Marques de Algarve Branca's clutches, and had decided to be generous. Mindful of that decision, he bowed courteously in her direction, carefully avoiding any direct glance at her shocking state of déshabille.

'Good morning, Lady Catherine. Your ladyship's maid has asked me to indicate that your ladyship's breakfast is waiting in your ladyship's *own* bedroom.'

Catherine did not dare to meet William's gaze. She

swallowed an almost uncontrollable bubble of laughter.

'Thank you, Benson,' she said. 'I shall go at once.'

'Very good, my lady.'

It was well into the afternoon before she saw William again. He came into her room and dropped a kiss on her forehead.

'My man-of-affairs tells me that the Marques de Algarve Branca boarded his ship at Tilbury almost two hours ago.'

'Thank God! I hope we may never see him again.'

'Amen to that! I thought you would also like to know that Mr Canning sends you his best wishes. He summoned me to the Foreign Office at midday. He wanted to ask me if any part of the extraordinary story he had heard about the Marques's party was actually true.'

'What did you tell him?' she asked anxiously. 'There must be the most outrageous rumours flying all over town. The butler has been turning away callers all day.'

'I told Mr Canning the truth. He already knew what had happened in Lisbon seven years ago, so the story was easy to tell. He seemed to find the events at the reception rather amusing, although he insists that we shall neither of us be able to show our faces in London for at least another two years. He plans to do what he can to help, by spreading the story that we were both engaged on some secret mission to save England from a deadly plot, spearheaded by the Marques de Algarve Branca.'

She grimaced ruefully. 'Will you be very bored if we have to stay at Long Acres? Two years is quite a long time.'

'No, I shall not be bored if you are there with me. But we do not have to stay at Long Acres unless you wish it. Canning has offered me the chance to accompany Bernardino Rivadavia back to Argentina in order to assist the Council in Buenos Aires to establish a government. I should enjoy the task, but we do not have to go, of course, unless you would like it.'

Her face lit up. 'I should like it above all things! But won't your family be very unhappy if you leave England again so soon?'

'We shall not be gone for long—no more than two years

at the most. And my mother will not worry if she knows that you are there to keep me in order.'

He strolled over to the window and glanced down into the street, fiddling with the tassels of the curtains as he did so. She sensed an unusual nervousness in his manner, and her impression was confirmed when he walked back towards her, extracting a gold-wrapped package from his coat pocket with very evident misgiving.

'Catherine, we have never talked about that abominable necklace I gave you, chiefly because I have never known how to apologise adequately for the insult. Can you believe me if I tell you that my affaire with Lady Annabelle was never of any significance and that it finished before we were married? The truth is that I was appalled when she turned up at Canning's reception wearing those dreadful emeralds. It may give you some satisfaction to know that I not only spent the entire evening cursing myself for my gross stupidity, but I also had to endure a tongue-lashing from my mother unlike anything I have suffered since I was fifteen and she came upon me kissing one of the milkmaids. My only excuse for giving you that tasteless bauble on our wedding night is that I was half-crazed with frustrated love at the time. You see, I already knew that I loved you, and I was certain you did not love me in return.'

'Hush,' she said, placing her fingers on his mouth. 'We both have far too many things to apologise for. I think it would be better if we simply declared a general amnesty.'

'You are too generous, Catherine.' He held the gift-box towards her. 'I commissioned this for you before we were married, and I have never had the courage to give it to you. I think I was afraid that you might reject it.'

She unwrapped the gold paper and opened the black leather case that lay inside. An emerald necklace, exquisite in its delicate workmanship, nestled on a bed of cream velvet. She picked it up and held it against her throat. The fragile gold links quivered with every breath she drew, causing the emeralds to shimmer in unison with her breathing.

'It is simply beautiful,' she said, when she was able to speak. 'Thank you, William.' Her eyes twinkled with sudden laughter. 'What a pity that we are in such deep social disgrace! I shall have to wait until we are in Buenos Aires before I can wear it.'

There was a knock at her door, and in response to her command, Mary came into the room.

'My lady, there is a letter for you that came this very minute from Richland Towers. It is from Lady Jane as you can see from the writing. Perhaps she sends news of the Countess's baby, my lady.'

'Perhaps,' Catherine said. She walked over to her desk and found a knife to split open the letter. Half-way through the first page she began to smile. By the time she had reached the end of the letter, she was laughing helplessly.

'I am delighted that your sister writes so entertainingly,' William said. 'What news does she have to impart?'

'My stepmother has been safely confined. The birth took place in the early hours of Monday morning.'

'I am happy for her and for your father,' William said, clearly puzzled by his wife's amusement. 'I assume that she has produced the son and heir your father longed for?'

'No.' Catherine struggled to overcome another fit of giggles. 'My stepmother has presented the Earl with twin daughters! Jane reports that they are exceptionally chubby for twins, and very noisy! Despite red cheeks and bald heads, she assures me that they show promise of great future beauty.'

William grinned. 'Is the Countess very disappointed?'

'Jane says that she is taking it surprisingly well. She was overheard to remark to the midwife that there were plenty more where those two came from, and that no doubt the next pregnancy would result in twin boys.'

'I trust your father is equally optimistic?'

'His opinion is not officially known. He came downstairs after speaking to the doctor and immediately shut himself in his study. He summoned the butler in order to demand two bottles of the best burgundy, and at the time this letter was written, had not yet emerged from his study. The butler did report, however, that when he carried in the wine, the Earl was sitting in his chair, muttering "Five daughters. Four shots at a son and I already have five daughters."'

Mary laughed, then hastily converted her laughter into a cough. 'I am pleased to hear that the Countess is well,' she said primly. 'Do you need me for anything else, my lady?'

'No. The Captain and I will be dining informally tonight and alone. I shall not bother to change.'

Mary bobbed a curtsy and left the room. William gathered Catherine into his arms, laughter still warming his expression.

'Well, I must say that I am beginning to feel sadly inadequate. Here is Edward, only a few years my senior and already the proud father of two and a half children. Here is the Earl producing his offspring two at a time, and no doubt preparing himself for the simultaneous production of infants numbers six and seven. And here we are, married for three weeks and virtually nothing to show for it.'

'I wouldn't say that, precisely. We have, after all, survived an abduction, saved ten thousand pounds of your fortune and you have been offered a post in Spanish South America. We have also discovered that we love each other. Some people might consider those quite significant achievements.'

'Everything you say is true. Still, I cannot help but feel that we are getting sadly left behind in this race for progeny. We have obviously not been devoting nearly enough time to the essential first steps of the production process.'

Catherine walked over her desk and pretended to examine her engagement calendar. 'It just so happens, Captain Moreton, that the rest of my afternoon is free . . .'

William swept her into his arms, his manner jesting, but his gaze achingly tender. 'I am delighted, Lady Catherine, to see that you are according this serious matter the prompt attention it deserves.'

Benson, having ascertained from Mary that Captain Moreton was in her ladyship's bedroom, carried an urgent note from the cook on a silver salver. Despite the fact that it was not yet dark, Benson had been so overcome by his early morning experiences that he had actually hesitated before taking the missive upstairs. However, a few discreet enquiries elicited the reassuring information from Mary that both Lady Catherine and the Captain were fully clothed and much occupied in discussing the recent news from Richland Towers.

His first knock at Lady Catherine's door produced no response. His second, louder knock, was similarly ignored. Benson opened the door a few inches and peered round the crack. He wished immediately that he had not done so. Captain Moreton and Lady Catherine were indeed fully clothed. Even Benson, however, could see that this happy state of affairs was not likely to persist for long.

He closed the door and stared disconsolately at the note on his silver tray. Life, he reflected morosely, had certainly been much simpler when the Captain was a bachelor.

Catherine, lost in her husband's kisses, vaguely heard the click of the latch. 'William?' she murmured. 'Did someone come in?'

'It was Benson,' he said resignedly. 'Now we shall have absolutely no credit left with him whatever.'

She moved reluctantly out of his arms. 'Oh William! We have already scandalised half London; now we are scandalising the servants as well! Benson is quite right. We should not be making love in the middle of the afternoon. It is vastly improper, and anybody might come in.'

William walked over to the door, threw the bolt and turned the key with a decided flourish.

'My dear, you have only just begun to discover how resourceful I became during my years in the South American jungle.' He grinned. 'Now, where were we?'

She put her arms around his neck and drew his mouth down until it covered her own.

'I think,' she whispered, 'that we were just about here.'